FIGHTING SHADOWS

FIGHTING SHADOWS

Sumanta Ganguli

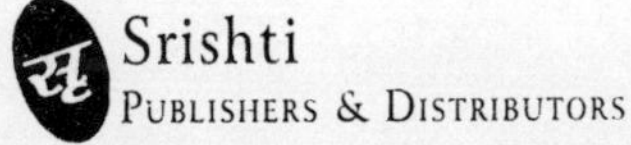

SRISHTI PUBLISHERS & DISTRIBUTORS
64-A, Adhchini
Sri Aurobindo Marg
New Delhi 110 017
srishtipublishers@forindia.com

First published in 2002 by
Srishti Publishers & Distributors

ISBN 81-87075-78-3
Rs. 195.00

Cover Design by Arrt Creations
45 Nehru Apartment, Kalkaji, New Delhi 110 019
arrt@vsnl.com

Printed and bound in India by
Saurabh Print-O-Pack, Noida

"To Dadamoshai; I'm living your dream."

ACKNOWLEDGEMENTS

A first novel is like a fledgling; it needs a lot of encouragement and support for its flight of fancy.

I am indebted to my publisher, for his faith and support. Sonali Prakash and Dr Rani Roy were patient and ever helpful editors. I am thankful to Sarah Dunant for her advice and encouragement. The British Council helped me gain insights on creative writing, by allowing me to participate in the Writers Eye Workshop at Kolkata. Dr Basudeb Chattopadhyay and Rimi B Chatterjee offered valuable suggestions. Brigadier S.K. Bhattacharya and Dr (Col.) S.N. Bhattacharya helped me get closer to life in the army. Paramita Saha flagged it off with her first-reader-enthusiasm. Joy Bhattacharya and Ashok Malik helped me find my publisher. Annirudha Bhattacharya, Samir and Aditi Talapatra, B. Mukherjee and Somnath Dutta offered a very sensitive reading of the book.

And, this book would have never seen the light of the day without the encouragement and support of my wife and family.

God created man, to live in his garden,
But the intelligent clan soon became a burden.
They chopped the trees, cut the plants,
And ate everything save the ants.
They built dams over the river,
And blasted the rocks, making them shiver.
God was patient, understanding and kind,
And hoped man would embrace peace in the mind.
But man defied God and devised religion,
To barter the Lord, in rupee, pound and yen,
Man made swords, guns and the Bomb,
To fret, to fight and carve his own tomb.

CONTENTS

CHAPTER

One

The shell destroyed the silence of the mountains. It was to herald a volley of blasts from both sides. Even God could not predict how long it would continue – mankind was beyond salvage. A shell exploded nearby, charring the barren land. Avijit wondered what his artillery was doing at the base. They were yet to respond. Had they fallen asleep? One couldn't blame them if they had. Most had been deprived of that luxury for the past few weeks, throwing up killer powder by the tonne every minute, from those huge monsters, ever since the enemy was spotted within the nation's territory.

Well, it had looked like God's own country. Its beauty had stopped Avijit dead in his tracks, the first time he had set foot on this land. The truck carrying them from their temporary quarters had started in the evening and travelled all night through the hilly terrain. The driver took too many risks for comfort to ensure they reached the base camp before dawn. The enemy occupied the superior positions on the hills and ridges and could target a convoy of trucks easily in the daylight. They heard the thunder of guns echoing from the mountains; saw flashes of orange tearing through the dark sky. Their truck reached the base camp, the operational headquarters, around three in the morning. Not a light could be seen from the outside and it comprised around a hundred tents, along a mountain face. They could see a battery of guns targeting the enemy on the mountain peaks, away to the right. The sound was deafening every time a gun fired, and the ground shivered under its strain. Their company was ordered to rest and be ready by five a.m.

Avijit was tired. He tried to get some sleep, but his mind wandered aimlessly. He wondered what his mother thought a thousand miles away. Was she filled with the dread of another dear one deserting her? He still remembered the fateful day that shaped his life as no other day had.

He was born into a Bengali middle class family in Rajpur, a small industrial town, around a hundred kilometres from Calcutta. His first memory of Rajpur was the vast barrage built over the river Bhairab. His father, who was a blast furnace operator in the local steel plant, would take Avijit on a cycle to the barrage during weekends. He was then so small that his father had to raise him up over the railing so that he could see the water falling down. He would stare at the cascading water with a sense of wonder, as man and nature battled for supremacy; the latter covering Avijit's face in a thin wisp of vapour, as it toiled and roared over the man made barrier to freedom. His trance would only be broken, once his father tired of holding him up, would put him down. They would have misti-doi on the way back. That had been the only thrill in his otherwise routine and mundane life. Theirs was not a life of plenty but his parents were determined to give their only son the best. So Avijit went to the best school in town, the only school that had a permanent building and a playground of its own. His father wanted him to be an engineer, having had to work under one all through his career. His mother wanted him to be a doctor, as she was fed up with their local doctor who invariably prescribed medicines for malaria when a patient went to him with a mild fever. Avijit wanted to be a football player.

He remembered an early morning in June. He was only ten and

taking a growing interest in sports. They did not have TV at home and his father would take him to his colleague Nalu's house, to watch a football or cricket match. It was the football world cup quarterfinals and Argentina was playing England. He was mesmerized by a five foot odd player, who reigned the field like an emperor. The opponents were caught on the wrong foot everytime he had the ball. It was no surprise his team won and advanced to the semifinals. That match was even worse for the opponents. Avijit watched with awe, how a player could dribble the ball from his own half into the opponent's net. Argentina became the world champions and the biggest poster of Diego Maradona available in the whole of Rajpur, adorned the walls of Avijit's small bedroom within a week. He yearned to emulate his idol and started playing the game. Determination and hard work earned him a place in the best team in Rajpur within three years.

His parents did not stop him, but ensured that studies didn't take a back seat. His father would sit with him every evening, in spite of working a ten hour shift in scorching heat at the plant, and guide him through his daily homework. And the hard work paid off. Though Avijit never topped his class, he was always within the top five. As the school finals approached, his parents persuaded him to concentrate only on studies and forget football for a while.

"It is now that you shape your destiny. No one can deprive you of a good life if you study hard and get a good score. If you fail to do so, don't blame God."

Avijit decided to be an obedient son. It helped him secure a first division in the secondary examination as well as the higher secondary examination that followed two years later. However, he narrowly missed admission to both the engineering and medical streams. His parents were disappointed and wanted him to try again the next year. But Avijit was happy. He could pursue his first love football with a little more vigour, after joining college.

He soon regained his glory in the playing arena and was selected to represent his district in the annual competition in the state. He played his best, but they lost in the semifinals. Later, as he was resting on the field after the match, his team manager introduced him to Mr Bhowmick.

"He is the chief recruiter for a top club in Calcutta," the Manager informed him.

"I liked the way you played. A little grooming can see you a better player. Would you like to play in the Calcutta League? I can arrange for your stay," Mr Bhowmick said, and waited.

"I will ask my parents," was all Avijit could say.

"You do that and let me know by tomorrow. I know a good player when I see one."

Calcutta was considered the Mecca of Indian football. Players from all corners of the country dreamt of making it to the final eleven of a top club there and Avijit was no different. He couldn't believe that an opportunity would present itself so soon.

"Are you out of your senses! How can you live all by yourself in such a big city? And what will happen to your studies?" his mother was dismayed.

"Did Mr Bhowmick confirm that you would be in the playing eleven? You may end up on the reserve bench for the whole season and nobody will bother about you next year. Tell Mr Bhowmick you will meet him in Calcutta after finishing your studies," his father reasoned, "I will make sure you get a job in the steel plant, if they refuse to take you then."

And it went on and on. His parents stood their ground and Avijit decided not to hurt them. He met Mr Bhowmick the next day and told him the decision.

"You're wasting a great opportunity. Anyway, keep my contact address. Get in touch if you change your mind."

And Avijit continued his life at Rajpur. His parents were relieved that a major crisis had been averted. They hoped their son would see reason and concentrate on building a career. But little did they know what the future had in store.

The steel plant his father worked in employed more than a thousand workers. They were represented by a few trade unions. The unions had regular interaction with the top management for the welfare of the work force. They also had control over decisions like ordering for machinery spares, allotment of jobs to contract labour and the fate of scrap generated in the plant. Avijit had overheard his father narrating tales of increasing tension in the steel plant to his mother. Rival unions were at loggerheads over the selling of scrap, which involved millions of rupees. His father had mentioned that money was being swindled and threats were being made.

It was nearly evening. Avijit was resting after a practice session at their club, when his neighbour, Naluda, came running.

"You must come with me to the hospital immediately," he shouted.

"What's up?" Avijit was exhausted after the strenuous workout and didn't want to move an inch.

"Let's go before it's too late," Naluda didn't elaborate, but his tone made Avijit jump up and get his cycle.

It seemed the longest journey in his life, that ten-minute cycle ride. He thought his mother must have fallen seriously ill, as she had not been keeping well for the past few days. An unknown fear gripped him when he reached the only hospital in town. A few known faces were strangely silent, as he followed Naluda into the casualty ward. His father's body was lying on the floor at the far end, covered in a white sheet with red stains. He was dead.

Avijit woke up with a start. Gurinder was shaking him.

"Get up son, or the Captain will come in and kick your ass." Gurinder, nicknamed Guri, was a lanky *sardar* in his regiment. Avijit never knew friendship could weld souls. Now they were inseparable. Guri, the happy-go-lucky guy; Avijit, shy and reserved. They complemented each other brilliantly.

Avijit felt tired, but everyone had to be ready. The air was biting cold and the wind was like a blade of ice on the bare skin. They stumbled through the darkness and entered the tent where the briefing would be held. The Captain was immaculately dressed as ever and looked his usual self. He explained in detail the operation they were to undertake. They were to recapture peak 4987 at the earliest. It was a vantage point from where the enemy had a clear view of the highway, the only road for the army to maintain supplies to the forward posts all along the border. The army was planning to attack the enemy from the three sides of the hill within their control. Their platoon was to attack from the steepest side. It was the path of maximum difficulty but also the path of least resistance, as the enemy was expected to be busy guarding the easier approaches to the peak. It meant Avijit would need to climb rock faces. The realization made him uncomfortable, as he hated heights. But then, a soldier was not allowed to be fanciful. He tried to concentrate on the Captain's instructions. The Captain finally asked them to collect the rations and snow boots from the store and be ready by eight a.m. And with that he left them. One by one they came out, men in the prime of their youth, ready to make the supreme sacrifice for their motherland.

The battle seemed to have ebbed with only occasional gunfire from positions further up. Both sides were resting their artillery, the machines overheated, their barrels puking smoke in the cold dawn. An enemy shell had hit an oil tanker the previous evening. It lay in a charred heap in the middle of the narrow road. But the first light of the morning had lit up nature all around and it looked like paradise. The rays of the sun had turned the snow atop the mountains to a bright orange. It reflected tranquillity and peace, in sharp contrast to the sense of panic and death prevailing below. They were in a lush green valley, the mountainsides dotted with pine trees. A small river flowed by, carrying the melting snow of the Himalayas. The army tents, the huge guns, the trucks and the humans looked misfits in this perfect world.

The sweet sound of the river gushing past was drowned by the drone of two helicopters approaching the base. They were coming back from the battlefront and Avijit and his colleagues inched towards the makeshift helipad to have a closer look. The medical team rushed forward the moment the helicopters touched down. They could hear someone crying in pain and the medics brought him out on a stretcher. The soldier's legs ended at the knees; the bones peeping out through mutilated flesh. He was rushed towards the temporary hospital. Occupational hazards, Abhijit mused. There were four martyrs too. Their bullet ridden bodies were brought out with great care. The stench of death was everywhere. The pilots told them that twenty soldiers had tried to recapture an enemy position the previous night. But the mission had been unsuccessful. Chances of any survivors were remote, as the enemy, being at a superior height, could target everything with ease.

Avijit and his colleagues decided to have a bath in the river before starting their ascent. The river water was cold, but washed away all the grime and tiredness from their bodies. They jumped around, some breaking into a song, while the others clapped. Guri danced the *bhangra* and for once the Captain did not play spoilsport. The *sardar* had enthralled Avijit's neighbours with his dancing too.

Initially, when they had joined the army as trainees, Guri had stayed away from Avijit. No one was able to open up a conversation with him, as Avijit only answered in monosyllables. However, he impressed his batch mates with his shooting prowess once they had been initiated into rifle firing. He saw his father's killer in front of him whenever he aimed a gun, and never missed a target. He also excelled in football, a mandatory discipline in the army to stay fit, and scored three goals in a friendly match. Guri was not doing badly either. He shot everything but the target and was warned. He also scored a goal in the same match, trying to make a clearance and putting the ball into his own net. His teammates heaved a sigh of relief, when he had to leave the field with a bruised leg. They lost the match four goals to three and everyone was upset.

Avijit went up to Guri's bed in the barracks later.

"Don't worry friend, we'll win the next time."

Guri couldn't believe his ears! It must have been the longest sentence Avijit had uttered since the two had met. They talked a lot about their lives that evening. Guri, the son of a farmer, about the life in his village and Avijit about his passion – football. Guri made Avijit laugh a lot as he shared his pranks at school; how he had learned ventriloquism from a local monk and made his teacher sweat in class. A peculiar voice would suddenly announce, "Hey Panku, your fly is open," or "Did you pee in your pants? It's all wet!" The class erupted in laughter and the teacher, red faced and unable to identify the offender, would end up asking the entire class to stand up on their benches. It had been a tradition in Guri's family, since the time of his great grandfather, that at least one son served in the army. His uncle had fought as a captain in the Punjab Regiment during the 1971 war and had always encouraged him to join the institution.

"There is no greater service than serving your motherland," he would tell Guri.

Sadly, he did not live to see his nephew honour the family tradition, as he had died of cancer the previous year.

The word *death* touched a resonant chord in Avijit. He decided to pour forth his cup of woes that night and found an empathizer in Guri. He spoke of his father's death, of the indecision and insecurity he had faced in its aftermath. His mind had ached with the desire to avenge the death, but no one knew who had killed his father. The police had come and gone, leaving assurances and doing nothing. There was no eyewitness, they had said. The rival trade unions had placed wreaths on the deceased, proclaiming that he had attained martyrdom fighting their cause. But nobody could say who killed him. The works manager of the plant spent an evening with them. He assured Avijit of a job in the plant at the earliest, only to forget his commitment as the dust settled down.

"The approval is stuck at the head office in Calcutta," he remarked on the couple of occasions Avijit went to his office to follow up. His mother, a social worker and a happy housewife, aged overnight. Her laughter, which used to resound from all corners of their little home, was replaced by melancholy and anxiety. She became over protective of her son and could not tolerate his absence for more than a few hours. Avijit, unable to get a job at the steel plant, decided to try his luck in Calcutta; he would take his mother to his uncle's place there and play football for a living. His father had not saved much and their only asset was the small two-roomed flat he had bought in Rajpur. Though they had a shelter, his mother's pension was too little to lead even a frugal life in the face of spiralling prices. His mother insisted that he complete his studies at Rajpur and they would manage with whatever they had. But that would have taken another year and only added his name to the long list of unemployed graduates in the state. Even engineers were being forced to take up jobs, which had little to do with their technical skills. Militant trade unions ruled the industry and productivity was at a historic low. Their state did not exist on the map of any industrialist. He hoped that Calcutta, the City of Joy, would not disappoint him.

His uncle was a chartered accountant; his aunt a school teacher. They had built a small house in Salt Lake, away from the bustle of the city. Their only son Khokon, a chemical engineer, had settled in the United States as a computer professional. They led a lonely life and welcomed Avijit and his mother with open arms. His uncle was yet to come to terms with the sudden demise of his younger brother. He wanted Avijit to continue his studies in Calcutta.

"Build up your career first. A job can come later."

"But I need to sustain my family. And I can't be a burden on you," Avijit reasoned.

He decided to go and meet Mr Bhowmick, the man who had offered him a chance to play football in Calcutta. It took him the better part of an hour to locate the club tent in the vast lush green Calcutta Maidan. Mr Bhowmick was not available and Avijit was asked to wait. He ventured out onto the field to find the players practising under the watchful eyes of their coach. They wore colourful jerseys and Avijit had a great urge to join them. But that was not to be. Mr Bhowmick returned shortly.

"Sorry son, you missed your chance," he said, after Avijit introduced himself, "we plan to recruit foreign players now; local players are no longer crowd pullers. Two students from Nigeria have confirmed their availability for the entire season. We hear they play well. Both are over six feet and have great hairstyles. Just watch, they will be big stars."

"But you saw me play," Avijit protested, "I can break through the best defence."

"Well, you didn't turn up last time," Mr Bhowmick reminded him, "what's the guarantee you won't vanish in the middle of the season?"

Avijit saw his dream go up in flames. He trudged back to his uncle's house and wanted to catch the next train back to Rajpur.

"Life isn't easy. Never give up after a single failure. Be determined and you will succeed," his uncle spoke, just like his father would.

His uncle was able to get him a job through his associates, as an office assistant in a small trading company. Avijit, dressed in his best clothes, reached his office sharp at nine thirty a.m. on the first day. He had always thought offices were large clean buildings with neatly placed chairs and tables, and people talking with each other in a polite tone. This office was on the third floor of a very old building in the midst of a commodity market. The ground floor had shops of all hues and colours, some selling automobile spares, while others sold fast food. The only lift was so old and worn out that Avijit decided to go up the dark and narrow staircase. It took him almost ten minutes to find *Dayaram & Co.* at room number 316. It was next to a dimly lit toilet and the stink filled the office whenever the main door was opened. The office was small, with a chamber for the owner and a sofa outside. The owner, Mr Dayaram, was a man of medium height with a bloated belly. A generous coat of oil made the sparse hair on his head glisten. He sat in a big chair in the cubicle, chattering continuously into the three phones on his table.

"Take off your shoes and come in son," he said.

His teeth were stained from chewing paan masala and he used a spittoon to spit out the betel nut paste from his mouth at regular intervals. The cubicle looked like a temple, with pictures of gods and goddesses all around. The owner gave him a stained-toothed smile and got down to business.

"I know your uncle – a very good man," he started, "since he recommended you, I have nothing much to ask. You are young and will have to learn the intricacies of business. Work hard with your heart and mind, as no one else will give you this opportunity. I will pay you fifteen hundred rupees per month as salary."

Avijit didn't know what to say and simply nodded his head.

"Clean the office every morning. Take all calls, note down the message and pass it on to me when I come. Take this spare key to the main door. Always lock it if you have to go out in my absence. Now take this flask and get me some tea from downstairs. Here is the money for the tea," Mr Dayaram finished his directive.

Avijit had another dream shattered; but he needed the money and decided to give it a try. He did not tell his mother about the office, lest she felt bad. She believed her son was going to work in a firm of repute and *Dayaram & Co.* was a far cry from that.

He was out of the house for six days a week, from eight thirty a.m. till evening, trying to meet the demands of his new job. There were a few dubious characters who came to meet his boss; Mr Dayaram would lock his chamber and go into a huddle with the visitor for hours. Later, he would hand over loads of cash to Avijit, to go and deposit it in a nearby bank. Avijit was fearful of handling so much money as snatching and robbery were common in the locality; he felt relieved once he was within the four walls of the bank. He often wondered how many years it would take him to repay Mr Dayaram, if the money got snatched from him. It could be at least one lifetime at his current salary.

He befriended Munna, Mr Dayaram's driver for the past five years. Munna had started off driving an old Ambassador and was driving a brand new Opel within three years. However, his salary had gone up a mere two hundred rupees since he had joined Mr Dayaram. It was Munna who told Avijit what Mr Dayaram's business was all about – he was a trader who dealt in commodities like chemicals and plastic granules. He made clandestine deals and Munna warned Avijit of the tax raids. The authorities came often and threatened Debashis, Avijit's predecessor. They only left after Dayaram came and offered a deal.

Avijit's mother had lost her zeal for life. She hardly spoke and only showed concern if her son needed something. She didn't want to be a burden on Avijit's uncle and aunt for long, and coaxed her son to find a new home. Luckily, they had found a tenant for their flat at Rajpur. The two thousand rupees they received per month could be used to rent a house. His uncle did not like the idea, but agreed in the end. They rented a house in the outskirts of the city. It was small – two pigeonhole bedrooms, a kitchen and a bathroom, with a small passage acting as their drawing room cum dining space – but a decent enough shelter for the two of them.

His day now started early. He went to the local market to buy their regular quota of milk and vegetables and sometimes fish or meat, if the price was affordable. His mother had stopped eating non-vegetarian food since her husband's death, as per the norms of society. Avijit felt uncomfortable asking her to cook the fish or meat for him. His mother reasoned he must have his daily intake of animal protein to stay fit, though she did not apply the same logic to herself. Avijit had to start at half past eight every morning to reach office on time, where he would clean the entire office including his boss's spittoon, and await Mr Dayaram's arrival. His boss normally arrived around half past ten and spent the first half hour lighting incense sticks and offering prayers to each and every god and goddess, who adorned the walls of his cubicle. Avijit was touched by the devotion and could never comprehend how such a pious man could run the business the way he did. Mr Dayaram had a lot more faith in Avijit now and often confided details of his business deals. He had learnt of a price hike in the international market for a particular chemical and immediately stored it up by buying it cheap from domestic suppliers. Prices had gone up in the local market within two months and the material was not readily available. Mr Dayaram made a quick profit. None of this sale was registered and he never bothered with the triviality of paying tax. Those in authority turned a blind eye once the thick envelopes reached them every month. The government continued to attract public wrath for its failure to generate revenues and the Dayarams of the world prayed with increasing fervour everyday so that God also looked the other way. The clients who came to meet his boss were not too honourable, though they always wore good clothes and drove expensive cars. They wined and dined at the best places in town. And people like his uncle, who had worked hard to get a professional qualification, still drove a fifteen year old car and calculated a hundred times before going on a vacation once in five years.

Avijit was finding it difficult to digest this hard reality. His mother wanted to go back to her familiar surroundings in Rajpur.

"You can finish your studies there and then get a better job," she would say.

But Avijit was not sure it would work out. He still nurtured hopes of joining a football club at the start of the next season. He did play a couple of matches for the local club, on Sundays, and won a few friends with his fleet-footed passing. It made his evenings less monotonous.

They met after office, Avijit, Chandan and Ujjal. Chandan was a budding singer and Ujjal a bank employee. All three wanted to live a worthy life. Their meetings were a time for stock taking. Chandan had a melodious voice and often livened up the dull air by singing popular old songs. His voice effortlessly touched various octaves, as also the heart of his friends. It killed the frustration, which had piled up throughout the day. They discussed sports, politics, life – agreeing on the need for change, but unable to decide how to precipitate it. They retired to their homes with many questions in the mind but no answers, to rest the body and be ready for another tough day, to be at the mercy of an enigma called office.

CHAPTER

TWO

Avijit saw her for the first time at the bus stop. He took the eight forty a.m. bus every day to office and that day was no different. The bus was leaving when Avijit turned the corner near the bus stand. He broke into a run as otherwise he would be late for office and face Mr Dayaram's wrath. He almost caught the bus but for the girl running into him from nowhere. He lost his balance and sprawled on all fours on the hard road, his lunch box flying off and landing in the drain next to the road, his nostrils full with the misty grey exhaust from the departing bus. He was shocked into silence. The fairer sex was an unknown entity in his life but for his mother, who had never made him kiss Mother Earth publicly. He felt humiliated. The sweet smile followed by an "I'm sorry," put him in no-man's-land. Loud laughter all around brought him back to his senses. He realized he was still on all fours and the people at the bus stop were enjoying his state. He got up and dusted himself clean. It was useless to retrieve his lunch box, as the slimy water must have invaded its innards.

"I'm sorry," the girl apologized again.

Avijit looked at the dark eyes that stared back with a glint of fear.

"I was in a hurry to catch the bus, as I am late for college," she explained, "I didn't mean to bump into you, I'm really sorry."

Avijit was at the crossroads. He was upset and wanted to tell the girl not to dash into people blindly. But he lost himself to the smile and questioning dark eyes.

"It's okay," he forced a smile. "It was my fault. I also ran without looking. Hope you aren't hurt."

"No, no."

She smiled and the ice was broken. Both struck up a conversation, as the next bus was not due before another ten minutes. Her name was Sraboni and she was in her first year in college. She normally took the eight a.m. bus, but had overslept today. Now she was certain to miss the first lecture.

No young girl had ever spoken so many words to Avijit. He quickly looked around, relieved that no one was looking at them. He stammered trying to explain what he did for a living. The girl listened intently, those dark liquid eyes fixed on him, and he felt dizzy. Fortunately, the next bus arrived and their conversation was broken. He got a seat two rows behind her and took the opportunity to catch his breath.

"I'm buying your ticket," she turned around and told him. The conductor handed him the ticket before he could protest.

"Thank you," he muttered.

He kept on glancing in her direction, but she didn't look back. Her hair, tied into a ponytail, bounced gently with the motion of the bus. She sat quietly, staring out through the window at the dusty dawn. Avijit wanted to sit next to her and continue their conversation, but an elderly lady had taken the seat. His hopes soured, once Sraboni got up. She waved at him before alighting from the bus. Avijit suddenly felt a void. She had arrived like a breath of fresh air and her departure made him look back at the entire episode again and again.

His first hour in office was a disaster. He received two calls from potential buyers and noted their phone numbers incorrectly. He forgot to clean his boss's spittoon and was rebuked. He was in a trance and forgot to have lunch till his rumbling stomach reminded him that a meal was overdue. He went down in search of some food, only to leave it half eaten when he remembered Mr Dayaram was not in office and he hadn't locked the office door. Luck was on his side and no one had entered the office. Avijit sat down and took a few deep breaths. He was surprised that a trivial incident could induce such reactions in him. But try as he might to shut it out, those dark eyes and the smile continued to haunt him. He reached home after office and sat in his bedroom all by himself, trying to recall every detail. His mother retired to her room when he refused to enter into a lengthy conversation. He had an early dinner and went to sleep, the only way to stop thinking about the intruder in his life.

His first thoughts were of Sraboni, when he woke up in the morning. He had his heart in his mouth as he turned the corner at the bus stand. It was eight a.m. and he stood expectantly, hoping to meet her, but she didn't turn up. He reached the bus stop an hour earlier the next day and waited eagerly. She came a half hour later with two other girls in tow. Her laughter filled the air all around Avijit. He felt stiff and uneasy and avoided looking at the girls. But time was running out. He was about to turn around and approach her lest the bus should arrive, when she came up and stood in front of him.

"Hello, how are you?" she smiled, "I hope no one has bumped into you again?"

The dark eyes and the smile made his heart beat faster. Avijit could only manage a thin smile. They stood awkwardly for a few moments, before Sraboni decided to introduce her friends. The names didn't even register in his mind.

"Is your office starting early now? Its only eight," Sraboni asked with a sparkle in her eyes.

"No, no. I've an important appointment."

The loud honk of the approaching bus broke their conversation. The girls got a seat, but Avijit had to stand a little further down. Sraboni chatted with her friends and was unaware of Avijit's gaze, till she looked up suddenly. Avijit felt like an eavesdropper, but held his gaze. He, trying to fathom what the future held for him in those dark eyes; she, a little amused at this sudden interest from an acquaintance of a day.

His friends called on him in the evening. The annual football match between their club Banani and their arch rivals Redstars would be held on Sunday. Avijit was in the playing eleven. There was intense rivalry between the two clubs and the event was a matter of prestige for both. Supporters of both clubs thronged the venue, each wanting their side to win. Banani had lost in the last two years and the Redstars wanted to celebrate a hat trick by winning again this year.

"They have a few divisional players on their side," Ujjal informed him, "you must join the practice from tomorrow morning to build up cohesion in our team."

Avijit had to agree, though it meant he wouldn't be able to reach the bus stop early to catch a glimpse of Sraboni. The thought made him morose but he decided to make the sacrifice. An opportunity to play in front of a big crowd didn't come every day. Who knew what it could bring? Spotters from big clubs normally attended such matches to scout for new talent.

Sunday arrived and Avijit reached the venue an hour before the kick-off. A huge crowd had already gathered and there was festivity in the air. Avijit's team was ready and raring to go. Chandan introduced Avijit to their club's President, Mr Ghosh.

"Play like a true sportsman. Winning or losing is a part of the game," he told them.

Avijit realized within the first ten minutes of the match that the Redstars were a much stronger and more balanced team. His own team had a brilliant goalkeeper, who brought off some spectacular saves, and a solid defence. But their midfield was a letdown. As a result, the ball was not passed on to the forwards and they were playing mostly in their own half. They managed to survive the first half, but defeat loomed large unless their midfield play improved. Mr Ghosh came and told them as much during the break. The crowd was also impatient, as no goals had been scored, and egged them on once the second half started. It was almost a repeat of the first half, till Avijit got a loose ball in his half, mid-way into the session. He quickly dribbled past two players and looked up to find the opponent's goalkeeper standing at the edge of the penalty box. Avijit had a clear view of the goal and let fly a right footer from a distance of around thirty-five yards. The Redstar goalkeeper who had hardly faced a tough shot till then, was taken by surprise. He dived in vain to stop the ball. The sheer power of the shot took the ball into the far corner of the net. Their fans went delirious and a few even came into the playing arena and hugged Avijit. The Redstars, stung by this reverse, stepped up their attacks and their defenders also joined in. It opened up huge gaps in their defence and with only five minutes remaining, Avijit received a pass and ran a solo through one such gap. He only had the goalkeeper to beat and did it in style, wrong footing him and dribbling past, before slamming the ball into an empty net. The Redstars fought valiantly, but were defeated. The fans carried Avijit on their shoulders, all the way from the venue to their club. There was shouting and cheering all around, and crackers were burst. Mr Ghosh came up to Avijit and hugged him.

"Well done, you were simply unstoppable."

He invited Avijit and his friends to his home for dinner. Avijit, too tired to speak, simply nodded and accepted the invitation. His mother's face lit up when she saw him. She had already heard how her son had single-handedly thrashed the Redstars.

Chandan and Ujjal coaxed Avijit out of his home in the evening, to accompany them for dinner at Mr Ghosh's residence. It was a small house, a few blocks down the road with a flower garden in front. They entered a drawing room elegantly decorated with cane furniture. Mr Ghosh welcomed them and wanted to celebrate the win with beer. Avijit had never tasted beer before. He settled for a soft drink, while the others made themselves comfortable with a mug of the frothy liquid. Mr Ghosh wanted to know more about the player who had salvaged their club's pride. He fell silent once Avijit spoke of his father's death and their last days at Rajpur.

"What do you plan to do now?" he asked, to which Avijit had no clear answer.

The party continued and the beer flowed freely. Avijit came to know that Mr Ghosh was a retired army officer, who had been posted all over the country during his service period. He had built this house after his retirement. Mr Ghosh was a member of a leading football club in Calcutta. He assured Avijit that he would try and get him into the trials for selection of the team next season. The alcohol had set free the spirits of the other three and they shared jokes and laughed aloud. Avijit was tired and wanted to leave.

Dinner was finally announced and the array of food on the table set his taste buds tingling.

"These are all home made," Mr Ghosh announced, "so eat without a worry."

Mrs Ghosh made her appearance for the first time and served the food on each guest's plate.

"Don't be shy and enjoy the dinner," she told Avijit.

It had been a long time since Avijit had tasted such culinary delicacies. After having finished the fish fry, vegetable fried rice, chicken korma and pineapple chutney, he tried the dessert and found it to be delicious. He said as much to Mrs Ghosh who shook her head.

"It was prepared by my daughter. Wait, I will call her," she went inside and came out with her daughter in tow a few minutes later.

Avijit froze with a spoonful of the payesh halfway to his open mouth. Standing next to the door besides Mrs Ghosh, was Sraboni! She gave him an enchanting smile when their eyes met.

"This is my daughter Sraboni," Mrs Ghosh made the introduction.

"How are you?" Sraboni asked innocently, putting Avijit further on the wrong foot.

"Do you know my daughter?" it was Mr Ghosh's turn to query.

All eyes had turned towards him and Avijit felt weak.

"Yeah, no, I mean ...," he couldn't finish. The spoonful of dessert missed his mouth and landed on his lap instead. In a hurry to clean it, his hand hit the glass of water on the table, spilling it and the water started flowing all over. Mrs Ghosh came to his rescue by quickly dropping a dry cloth to stem the tide.

"It seems the smell of the beer has knocked out our dear friend," Mr Ghosh joked and there was loud laughter all around.

Only Avijit knew who had thrown the knock out punch and stole a glance at her. She looked back quizzically. The others finished their dinner and thanked the host for the excellent evening. Avijit, who was eager to leave a half hour back was now desperate to stay on. His tiredness had eased and he felt he could stay awake all night. Sraboni had taken a seat at the far corner of the drawing room and a wry smile creased her beautiful face. It was as if she understood the reason behind his discomfort and enjoyed it.

"Well, the door to our house is always open. Come down any time you want to," Mrs Ghosh remarked.

The others were ready to leave and Avijit reluctantly followed. He darted a furtive glance at Sraboni, who seemed to look back with equal interest.

"How long have you known Sraboni?" Chandan asked the moment they were on the road, "she was looking at you with a lot of interest."

Avijit knew he had to say something before his friends jumped to a conclusion. He spoke of their first meeting.

"Good. She's still single and not in love with anyone. Give it a try," Ujjal patted him on the back.

Avijit felt a strange sense of relief but wanted to know how his friend knew so much.

"He keeps track of each and every good looking girl in this neighbourhood," Chandan replied. "Be assured, his information is correct."

"How do you manage? Must be a tedious job! Are you in love with anyone yet?" Avijit asked jokingly.

"Hah! He's in love with all of them. But does he have the courage to talk to even one?" Chandan laughed.

"Love is a disease I would like to avoid," Ujjal added philosophically.

Avijit's job responsibilities increased as the days went by.

"My brother is getting married," Mr Dayaram stated one morning, "this is a list of customers and acquaintances I need to invite. But I've no time, as the reception is only twenty days away. You take Munna and complete the job. A man will deliver packets of sweets in the office today. Hand over a packet and the invitation card to each invitee."

Avijit's boss handed over a big list and a bunch of cards.

"But who will handle the office work?" Avijit asked.

"Who asked you to worry about that? Do as you are told," was the terse reply.

Avijit suspected his boss suffered from chronic dyspepsia. Mr Dayaram had hardly smiled after their first meeting. Munna though was happy to be out of the clutches of his master. He told Avijit that the Dayarams had been on a buying spree over the past few days – sarees, jewelry, furniture and even a brand new flat for the newlyweds. Munna had been a witness to a flurry of activities between the two families of the bride and groom, each trying to eclipse the other in a vulgar exhibition of wealth.

"Guess the cost of the invitation card?" Munna asked him.

Avijit had only one previous experience of buying invitation cards, for his father's funeral. That card had been much simpler.

"One hundred and seventy five rupees each." The price shocked Avijit. "And he ordered more than a thousand! The miser would not give me five hundred rupees I wanted for my father's medicine."

One by one, the invitation cards and the sweets were distributed. Some asked Avijit into the house and offered him a glass of water. Most did not open the door more than the few inches needed to squeeze in the box of sweets. Avijit was too tired to even eat the frugal meal his mother had prepared by the time he reached home late at night.

In spite of the pressure, he made it a point to meet Sraboni every day in the morning. She seemed to understand why he was there so early and was not surprised any longer. They exchanged only a few words and always sat separately on the bus. But it kept Avijit refreshed throughout the day. In between, he met Mr Ghosh at the club one day.

"Well young man, where have you been? I was expecting you at my house."

Avijit explained that he had to stay late in office and could not come down.

"Let's go and sit somewhere," the elderly man remarked and led the way.

Avijit hoped the armyman was homeward bound. He could then meet Sraboni. But that was not to be.

"War has broken out at home! Both mother and daughter are on a cleanliness drive. All corners are being dusted clean. I came out in fear of getting dusted too," Mr Ghosh chuckled. "Can we go to your home instead? I want to meet your mother and have a cup of tea with you all."

Avijit's mother was surprised and a little embarrassed at this sudden visit. She had not received a single visitor for the past few months and was at a loss for words. A vibrant personality, she had withdrawn into a cocoon since her husband's death and did not care much for the outside world. Her whole world now revolved around her son. She welcomed Mr Ghosh only because he was her son's guest. Mr Ghosh, being an armyman was very outspoken. He questioned the wisdom of confining herself in the house and not venturing out.

"I know your loss is irreparable, but you need to live a normal life for your son," he reasoned "what would he do if you fall ill? I will ask my wife and daughter to come over. They have a ladies club here and you will feel a lot more comfortable by engaging yourself there."

Avijit's mother knew she couldn't carry on living the way she was for long and did not disagree. Avijit's heart soared at the prospect of meeting Sraboni at his home. Mr Ghosh spent some more time with them. He took leave with a promise to come over with his family soon.

Mr Dayaram imposed a new responsibility on Avijit every morning as the day of his brother's wedding drew near. Mr Ghosh had come down with his family one evening but Avijit was not at home. He was busy with the florist, handing over the list of flowers needed on the wedding day. His mother seemed to have taken a liking to Sraboni and they had a common love, Rabindrasangeet. Sraboni had sung a few songs of Tagore to enthrall her. Avijit was called to Mr Dayaram's residence, the day before the wedding, to help out in the preparations. They had a bungalow in a posh area of Calcutta. It was a beautiful house with a big lawn and a flower garden. A line of expensive cars stood near the entrance.

"What took you so long?" his boss was his usual dyspeptic self. "Arrange the chairs on the lawn in rows of three immediately. The guests from the bride's house are expected any minute."

There were a few hundred chairs stacked in one corner of the lawn. Avijit was sure the agency which supplied the chairs could have arranged them better. But Mr Dayaram must have refused to pay their charges. There was always Avijit to fall back on. Avijit hoped he would not be asked to clean the toilets too. Expensive cars came in at regular intervals and disgorged passengers; the ladies glittering in jewelry, while the men wore smart kurta-pyjamas. They quickly entered the house from where the sound of singing and cheering could be heard. There were close to a thousand chairs and Avijit was tired by the time he was able to line up about half of them. He decided to go into the house for a glass of water. The main entrance led to a large hall, full with the invitees. His boss was nowhere in sight and Avijit didn't know whom to approach. He had almost given up the thought of the water, standing awkwardly in the midst of the singing and dancing, when a young lady approached him.

"Can I help you?"

Avijit introduced himself and asked for the glass of water. The lady left him, only to reappear with a plate full of sweets and the water.

"Eat it," she said and offered him the plate.

He looked hesitantly at the lady. Did she know Mr Dayaram? She wouldn't have offered him the sweets if she did.

"I will only have the water," he answered.

"No, no, don't feel shy, you must have the sweets too," the lady insisted and forced the plate into his hand. "I'm Mrs Dayaram. Have lunch with us today," she smiled and vanished into the crowd.

Avijit was surprised. Mrs Dayaram was smart and beautiful. She looked much younger than her spouse. He wondered how she tolerated her ill-tempered husband. The sweets were delicious and he gulped them down. He was called in for lunch after he finished arranging the chairs and had dusted them clean. The lunch was a grand affair. There was an array of vegetarian delights and Avijit never imagined so many delicacies could be prepared without his usual fish or meat. Munna arrived in the afternoon and his boss immediately asked the two of them to go to the furniture shop. The bed and the dressing table for the newly weds had to be installed in the new flat.

"You go home after that," Mr Dayaram was all benevolence.

Avijit loved the thought of reaching home early. But it was a full two and a half hours before they reached the flat. A political meeting was in progress and the roads were clogged with traffic. The flat was on the second floor of a beautifully painted building and it took another half hour to pull up the furniture. They had to be careful not to damage the walls or the marble stairs. Once in the flat, Avijit and Munna rested on one of the plush sofas whilst the carpenters got busy setting up the furniture.

The flat was fully decorated except for the bedroom and had all the comforts the rich were privileged to own. Avijit wondered how it would feel to stay in a house as luxurious as this. Not very gratifying, he concluded. He would be scared all the time of staining the walls or breaking valuable furniture. His home was much better. He had no fear of falling off the bed during sleep, as there was no space between the bed and the wall on three sides. It was a short hop to the bathroom and the main door. In a house as big as this, one's legs would ache in trying to move from one end to the other. He had no telephone at home to disturb him in the night and no wealth to conceal and sweat over, every minute of the day. Avijit was convinced God needed a crash course in distribution management. The Lord had made a mess of it. There would only be glitter at one end of the city and gloom over the rest if things continued this way.

He had to report again the next day at his boss's residence. It was the day of the wedding and the house was crowded with relations and well-wishers. Avijit was asked to help in parking the cars. The day was sultry and the guests came in droves. Avijit found it difficult to manage the traffic on the narrow road, as vehicles came from both sides. The line of cars parked at one end made it even narrower and led to commotion. There were loud honks all around. Mr Dayaram's neighbours unlike those of Avijit's locality, were not too cooperative. They were egotistical islands in this ocean of wealth. A few even came up to Avijit to enquire what was going on.

"Your stupid car is blocking my door. Move it or else ..." a man threatened from a verandah.

A car was indeed parked near the door, though there was enough space between the two for an elephant to pass.

"I'm calling the police," the man ran back into his house, when the driver refused to move his car in spite of Avijit's request.

Avijit ran from one end to the other, trying to direct the crowd and the cars. He could appreciate the difficulty of a traffic policeman's job and vowed not to curse them again while stranded in a traffic jam. The guests started leaving in the late afternoon, to dress themselves up for the evening and flaunt their wealth. Avijit hoped to be a witness to all that. But Mr Dayaram didn't want to waste an extra meal on an employee.

"You must be tired, so go home and rest. Report to the office tomorrow morning and finish the pending work. I may be late."

Avijit heard the sound of the harmonium and then his mother's sweet voice the moment he stepped through their door. His mother was singing! He couldn't believe his ears and slowly tiptoed into the room. His mother, her eyes closed in concentration, was singing in the soft voice that lulled him to sleep in his childhood. The person who had coaxed it out from its exile was busy playing the harmonium. Sraboni stopped the moment she saw Avijit. It made his mother open her eyes and stop singing. She seemed a little embarrassed and immediately got anxious about him.

"How was the day son? You look tired. Will you have some puffed rice and tea?"

She told him that Sraboni wanted her to participate in a musical soiree to commemorate Rabindra Jayanti. She could not make up her mind and wanted Avijit to decide for her, whether she should sing at Tagore's birth anniversary celebrations.

"But what is there to decide?" Avijit was happy to see his mother her normal self. "You must participate."

Sraboni informed her that rehearsals would be held every evening at the Ghosh residence and invited Avijit too.

"But I can't sing!" Avijit was terrified.

"I know that silly. Be an audience."

'Let me get you some tea," his mother left for the kitchen.

Avijit did not feel uncomfortable talking to Sraboni in the confines of his home. She was busy covering the harmonium, a few beads of sweat plastering the hair onto her forehead. She looked up and caught him staring.

"Don't stare, silly. You'll strain your eyes." Her laughter reminded him of tingling bells.

"I will if I wish to."

"Why?"

"I like you."

Sraboni lowered her eyes and blushed. "It doesn't give you the right to stare. You look dumb," she crossed her eyes and wagged her tongue at him. "I never knew you could be so silly," she added.

"Why?"

"*Why*? We could meet every evening during the rehearsals. But no! You would rather follow me to the bus stop every morning!"

"What makes you think I follow you every morning? What for?"

"Then don't disturb me anymore in the mornings. I don't like to see silly faces after waking up. It spoils my entire day."

"Well, you stupid girl, I never disturbed you in the first place. You forcibly bumped into my life. And I am not desperate to meet you, I never was."

His words made Sraboni serious. She refused to look at him and Avijit was worried she might cry. His mother returned with two bowlfuls of puffed rice and tea for them. She seemed oblivious of the charged atmosphere. Sraboni did not speak to Avijit for the rest of her stay. He offered to accompany her home, but she refused and stomped out all by herself. Avijit was too tired to bother and decided to have an early dinner and sleep off his tiredness.

CHAPTER Three

Avijit didn't meet Sraboni for the whole of the next week. The days passed by in monotony. In between, he and Ujjal paid a visit to Chandan. The latter seemed to be in a great mood and herded them into his room.

"I've made it," he exulted, even before they had sat down on the bed. "My cassette should be out within a month."

Before the others could react, Chandan had turned on the expensive music system, the lone item in the room that looked clean. A familiar voice was singing and it took Avijit a while to identify it as his friend's. Chandan had recorded ten of his own compositions with a music company. They had given him a demo-cassette and three thousand rupees as the first installment.

"You can have my autographed cassette later," he beamed, "let's celebrate."

"How much is the contract for?" Ujjal had asked.

"Well, I will know when I sign it. I'll be rich and famous soon."

"But you recorded all the songs without a formal contract!" Ujjal couldn't hide the surprise in his voice, "that's not very clever."

Avijit was happy someone close to him had realized his dream. He thought Ujjal was too skeptical. The songs were well composed and beautifully sung. Chandan had responded to an advertisement in the papers by a music company, promising to promote young talent free of cost. His work had been selected from a few hundred.

"It was a great experience. The music playing through my earphones and I singing into the microphone. I had never felt so good. It was even better than having an orgasm!" Chandan sighed deeply.

Avijit and Ujjal exchanged knowing glances. All three being bachelors, had to depend on their own trusted hands, to bring them occasional relief from the cruel world. They never thought anything could be better than the momentary pleasure, except possibly the real thing. Though Chandan insisted, Ujjal agreed to celebrate only after the contract was signed. That it was prudent was to be proved later.

Avijit got busy with his office again and decided not to meet Sraboni on his own. It seemed the ice had not melted at her end either, as there had been no attempts at reconciliation. He felt morose and lonely, but knew they would meet on Sunday during the Rabindra Jayanti celebrations. It was Wednesday night when Ujjal came and knocked on his door. Avijit had just finished his dinner and was thumbing through a sports magazine. Ujjal looked tense and wanted Avijit to come with him.

"The music company has cheated Chandan and he has broken down," Ujjal said glumly.

Chandan looked tired and weary indeed.

"I have no reason to live anymore. It took me two years to compose those songs and in two days they have been credited to someone else," Chandan couldn't hide the disbelief in his eyes.

He had gone to meet the owner of the music company for his formal contract. The man had initially dismissed him, giving one excuse or the other.

"The compositions are not as good as I had thought. We have decided not to bring out the cassette."

But Chandan had persisted and was almost on his knees, when someone had barged into the room.

"Boss, it is good," the smart looking young man hugged the thick set owner. "How could a diabetic like you compose such sweet songs! What was the first song...... yeah....." and he had started singing the first few lines from one of Chandan's compositions.

It had taken Chandan a while to realize that it was Kumar Probir, a singer of repute, who had come into the room. The owner had not been flustered. He had calmly requested Kumar Probir to wait outside and turned to Chandan.

"Look, your songs are good, but no one buys a cassette unless it is by an established artist. Probir will do justice to the songs and I paid you for the singing rights. I have your signed receipt to that effect. So don't disturb me again."

Avijit realized the world was no more a place for the true and the simple.

"Don't give up," he warned Chandan, "if you could compose ten songs in two years, I'm sure you can compose a few more. Try again, you may be lucky the next time."

Ujjal wanted to go and meet the owner and thrash him, but desisted in the end. The incident had a depressing effect on all of Avijit's activities. He went through the motions of his daily chores for the next couple of days. His only joy was his mother, who was cheerful after a long time. As the day of her concert came closer, she became a little nervous, but shed it the moment Avijit reminded her that she would be singing in a group.

They had an early lunch on Sunday and his mother left for the venue at around three in the afternoon. The soiree was in the evening and Avijit decided to listen to some music to kill time. He must have dozed off and woke at the sound of loud banging on their front door. He glanced at the clock. It was almost five. Who could be banging at their door? He put on a shirt over his jeans and hurried towards the door. The banging had not stopped and he was suddenly worried about his mother. Had anything happened to her? He quickly opened the door. Sraboni looked exasperated, having had to bang on the old termite smitten woodwork with her soft hands. She looked beautiful too in a red saree. Avijit kept staring at her and even forgot to ask her in. Sraboni brushed past Avijit and moved towards his mother's room.

"Just a minute lady. May I know what it is that you want? You are entering my house without my permission," Avijit couldn't believe his luck.

"Throw me out if you can," Sraboni sat down on his mother's bed, "well, it seems you have lost your job. I don't see the great employee of Dayaram & Company going to office early as he used to till a week back."

"My boss has hired a beautiful young secretary and my work load has gone down. I can reach office late."

"I see. So you report to your boss's secretary now? That's great. She must be making you run like an errand boy."

"I never said I report to her. She is junior to me and I'm busy teaching her the basics of office work."

Avijit wanted the conversation to last an eternity.

"Well, don't teach her to be silly," Sraboni took his mother's notation book, which was lying on the bed. His mother must have forgotten it in her hurry and sad sent Sraboni to collect it. But Sraboni was leaving!

"You seem to be in a terrible hurry. I was making some tea. You can join in," Avijit hated making tea. But he couldn't think of anything better to stop her.

"Okay, only if it is ready. The concert will commence at six and your mother will worry if I don't get back soon," Sraboni sat down.

Avijit ran into the kitchen and poured two cups of water into the saucepan. He fidgeted with the burner but couldn't light it.

"Let me do it for you," Sraboni had come into the kitchen. "You can't even light the burner! You are not only silly, but also equally lazy. God help the girl who marries you."

"And may the Almighty come to the aid of the guy who ties the knot with you. The lady with the rapier tongue."

They came back to the room, leaving the tea to brew. Avijit had never felt so good in his life.

"How was college last week?" he asked.

"Couldn't have been better. I didn't have to see silly faces in the morning. It helped."

"But you are with a silly person all alone in this house. What if he did something silly?" he took a step towards her.

"Oh, I don't think he has the guts to do anything, does he?" she seemed to challenge him.

Avijit caught her hand and pulled her up. She was surprised by his sudden move and was about to protest. But he raised her face towards him and kissed her deeply. She initially resisted and then slowly gave in. Her lips seemed to melt under Avijit's. They parted as suddenly as they had united, lest things got out of hand. Free mixing was not a virtue and sex between the unmarried was taboo in their world.

"Let me get the tea," Sraboni couldn't look him in the eyes.

Avijit followed her into the kitchen. He was dumbstruck by the experience and was worried Sraboni might be upset with his behaviour.

"I'm sorry. It just happened. I couldn't control myself," he blurted out, after they had finished the tea silently.

Sraboni took the book and moved towards the door. She turned back and gave him a captivating smile. "Don't be sorry silly! It felt good," and with that she flung open the door and quickly departed.

Avijit felt ecstatic! Sraboni did care for him then. He quickly dressed and reached the venue. It was a full house. The participants sang with devotion and the event was a success. He went backstage and found his mother with a couple of ladies, basking in the satisfaction of a job well done. He left her with her friends and was about to turn for home, when Mr Ghosh called out to him.

"Your mother sang so well! Such a talent would have remained behind your four walls had I not visited your home," he smiled proudly.

"I must thank you sir. It was you who could get her out of her shell," Avijit replied.

"But I'm still worried about you. My club is yet to decide on recruitment for the next season. I'll be a happy man the day you start playing for my club," Mr Ghosh seemed to have taken a particular liking for Avijit.

Avijit wondered what the armyman would do, if he came to know that his daughter had been kissed passionately by the vagabond standing in front of him. Would he blow his nut off?

"Where the hell have these people gone?" Mr Ghosh looked around in frustration, "they asked me to give them just five more minutes. Really, women can never be trusted."

But mother and daughter did seem concerned as they arrived together shortly.

"Where had you been?" Mr Ghosh couldn't hide his displeasure, "don't you know its time for my dinner?"

"Why?" Mrs Ghosh retorted, "you asked us to wait near the podium. We wait for you and you chatter here. Don't you ever get tired?"

Sraboni raised her eyes and looked skywards.

"Now, don't you two get into a fight again! Let's go. I'll have to catch the eight o'clock bus to college tomorrow," she pulled Mr Ghosh by the elbow.

"I'll also take your leave. I've to go to office early too and I better get back now."

And thus their morning rendezvous was confirmed.

They sat together on the bus for the first time the next morning.

"Do you watch movies?" Sraboni asked, after the conductor had given them back the change.

Avijit couldn't remember the name of the last movie he had seen. It must have been well over a year back, before his father died.

"Would you like to watch one with me?" Avijit felt a lot more confident with her now and his voice didn't quiver.

"I can, but only if it is in the afternoon. Dad could end up calling both the ambulance and police if I don't reach home by evening. I can come with you this Friday," Sraboni suggested.

"But what movie would you like to see?" Avijit knew nothing about current movies.

"Well there is an English movie running at the hall near our college. I hear it's a great love story. Let's go and watch it."

Avijit's heart soared. At last things were moving his way. Sraboni was definitely in love with him. Otherwise why would she suggest watching a love story?

"First let me get my boss's sanction," Avijit was never sure with the man.

Mr Dayaram was in a very foul mood and shouted at him without provocation. But Avijit would have forgiven his boss even if he had slapped him. Everything felt so good after a long time and the hours swept past. He realised it was time to go home, once his boss marched out of the office with Munna in tow. Avijit followed. He was dreaming of Sraboni in one corner of the bus when a woman, seated a few seats in front of him, cried out. It jolted him out of his stupor. A lanky youth was trying to snatch the lady's purse, in full view of her fellow passengers. The lady was protesting and begging for help, but no one dared to challenge the thief. He would have got away with the booty had not a big fist slammed into his face. Avijit felt he was facing his father's killer and followed up swiftly with another punch. The thief collapsed under the sudden impact and Avijit handed the bag back to the lady. But he was not ready for the violent kick from behind. He sprawled on top of the body that was yet to recover from his vicious punches. Three youths, who all along had been posing as innocent passengers, surrounded him.

"Bastard, want to be a hero? We will make you a martyr instead," one of them shouted, brandishing a knife.

The other passengers in the bus were mute spectators. The bus was still moving at it's normal pace, the driver oblivious of the happenings within. The youth, who was punched by Avijit, had recovered. He brought out a razor without a warning and slashed Avijit on the arm. He would have inflicted more bodily harm had one of his accomplices not stopped him. They shouted at the driver to stop the bus, took the bag and got down calmly, vanishing into the crowd on the pavement. Avijit's arm had gone numb, after he had felt something hot tearing at his flesh. He was still on the floor of the bus and blood was flowing freely from the deep gash. His co-passengers, assured that the threat was no more, rushed up to him for a closer look.

"Why did you get involved with such dangerous people?"

"Are you mad? Don't you know these people carry weapons? Could you stop them?"

"They did not rob you. Who the hell asked you to put all of us in mortal danger?"

It would have continued had not the lady, who had lost her bag, pushed them aside and knelt down beside him.

"He needs a doctor," she shouted.

"Hey, stop the bus at the next crossing. We will get a doctor there," an elderly man requested the driver.

He got down with Avijit and led him to the dispensary. Only the lady thanked him and advised him not to take such risks alone in the future. The rest of the passengers in the bus seemed relieved that the real threat was finally getting down and they could now finish their journey without further trouble.

Avijit got his arm stitched and bandaged. His mother, initially hysterical at the sight of his torn and bloodstained shirt, calmed down after he explained that it was a minor cut. She ordered him to rest and went into the kitchen to cook dinner. Avijit was still in a state of shock. He was appalled at the reaction of the passengers on the bus. Had even a few of them helped, the four dacoits would have been behind bars. The new age heralded an obsession with the self, forcing people to distance themselves from the distressed. It was easy to terrorize the common man today and the scum of society could rob or rape with ease. Qualities like courage and chivalry could rarely be found outside of books.

Mr Dayaram agreed to let him off on Friday afternoon after much persuasion. The workload was not too high and Avijit could easily manage the backlog the next day. He reached the movie hall only to be disappointed. All the tickets were sold! He wanted to kick himself for not having bought them the previous day.

"You want tickets?" a youth asked him.

"Yes, two," Avijit couldn't believe his luck.

The youth brought out a thick bunch of tickets from his pocket and handed Avijit two after pocketing a hefty premium. The box seats were expensive enough to cost him a tenth of his salary, but Avijit wanted to impress Sraboni. She arrived just before the show was to start and they bought peanuts and potato chips. The movie was a touching love story, but had a few steamy scenes. Avijit felt terribly embarrassed whenever the screen showed the couple making frenzied love. The audience broke into cat-calls and whistles. He was relieved once the show was over. Sraboni seemed to have enjoyed the film and suggested they come again the next week to watch a new one.

His uncle was waiting for him when Avijit reached home.

"Since you have forgotten me," he remarked the moment Avijit touched his feet, "I came over."

It was true. His uncle maintained regular contact by calling him up at office or dropping by at their home at least once a month. But

Avijit had not paid him a visit ever since they had moved out.

"Thanks to the job, I've no time for myself," Avijit said.

It felt good to have his uncle at their home. But for him, they would have been swept away to oblivion by the currents of the acquisitive world. They chatted about his office for sometime, before his uncle broke the news.

"Khokon is coming home tomorrow. Both you and Avijit must come over on Sunday morning," his uncle told his mother. "He will be here for a month and I plan to find a match for him. At least someone who can give him company in the far away land."

Khokon was almost a half decade older than Avijit. In his early years in school, both families met twice in a year – once when his parents came down with him to Calcutta and again when his uncle reciprocated by visiting Rajpur. His father and uncle thus spent some time together, and Avijit and Khokon developed a friendship of their own. His uncle had not built his house then and they stayed in the southern part of Calcutta. Avijit was always over-awed by the big city and it was Khokon, who took it upon himself to educate the village boy. He was the first to inform Avijit that God did not gift babies, as was the popular belief amongst his classmates. It was the teenie-weenie thing between his legs, which had a major role to play. Khokon showed some pictures to convince the hapless kid that his wisdom was beyond doubt. Avijit was in class five then and became the most sought after guy in school. A friendship with him meant a peek at those pictures, proudly gifted to a loyal disciple by the resourceful guru. The guru mesmerised Avijit's friends at Rajpur with his wisdom. Avijit could never forget how he got initiated into masturbation. Khokon had brought a book full of lewd pictures and Avijit and his closest friends were gawking at them in his bedroom. It was afternoon and their parents had gone to watch a movie. Khokon mentioned something about "jacking off", at which the others stared blankly.

"Don't tell me you don't know how to jack off!"

The silence and the dull stares made Khokon realise that the creatures in front were truly deprived and he needed to pass on his wisdom.

"Okay, do you know the six steps to peeing?" the dull stares did not waver "shit, what place is this? A village?"

And he imparted the knowledge in a very professional way.

"Look, step one is unbuttoning fly. Step two is taking out 'Moby Dick'. Step three is uncovering the skin. Step four is pissing. Step five is pulling back the skin. Step six is putting the treasure back and buttoning up fly. Well, start and go up to step three. Then only repeat step five and three as many times as you need."

All the disciples had a look of enlightenment in the eyes and a smile on the face, the next day. It was in Rajpur again, a few years later that the unrelenting guru introduced Avijit to a new wonder. It was another hot afternoon. Avijit's father and uncle had gone out and the ladies were having a short nap. Avijit was reading a Tintin comic in his room. He suddenly noticed Khokon, peeping out of the window in a curious way.

"What are you doing?" he got up and approached the window.

Khokon wanted him to peep out. Their room was adjacent to another flat in the next building. Avijit peered through the curtains to find he was looking directly into the bedroom. The curtains of the room were not fully drawn and he could clearly see inside. The lady of the house was standing in front of a mirror, with her back towards them. She was completely nude and busy looking at herself, oblivious of two roving pairs of eyes which were equally critical, and took in each and every curve of her young and luscious body. She turned towards them, her assets in clear display and Avijit ducked to escape notice. He couldn't breathe. It felt as if he had run a mile. He was in a moral dilemma; one part rebuking him for having sinned and violated someone's privacy; the other urging him to have another look. Khokon was unperturbed and continued on his voyage of ecstasy. Avijit vowed many times not to repeat it, only to break the vow. It remained a dark secret in his otherwise ascetic life.

Khokon became serious about his career after joining the engineering college and they met less frequently. They had met for the last time in Rajpur, three years back. Khokon, a graduate chemical engineer, was taking up a job in the United States as a software programmer.

"There are no decent jobs for my discipline in this country," he had mentioned, "I might land a job in sales and marketing – possibly developing strategies to sell tampons!"

They were sitting on the banks of the Bhairab and Khokon threw pebbles absentmindedly into the gushing waters.

"What a waste of four years of pain and hard work," he had shaken his head sadly.

Khokon had gone away to the faraway land and there had been no more communication. Avijit was eager to meet his childhood hero.

CHAPTER Four

His uncle was having breakfast when they reached his house on Sunday. Khokon was asleep, yet to adjust to the time lag. Avijit's uncle and aunt looked excited. The return of their son seemed to have removed the veil of loneliness and melancholy that had enveloped their lives. The prodigal son woke up only around noon, when the others were ready for lunch. He had put on weight and his face glowed with the shine of fulfilment. They hugged each other, the guru and his disciple, both with a full heart, ready to pour out the joy and sorrow of the years of separation.

"It was terrible to hear of uncle's death. Have the killers been caught?" Khokon asked, once they had finished an extravagant lunch. "Is this democracy? A person is killed in broad daylight and the murderers move around freely. This is simply crazy!" he exploded, after Avijit shook his head.

Avijit didn't want to open up the unhealed wound, as it always led to pain. He never understood why somebody should kill a simple person like his father.

"Well, how is life in the States?" he asked instead.

They were sitting in Khokon's room, the elders in the drawing room were watching television.

"It certainly is different from this place. Fresh air and lot less people on the roads. Its stuffy here with all this pollution," Khokon sniffed the air suspiciously and decided to add his part to the environment by lighting a cigarette. "The first thing that hits you there is the cleanliness. Its spic and span and no one urinates on the roadside. There is discipline, which is sadly lacking here. Life is very comfortable," Khokon finished in one breath. It certainly showed in the pinkness of his health. "But tell me, what have you been up to all these years? Where all have you been sowing your seed? Not into space I hope!" Khokon was sounding his old self.

He was disappointed to hear of Avijit's austere life style and described his own escapades.

"Free mixing is the buzzword there. If a girl likes you, it is natural to bed her. Why create inhibitions all around and be a mental wreck when you have been born free? I think marriage and all is a sham."

Avijit was feeling uncomfortable. He had never thought of sex without a feeling of love. Ever since meeting Sraboni, he could not imagine falling for another girl. And his mentor was busy perpetuating the virtues of free sex.

"But uncle is finalising your marriage," he informed Khokon.

The latter was reclining on the bed and the news made him sit up. He looked at Avijit in disbelief.

"Don't tell me! He must be mad. How can he decide about my marriage without asking me? I must stop him," Khokon got up and went towards the drawing room to confront his father.

Avijit rushed up and pulled Khokon back into the room. He didn't want his uncle and aunt to be shaken out of their temporary bliss.

"Relax, nothing is final yet. I'm sorry. I shouldn't have raised the topic."

Avijit's worry reduced only after Khokon took up his earlier position on the bed.

"Look man, I thought I'll tell you later. You'll have to convince my parents that I cannot marry."

Avijit's worry returned. He had heard stories of fingers being cut off as a penalty for adultery in the conservative countries of the world. Had a similar fate befallen Khokon? Had something precious been cut off? Khokon doubled up on hearing this and had tears in his eyes by the time he could stop laughing.

"Silly goat, I'm not in a jungle but the US of A. Even if something is accidentally cut off, they can put it back before you can blink. I cannot marry because of Sally," he said.

"Who is Sally? Your girlfriend? Oh, great. Then you are in love!" Avijit was happy for his bohemian guru. "So when is the marriage?"

"Dear Avijit, don't confuse your world with mine. You need not be in love to stay together. Sally is from Australia. We went to the US around the same time and worked for the same company. I have left the organization, but we are still friends. You see, I save half the money on rent by staying together. Yeah, we did make love a few times, but that doesn't mean we are in love and will marry."

Avijit was very confused. He still could not understand why it was difficult for Khokon to marry. His mentor seemed to read his mind and continued while puffing on a second cigarette.

"I cannot ask Sally to leave for nothing. If I marry, my wife may not agree to share the apartment with her. Imagine the increase in my expenditure then! I must stop Dad," Khokon was getting agitated again.

"Don't worry. You simply reject each and every girl. Give some excuse or the other."

"Ah, that's clever I say," Khokon seemed to like the idea, "anyway, forget it. Let me show what I got for you."

Khokon got up and opened one of the two suitcases lying near the bed.

"I hope you like it," he handed over the goodies to Avijit – a pair of sneakers and a bottle of perfume.

Avijit still wore the sneakers gifted by his father four years back. It was worn out and uncomfortable. He thanked his cousin.

His week at the office would have been uneventful had not a tall man, wearing a grey safari suit, visited on Friday afternoon. Avijit was sitting opposite his boss, when the man arrived unannounced.

"My name is Dastidar and I own a company manufacturing plastic houseware. I need five metric tonnes of polypropylene urgently," he sat down without being asked to.

"Well, let me see if we have any stock."

Avijit was by now adept at predicting his boss's replies. Mr Dayaram always tried to judge the customer's urgency before quoting his price. The more the desperation, the higher the price.

"Sorry sir. We do have some stock but it is already booked for one of our regular customers. I cannot offer you anything today," Mr Dayaram told the man, after glancing through the register that maintained the electricity and phone bill payments.

"I'm willing to pay any price for the material. I need it badly. You must help me out," the man pleaded.

"But how can I ditch a loyal customer?" Mr Dayaram seemed pained at the plight of his fictitious client.

"So that's final then? You can't help me?" the customer looked disappointed and ready to leave.

"Um, well, if you insist then I have to find a way out," Mr Dayaram seemed lost in thought, "but you will have to lift seven metric tonnes, as that was what my customer had booked. He would never lift the remaining two tonnes if I give you five."

Avijit sometimes wondered who had trained his boss into the cunning and ruthless businessman that he was.

"Okay, I agree, but you have still not quoted your price," the customer was almost won.

His boss quoted a ten percent higher price than the prevailing market rate.

"I accept but I need to discuss something else," the customer looked around suspiciously, glancing at Avijit and then back at Mr Dayaram.

Avijit knew what was coming and waited for his boss's signal to leave. But Mr Dayaram wanted to put up an united stand.

"Don't worry. He is my employee. You can discuss anything freely." he said.

"I don't want to pay tax on the purchase. Can it be organized?" the customer was matter of fact.

"Oh sure," Mr Dayaram's face lit up, as he smelled an extra profit.

"But how is it possible?" the customer asked in a low voice, "what about the tax authorities?"

"Well, that's my problem. You pay me cash and take the material from my warehouse. There won't be any records," Mr Dayaram was eager to settle the deal quickly.

"No, no. Please don't misunderstand me. But I must know the procedure. It will help me avoid the nuisance on my sale too. Just how can you do it so easily?" the man seemed to marvel at Mr Dayaram's expertise.

The latter spat out the paan-masala paste and smiled in sympathy for the guy, who in spite of being in business, did not know the road to easy profits. He poured some more of the betel nut powder into his mouth and proceeded to enlighten the customer.

"How often do you do this?" Mr Dastidar asked in a stern voice when the sermon was over. His sheepishness had gone and he had a stern look on his face.

"What do you mean?" Mr Dayaram was a trifle perplexed.

"I asked how many times have you done this before?" the customer got up and leaned towards them over the table.

"Never," Mr Dayaram replied flatly, "and may I know who the hell you are to ask me this?"

The tall man stretched up to his full height and produced his identity card. He was from the vigilance department. He repeated his question. Avijit, who was sweating profusely in the air-conditioned room, got up to leave.

"Sit right where you are, young man," the sharp command made him drop back on the chair.

The officer walked up to the door and called in three more men. One of them sat with Avijit, while the others entered Dayaram's cubicle. Avijit had nothing much to offer, as he had never been a party to the shady deals his boss struck with the clients. The man got bored and picked up a glossy film magazine lying on the table. The ordeal continued till late evening and Avijit was scared that he might be arrested. He was finally called in. Files were lying scattered on the table, but the four men looked calm.

"Get some refreshments quickly. Should I arrange some hard drinks sir?" Mr Dayaram was all smiles.

"Don't bother. We are on duty," Mr Dastidar said in a mocking voice.

Mr. Dayaram came out and gave him the money. Avijit's first instinct, the moment he was outside, was to run away. But then he would lose his job. He decided to stay calm and went down for the snacks. The food smelled good and he served it to everyone. The officers munched on the food, while he sat silently on the sofa biting his nails. It was a tense half hour wait before he was asked to clear the plates.

"You need to pay us the full amount now. We cannot wait till tomorrow, as we have to file the report today," Mr Dastidar said.

"But sir, how can I arrange so much money at such short notice?" Mr Dayaram pleaded.

"Fine. We seal the office now."

The officer noted Avijit's presence and paused. Mr Dayaram looked on impatiently as Avijit cleaned the table. No more words were spoken till he was there. It was another hour before they came out.

"I have a request sir," Avijit overheard his boss, "you need not come again. I'll honour your request, but you must promise me total freedom in my business. There should be no raids from your department. I am a weak hearted person and cannot bear rude shocks."

It was one vulture trying to extract as much of the carcass possible from the other, each ensuring the death of a nation in their own small way.

"You keep your commitment and we will keep ours."

"Bastards!" Mr Dayaram exploded, the moment they had left, "come with me, I will drop you home."

They locked the office and went down.

"It might sound strange, but I also started this business as innocent as you," Mr. Dayaram seemed smitten by his conscience, "I wanted to be honest and sincere. I moved from office to office, table to bench, for a sales tax registration, but could not get it in six months. Then someone told me to pay three thousand rupees and got me the registration in two days. That's when I understood the power of money. You may be a great scholar, but without money you do not exist. I know this is wrong. But it is the rule. Follow it or you perish."

Avijit was surprised at his boss's words. It seemed the loss of money had made him self-righteous. But for how long? He was afraid Saint Dayaram might suddenly decide to close shop and become a sage. Avijit would then have to fend for his family by begging on the roads.

Avijit spent the weekend with Khokon.

"Let's have dinner outside," Khokon suggested, "I've missed Calcutta all these years."

They set out for the city in a hired car. The sun's last rays made the sky blush pink like a new bride. It had a tranquil stillness, in sharp contrast to the commotion of the evening traffic.

"What are your thoughts on the future? Have you made any plans?" Khokon seemed to have been effortlessly transformed into his childhood guru again.

Avijit was never comfortable with such questions. He wanted to be a footballer and had never really thought ahead of that. But it looked a distant dream. He had not completed his studies and was slowly realizing that without a formal education, society would pull him down. It would also mean a bleak future for his relationship with Sraboni. He hoped Khokon could guide him out of this impasse.

"Well I'm totally lost; I cannot hope to grow in my current job, but have no option either," he summed up.

The Calcutta summer had set in and the air was hot and humid. Khokon asked the chauffeur to drive down to the riverbank. They bought ice creams and sat on one of the empty benches. The Ganges flowed below them, an eagerness to reach the sea palpable as that could mean an end to its long journey. They sat in silence, the peace and quiet occasionally broken by the distant rumble of a ship's siren or the excited voices of revellers.

"You learn software," Khokon said, after slurping up a small portion of the ice-cream, which threatened to spill over the biscuit cone. "There is a great demand for software professionals abroad. Computers are an essential part of human life today. New developments are taking place everyday, which leaves a lot of scope for new entrants. I suggest you join a full time course."

"Then I have to give up my job!" Avijit's meagre salary sustained the family. Without it, they could be on the streets. "That's impossible. And where do I get the money to complete a software course?"

"Money is no problem," Khokon wiped his mouth with the paper napkin and threw it into the Ganges. "You take a loan from me. Return it once you are settled in life."

Avijit was touched by the gesture. But he didn't want to burden himself further.

"I'll think it over," was his non-committal reply.

"You do that and let me know," Khokon consulted his watch. "Hey, I'm hungry. Let's go and have dinner."

Khokon got down on Park Street and marched towards one of the many restaurants located on both sides of the road.

"This used to be my favourite joint. Just try out the Baked Alaska once and you will fall in love with it."

Khokon though was not ready for the rude reception inside.

"Do you have a reservation, sir?" a smart young man stepped forward and blocked their way.

"Not exactly. I would need a table for two," Khokon tried to move in, but the man stood his ground.

"I'm sorry, sir. All our tables are reserved tonight," the man shrugged.

"But I used to be regular here and am coming after a long time. Surely, I deserve better service than this," Khokon smiled at the man.

It worked.

"I can arrange a table if you kindly wait for sometime, sir."

"The biggest problem in this country is population," Khokon exploded, the moment they were outside again. "This is simply crazy. There is a queue everywhere; wherever you go, whatever you do. I think we spend a third of our life waiting in queues. Imagine the hours lost! But then no one is bothered." They were standing on the pavement along with a few other hopefuls and Khokon was fuming.

Luckily, they got a seat within twenty minutes and Khokon's anger subsided only after a sip of the expensive scotch. Avijit had settled for an orange juice and helped himself to the fried prawns they had ordered. The restaurant was full with the weekend crowd and the air was charged with high notes of excitement. He noticed a couple occupying a table to their right. The young and smart looking man had put an arm around his lady love and both were absorbed in each other. He too hoped to sit like that with Sraboni someday. Khokon ordered a lot of food ignoring Avijit's protest; the latter worried that the bill might cross his monthly income.

"Are you on a diet or something? You must try out the kebabs at this place," Khokon orderd dishes Avijit had never tasted before.

Khokon was sipping on his third whiskey and Avijit had just finished the last of the boti-kebab when it happened. A man, who looked in his late thirties, rushed in and went up to the couple Avijit had noticed earlier. He slapped the girl full on her face without a provocation. The sound of the slap and the girl's cry silenced the noisy diners.

"You dirty bitch, you are enjoying yourself here with this bastard!" the man shouted at the top of his voice.

A few diners had overcome the shock and rushed towards the table to prevent the man from hitting the girl again. The young and smart looking man who had been sitting with the girl all along, was strangely silent.

"Believe me, she's my wife. I've been trying to locate her for the past hour. My three-year-old daughter is crying herself hoarse for her. Wait, I will get my daughter," the man ventured out, only to be back with a little girl in his arms a few moments later. The couple across the table got up to leave, but sat down the moment they saw him coming.

"Oh Mummy! I was waiting for you all evening. You promised to read me Red Riding Hood after dinner. I'm hungry," the child wailed.

"I'm waiting outside. You come immediately," the man walked out of the restaurant, leaving the other diners in peace.

But the peace was short lived. The young lady had covered her face and wept silently. The smart looking young man seemed nonchalant, till one of the diners who looked a little drunk, moved threateningly towards him.

"You leaking-nut-hole, enjoying the forbidden fruit. I will cut off your balls."

Thankfully, he didn't quite carry out his threat though he poured a glassful of water on the guy's head. All hell would have broken loose had Khokon not sprung up from his chair and positioned himself between the two.

"Just relax," he told the young man. "Move out from there," Khokon seemed familiar with the rear exit. The couple didn't waste another minute and went out.

Avijit had lost his appetite and wanted to leave, though Khokon looked unperturbed.

"Oh, it happens, don't worry," he sounded experienced in such matters.

"How can you be so cool? I can't believe a lady leaves her husband and child at home, and enjoys dinner with another man!"

"Tell me, why didn't the father cook the child's dinner? This is the problem with Indian males. You guys consider the wife as an all-purpose servant. She has to do all the boring things like cooking, washing and cleaning at home, while you guys have official lunches and dinners at the best places in town. I know of people who even expect their wives to massage their bodies when they come back home. And then you throw her on the bed and get between her legs for instant release," Khokon shook his head sadly.

"Don't you believe the girl was at fault?" Avijit protested.

"What is wrong if she enjoys a meal with someone?" Khokon

shocked Avijit. "How do you know the man takes good care of her? Don't believe everything you see," his guru seemed to have the ultimate wisdom in such matters.

But Avijit could not forget the child's anguish. What wrong had she done to deserve this? He decided not to have the famous *Baked Alaska* for dessert, in spite of Khokon's insistence. The other diners continued with their meal and enjoyment, as if nothing had happened. He already hated the place and felt relieved, once Khokon settled the bill.

"It's sad but we are blindly aping the west," Khokon seemed sober even after the three whiskeys. "Why can't we pick up good things like discipline, punctuality and work culture? I have seen a lot of my college mates getting hooked on drugs. Most must be leading a life in darkness today," Khokon seemed genuinely pained.

They had got into the car and were homeward bound.

"You will be surprised how much respect the West has for Indian culture. Sally always asks me about yoga and spiritualism. She believes every Indian has mastered them. God help us if she comes down here!" Khokon chuckled.

"But I thought you were all for free sex and the West," Avijit mocked.

"*I salute thee my motherland, I am your long lost son*," Khokon suddenly shouted.

It made the chauffeur brake with all his might. He continued only after Khokon assured him that every thing was fine.

"It really hurts when I see my City of Joy dying this cruel death,"

Khokon continued in a lower pitch, "its people famed for their humanity and hospitality, gradually becoming an unknown race. Their unique culture of brotherhood and empathy, under threat from the selfish and commercial. The green getting covered by concrete. The romantic being pushed behind by the lustful. I could not remain a mute spectator to this destruction of my birthplace, but neither could I stop the vandals. So I charted out my self imposed exile. It's not easy to stay away from your dear ones. But then I need not face it every day. That's a big relief."

Avijit saw Khokon in a new light. He had never imagined so much anguish beneath the cheerful face. They finished the rest of their journey in silence.

"Do not plan anything tomorrow evening. We will be visiting the Chatterjees to introduce you to their daughter," Khokon's mother announced, the moment they set foot inside the house.

"What for?" Khokon asked innocently.

"The Chatterjees have proposed their daughter's marriage to you," she answered carefully, "see if you like her."

Khokon's parents were concerned about their son's lonely life abroad and wanted him to marry. But they didn't want to push him into a situation he wouldn't endorse. The subject was not discussed again till the next morning.

"This is not right. I should not join this circus," Khokon was visibly upset, "how can I give an impression of willingness by visiting these people, when I know I can never marry the girl?"

"But how are you so confident that the girl will like you?" Avijit tried to make it easy for his otherwise exuberant guru.

Khokon looked tense throughout the day. It was perhaps the only occasion when Avijit had seen his cousin so nervous. The four of them set out in the evening, with his uncle at the wheel.

"Get rid of this armoured car dad. We can afford to buy the best car in town," Khokon remarked, after his father had difficulty in changing gears.

"You'll never understand what this car means to us," his father remarked, "it was our dream come true. Certain things are priceless. I cannot change this car just like I cannot re-marry, though your mother has grey hair and lost a tooth."

They reached their destination shortly, a two storied building. It had a little garden in the front and a bright thatch of bougainvillea on both sides of the main entrance. Mr Chatterjee welcomed them and took everyone into a large drawing room. They took their seats on the sofa.

"You must be feeling uncomfortable with all the pollution and traffic jams here?" Mr Chatterjee asked Avijit, who stared back blankly. "Old cars are responsible for all this dirty air," Mr Chatterjee continued, "which car do you drive?"

"I don't own a car."

"Then how do you commute?" there was a surprised look on Mr Chatterjee's face.

"By bus," Avijit felt stupid having to face an interview to select his cousin's bride.

"Where exactly are you staying in the States?" the surprise on Mr Chatterjee's face was now replaced by concern.

"No, no, he is my brother's son Avijit. This is my son Khokon," his uncle cleared the confusion. There was laughter all around and relief on Mr Chatterjee's face.

"So what are your future plans? When do you intend to come back?" Mr Chatterjee was trying to know as much about Khokon as possible during the short meeting. After all, it was his daughter's future.

"I've no plans of coming back for the next five years. I do not know what can happen after that," Khokon replied softly.

"But it must be terrible to stay in a country as a second grade citizen?"

"Life is so comfortable there that you don't feel an outsider. And with the approach of the new millennium, computer professionals will be in demand because of the Y2K problem. You can never get such opportunities here," Khokon made it clear that he was first a professional and then a patriot.

The lady of the house came in with her daughter shortly. Introductions were made and courtesies exchanged. Avijit glanced at the girl and found her to be quite attractive. She was fair, with a good figure and looked an ideal match for Khokon. Refreshments were soon served and everyone got busy eating the samosas and drinking the rich aromatic tea.

"Well, why don't we elders go and sit in the balcony? Let them be comfortable here," Mr Chatterjee suggested and led the others out of the room.

Khokon looked nervous and was engrossed in an old magazine. Avijit decided to break the silence.

"So, what do you do?" he smiled and asked the girl.

She looked at him for a full minute before answering.

"Well, I get up late, brush my teeth, have the tea my mother prepares for me every morning, go and have a bath, then dress and have my breakfast, go to the bus stand, catch a bus, reach college, do some classes, bunk the rest, go for a movie or a theatre or simply chat with my friends, come back home, sit with my parents and watch TV, have dinner and then go to sleep. This is what I normally do," the girl thankfully ended.

Avijit wanted to hide his face behind a magazine like Khokon.

"Do you have high blood pressure or are you simply uncouth?" Khokon came out of his hiding for the first time.

"How dare you call me *uncouth*?" the girl rasped, "you may stay in the States, but don't think you are smart and the rest are uncouth."

"I never said that," Khokon interjected, "our parents want us to marry and you abuse me! I don't want to stay another minute."

There was a smile on the girl's face, as Khokon got up to leave.

"Ah, the foreign tiger leaves vanquished. Try your luck elsewhere. I always pity these ninnies who settle in a foreign land, but always come back home to marry the girl of their parent's choice. You know no foreign girl will accommodate your bloated male ego like the girl in your homeland."

Avijit felt bad and wanted to leave too. But Khokon had sat down again! It seemed he wanted to wage a fair war.

"Look, I can also call you names," he started, "but I would rather not. If you don't like me, tell me; that's okay. But please don't criticize my life-style, as it's none of your business. And I would strongly suggest that you do marry a ninny." Khokon paused for effect. "Otherwise a guy even half as tough as me, would throw you out the moment you open your loud mouth," he concluded with a grin.

The girl narrowed her eyes, as if to measure up Khokon, before the final assault. A holocaust was averted, as the girl's mother walked in with a tray full of mangoes.

"These are from my ancestral place," she said, "we were zamindars. Everything is gone now, but for a few houses and mango gardens." "It's a lovely place. You can spend your honeymoon there," she added with a wink.

She put the tray down on the table and served the mangoes in small plates. Khokon refused and Avijit wanted to follow suit, but the lady would have none of it.

"You are our guest. Please have a few."

Avijit looked at the girl from the corner of his eyes and she looked ready to burst. He still couldn't comprehend the cause of her rudeness. He thanked the Almighty for not making him go through this rigmarole of choosing a life partner. Sraboni had only floored him once and there was little threat of a repeat performance. He decided to finish the mangoes quickly before further trouble. They tasted delicious and he said as much to the lady, who immediately served a few more. Then she did what Avijit was desperately hoping she wouldn't

– she got up with the tray and left the room.

"You enjoy your chat. I won't eavesdrop," she winked again.

"How could you eat those mangoes after what had just happened?" Khokon exploded.

"Maybe he has never been to the States like you," the girl suggested, "you seem to have forgotten the basic Indian custom – like not to refuse food offered by an elderly person."

"Hey lady, tell me, what are you trying to prove?" Khokon sounded exasperated, "I tell you, I have no intention of getting married. I'm just doing this to please my parents. But why are you repeatedly attacking me and the lifestyle in a country you have never visited?"

"But Dad told me this marriage is as good as fixed," the girl stated in a much softer tone.

"Believe me, I'm in no hurry to marry. My parents never asked my opinion and I promise they will get it today. I'd come hoping to win a friend. But you have still not answered me," Khokon was turning on his best charm, "what exactly is your problem?"

"Can I bank on you two?"

Avijit was thankful that the girl still acknowledged his presence.

"I don't stand to gain anything by discussing your problem elsewhere. You can clear up the confusion, as otherwise I will remember you as the most eccentric female I've ever met. You might become a central character in my memoirs," Khokon concluded.

"I'm in love with someone else and we plan to marry," the girl finally said in a subdued tone.

"Oh, that's fantastic. Congratulations. Then where is the problem?" Khokon was comfortably settled on the sofa.

"He needs a little more time, as he is settling down in his first job," the girl continued, occasionally throwing a furtive glance towards the door, "he is also from a different caste and my parents won't approve my choice. We plan to marry quietly and leave."

"How do you know your parents won't approve your choice?" Khokon reasoned, "they might like him."

"What if they don't and get me married forcibly to someone else?"

"I don't think that's possible. Most of your suitors would beat a hasty retreat, if you behave as well as you did with us today," Khokon chuckled. "Maybe, you can put on your vanishing act then," he added as an afterthought.

"I'm not too sure you are right," the girl looked perturbed.

"Look, your parents can never do anything bad for you. And you will regret hurting them for the rest of your life. So take my suggestion. Tell them everything. You might be in for a pleasant surprise," Khokon concluded, just as the elders walked in.

Mr Chatterjee wanted to spend a little more time with his would be son-in-law, but Khokon got up to leave.

"So, how was the girl?" Avijit's aunt asked Khokon, once they were in the car.

"She was real polite," was Khokon's short answer.

They completed the rest of the journey in silence.

"Whew! That was some visit," Khokon remarked, the moment

they were alone in the room. Avijit was planning to leave for home and his aunt had gone into the kitchen to pack some food.

"Can you imagine marriages still being decided on the basis of caste? I thought we live in modern times."

"But the girl was unnecessarily harsh," Avijit couldn't help mentioning.

"I don't blame her. She was being paraded as a commodity. What do you do when your parents stifle your desires? Maybe, I would have done the same under similar circumstances. These oldies must understand we are adults and can take our own decisions too."

Avijit's aunt came in with a packet of food and he was on his way home.

"Promise me, you won't fight with your parents," Avijit was not sure how Khokon would react after he left.

He boarded a bus for home and his mind wandered back to the past few hours. Both Khokon and the girl thought their parents were redundant. Living fossils. Neither had lost a father and understood the pain.

He could hear his mother's voice, talking to someone when he reached his home.

"Ah, here you are! You got me worried. Sraboni is waiting for the past half hour," his mother said, after opening the door.

"Oh mother, I'm famished," he lied.

It made her rush into the kitchen. He tiptoed towards his mother's room where Sraboni sat on the bed.

"Where were you?" she looked up, the moment he entered.

"Oh, I was busy," he tried to sound casual, "but what brings you here?"

"Well, we had not met for the last three days. I thought you might be sick and dropped by. I wouldn't have, had I known you were busy," she made a face.

It was true. Ever since Khokon had come, his attention had been divided.

"At least it made you come here," he sighed, "otherwise these floors hardly get to touch your feet."

His mother still seemed busy in the kitchen and it took a great effort on his part to resist the temptation to kiss Sraboni.

"Don't be jealous," she seemed to anticipate the mischief in his mind and got up quickly. "You and aunty are invited to dinner, the day after, at our place," she added, "may I request His Highness to kindly make some time from his busy schedule and oblige us by gracing the occasion?"

"And what might the occasion be?" he was suddenly worried. Was it her engagement?

"It's my parents twenty fifth marriage anniversary, which we have decided to celebrate with all our well wishers. Though I am not too sure what you're wishing now," she raised her eyebrows, as Avijit had blocked the way out.

"Since you want to know, I must tell you," he whispered back. "I wish I could wrap my arms around you for an eternity. But it might be a trifle chancy now. So a simple kiss would do."

Sraboni blushed and tried to push past him. She only managed to fall into his arms in the process. Avijit knew he was playing with fire. His mother could come in any minute. He decided to risk it.

"What are you doing, let me go!" Sraboni whispered. She squirmed for release and finally called out to his mother as the last refuge. "Auntie, where are you? It is getting late and I must leave."

Avijit let go, as if she was a hot coal! His mother came in with tea and a plateful of delicacies his aunt had sent.

"You must have these before you leave," she told Sraboni, "and Avijit, you accompany her home. It is indeed late and not safe for her to go alone."

Avijit was delighted at the opportunity and smiled at Sraboni. But she looked far from amused.

"You acted like a raging bull," she told him sternly, when his mother left the room to get a glass of water.

"What can I do? I lose all sense when I see you," he whispered in a dreamy voice.

They were on the road shortly and it was pitch dark. Half the streetlights had been stolen and the rest glowed weakly under the fluctuating voltage, waging it's own battle for survival. It did little to illuminate the potholes in the narrow lane and they had to tread carefully. Sraboni had not uttered a single word since they had ventured out of the house.

"What's the matter? Are you angry with me?" he asked.

"I need to avoid you, especially at your home. The rat on the road becomes a tiger in his house," she didn't sound too angry.

"You think I'm a rat on the road. Okay, let me show I can be a lion too!"

Avijit had made sure the road was deserted, before embracing her. She was shocked and beat into his chest with her fists.

"I think you have gone mad. Please let me go. Someone might come and see us," she begged.

"Give me a kiss and you are free," Avijit wouldn't let go.

The sudden slap jolted him back to his senses. He quickly let go. Sraboni was crying and his face stung from the impact of her slim fingers. He cursed himself and silently followed Sraboni, as she hurried back home. She didn't even look back once and quickly entered the house. Avijit stood on the road for a while, unsure what to do next. What if she complained to her parents? He would lose face in his neighbourhood and could never meet her again. Oh! What had he done? He had a quiet dinner and retired to his bedroom. Fear of the unknown gripped him. How would he face Mr Ghosh, if he came rushing to their door in the morning? What if he came with his gun? Army men were supposed to be hot-headed. He spent an agonizing night tossing and turning on the bed.

Day light increased his tension, which only reduced, when Mr Ghosh didn't kick down their door even at half past seven. He felt a lot more confident and decided to apologize to Sraboni at the bus stop. He would have missed her, as the bus was leaving by the time he reached. He ran and boarded the bus. She was sitting in the middle, the seat next to her empty. He sat silently besides her for the next few minutes, unsure how to begin.

"I'm sorry about yesterday," he finally managed.

She only glanced at him but did not reply. It made him more desperate.

"Look, I repent my deed. Please talk to me. I apologize. It won't happen again," he blurted out in a weak voice.

"It's okay," the ice was finally broken, "you must understand that I am a young girl. It won't do me any good, if I am caught frolicking with you in public. Your behaviour was irresponsible to say the least."

Avijit remained silent till she spoke again.

"I'm sorry. I slapped you. But I had no other option," she spoke in a whisper, her eyes averted from Avijit's gaze. "Forget the episode and come over tomorrow."

She got up and finally smiled at him, before getting down. Avijit felt a sweet flood of relief. He was forgiven at last.

CHAPTER Five

Mr Dayaram was already in office and he called Avijit in.

"I will be out of town for the next few days," he said, rubbing his chin. "I have an important job for you. Take this and keep it safely," Mr Dayaram handed over a soiled piece of paper.

Avijit looked at it closely. It was a receipt for five cases of rope. Below it was scribbled a telephone number.

"Call the number and say you have a chit for five hundred thousand rupees. You will be given an address. Munna can drive you down there. Hand over the chit, collect the cash and give it to my wife at my residence."

"But this is a receipt for ropes! Are you sure they will give me so much money against this?" Avijit was baffled.

"Don't be stupid. I know my business," his boss reprimanded him. "Look son, there is a parallel economy that runs in this country. Millions of rupees are transacted everyday. It is all based on faith as there can be no records. Your bank's cheque can bounce, but this hundi will never be refused," his boss added with a rare smile. He seemed to be in a good mood and hummed a popular tune, as he got ready to leave for the station.

Avijit looked at the small piece of paper in amazement – five hundred thousand rupees for this soiled piece! He was getting increasingly tense as he had never handled so much money before. He dialled the number tentatively and waited for an answer. It seemed an old man had picked up the phone. The man listened patiently as Avijit stammered to explain his objective. He expected a harsh curse and the line to be disconnected. But nothing like that happened. Instead, he was given an address and asked to come over.

"Don't forget to bring the receipt," the man warned amidst bouts of coughing.

The man didn't even bother to ask Avijit his name and address.

Munna arrived just as he had opened his lunch-box. They shared the lunch and later went down to have the delicious dahi-vada. Avijit appraised Munna about the job on hand, though the latter didn't flinch on hearing of the total sum.

"Oh, it's nothing new. Dayaram does this often and carries much more cash," Munna was unperturbed.

They ventured out in the afternoon, the receipt safe in his pocket. Munna switched on the music system and drove towards their destination. The address turned out to be a small shop in the busy commodity market of central Calcutta. The car had to be parked a little way down the road and Avijit, carrying a folio bag, entered the shop alone. He handed over the receipt to a middle aged man, who sat behind the counter. The man asked him to wait and disappeared through a door in one corner of the room. Avijit looked around the shop. It was small and had a few cans of lubricant displayed along a shelf. A thick layer of dust had settled on the cans. It meant there was hardly any business done. The shop gave no impression that its owner earned enough to hand over five hundred thousand rupees to a complete stranger like him. The man reappeared shortly and called him into a back room, dark and sparingly furnished, but a little bigger than the shop in the front.

"It's all there," the man indicated a bare cot, on which it was stacked.

Thankfully, they were in five hundred rupee notes and it should not have taken him more than fifteen minutes to count the amount. However, it was another hour before he could put the money into the folio bag, as he miscounted thrice in his hurry to get back to the car. The shop owner looked relieved when Avijit finally got up.

"Thank you," he wanted to leave quickly.

He felt like running, once he was on the road. His tension subsided only after he located the car, got in hurriedly and locked the door.

"So? How was your initiation in the art of clandestine dealings?" Munna mocked.

"Yes, very cool. Now, will you please start the car or we wait here till we get robbed," Avijit couldn't hide the irritation in his voice.

"Rest assured, this is not the last time," Munna remarked, once they were on their way, "you will have to do it more often, now that you have proved your mettle. You might even be promoted to the position of *Chief Collector* in our great company and your salary increased by a hefty rupees fifty."

Avijit felt uneasy at the thought of repeating the exercise and prayed to God that this be the last time. But he knew the Almighty rarely listened to him ever since his father had died. Munna honked once they reached Dayaram's residence. The huge iron gates were opened, only after the sentry had peeped through a slit and identified the visitors. Avijit walked down the lush green lawn towards the house, the bag gripped firmly in his hand. There was no one in sight. Was the lady of the house having an afternoon nap? Would she be upset if he disturbed her? He rang the bell. It seemed an eternity before a maid opened the front door.

"What do you want?" she demanded in a harsh voice.

"Please inform Madam that I'm from Mr Dayaram's office. I've something to deliver," he indicated the bag in his hand.

"Take off your shoes and come in," she commanded, "wait in the hall."

She disappeared up the stairs at the corner of the hall that led to the first floor. Avijit looked around in wonder. The hall was big, decorated with wall hangings and paintings all around. The plush sofas looked comfortable and inviting. A huge chandelier hung from the ceiling at the centre of the hall, ready to throw its sparkling colours and light up every nook and cranny of this paradise. Avijit initially marvelled at Mr Dayaram's taste, but quickly dismissed the thought as improbable. A man as unkempt as his boss could surely not conjure up such elegance even in his dreams. It must be Mrs Dayaram who maintained the house. The maid reappeared at the head of the stairs and asked him to come up. He walked cautiously on the tiled stairs lest he should slip. He could hear the sound of music filtering through, as he approached the first floor. The maid indicated the last room on the right, down a long passage. He knocked softly on the partially closed door.

"Come on in," a female voice called out.

Avijit pushed the door open and entered a large room. It looked like a gymnasium! He had spent enough time in them during his football days to know one. The equipment looked expensive. Avijit wondered how his boss could be so badly out of shape even after having the privilege of owning them. Mrs Dayaram was performing aerobics and a big stereo blared out foot tapping music. She wore tight blue leotards that clung to her body like a second skin, accentuating her trim but voluptuous figure. It was sure to stop most men dead in their tracks and Avijit was no sage. He only averted his gaze, when the lady turned towards him. She stopped jogging and moved towards the stereo to put it off. A pair of eyes followed her and took in the ripple of her derrière, as she moved gracefully. She turned suddenly to catch him gaping at her and gave a wry smile. Avijit felt uncomfortable and stiff. The voyeur in him wanted to feast his eyes on this uninhibited display of the female form. But his conscience constantly warned him not to do anything foolhardy - this was his boss's wife. The lady seemed oblivious of the battle within him and asked him to sit down next to her on the sofa. Avijit could smell her body odour, which mingled with the sweet perfume she had put on and it felt difficult to breathe.

"Tell me, what do you want?" her query broke his spell.

He was tempted to speak his mind, as the stiffness between his legs had drowned his senses.

"No, no. I do not want anything," he stammered. "I came down to give you the money," he handed over the folio bag carefully, "it has five hundred thousand rupees. Sir asked me to give it to you."

He was sweating profusely and got up to leave.

"Sit, sit," she advised in a sweet voice, "I'll be back in a moment."

She went out of the room with the bag, but not before turning on the air conditioner. Avijit relaxed and moped his brow.

The maid came in with a plate full of sweets and a glass of juice, and put it down on a stool near the sofa. She left as silently as she had come. Avijit didn't know what to do. He was stranded in this big house with a beautiful lady, who threw his senses out of gear. She had looked at him in a dreamy way and he was not sure what could happen next. He desperately wanted to get out of the house, as he felt stifled. But the fear of the lady complaining to his boss that he left without permission kept him glued to his seat. He sat there for almost ten minutes before Mrs Dayaram came back. She had put on a robe and looked the normal housewife.

"Well, the bag had five hundred thousand in it. I've kept it safely," she sat down next to him. "Why? You have not eaten! Is something wrong?" she looked at the untouched sweets and exclaimed.

She made sure he ate everything before allowing him to leave.

"My door is always open. You can come whenever you want."

Avijit knew something was wrong with him. He had misbehaved with Sraboni the previous evening and painted a wrong image of Mrs Dayaram. The lady obviously didn't know he would barge in during her aerobics session. She was definitely not in the skintight dress to seduce him. It was all in his dirty mind. He wanted to laugh out aloud as he remembered the weird thoughts which touched his mind while sitting alone in the gym.

His mother could not go to the Ghosh's house the next day.

"You go alone. I am not feeling well," she remarked.

"What is the problem? Should I call a doctor?" Avijit became tense whenever his mother fell ill. There was always the fear of losing her too and facing a lonely and disoriented future.

"No, no. I don't need a doctor. I'm feeling a little tired," his mother tried to calm him down, "you go ahead and enjoy yourself."

"No way. I am not going without you. There will be lot of strangers and I might feel lost. Let me spend the evening with you then," he sat down on his mother's bed.

"See, don't misunderstand me. I would have gone had your father been alive. It doesn't look good for a widow to attend someone's marriage anniversary," his mother pleaded with him. "It is the unwritten law in our society," she sighed.

"I don't care what society accepts or rejects," Avijit shouted, "your so-called society couldn't protect my father. It couldn't even catch the killers! Nor could it give me a decent job. You have given up your normal food habits, changed your dress code – all after Dad's death. For whom? Is it for a society that can't even guarantee a peaceful and comfortable existence? Why are you bothered with what they may feel or say?"

Avijit was angry. His mother's soft hands on his head did little to reduce his exasperation.

"You will only understand when you are my age," his mother smiled sadly, "now get ready quickly and go. Don't forget to buy a bouquet for the couple."

Avijit wondered how many mothers quarantined themselves and languished at home after their husbands' death. It was all to uphold the virtues written down by the wise men of society. He knew he could not win against his mother's will and decided to go alone, as he yearned to meet Sraboni.

Avijit expected bright lights, loud music and a big crowd. But he was disappointed. A single light illuminated the entrance and he found only a few people seated in the drawing room. The record player played a Tagore song and a refreshing whiff emanated from the big bunch of Rajanigandhas on the table. Mr Ghosh was wearing a white dhoti-punjabee, the traditional Bengali dress, and accepted the bouquet from him.

"*Swagotam.* Since you would never come to our house on your own, we had to celebrate our anniversary and invite you over. But where is your mother?" Mr Ghosh looked behind Avijit, expecting his mother to come in.

"She is not feeling well and has sent her regards."

The host didn't press the issue and requested him to join the others. Avijit sat down on one of the empty chairs. An elderly couple sat next to him and two middle-aged men sat on the far side. Mr Ghosh was called inside and they sat silently, as no one seemed to know the other. Avijit kept an eye on the door to the inside of the house. He had still not seen Sraboni. Mrs Ghosh walked in shortly with a tray full of savouries but there was no sign of her daughter.

"Oh! My husband didn't make the introductions. Typical of him," she chuckled and introduced everyone in the room.

The elderly couple, the Bhattacharyas were next-door neighbours. One of the middle aged men, Mr Sen, was Mrs Ghosh's brother. The other gentleman, Mr Sankaranarayan, was Mr Ghosh's colleague in the army.

"Only Ujjal and Chandan are absconding," Mrs Ghosh remarked.

Avijit was feeling uncomfortable amongst the elders and looked forward to meeting his friends. Sraboni was nowhere to be seen and he was getting desperate for a glimpse of his beloved. It seemed she was still angry and wanted to avoid him. Mrs Ghosh served the snacks. The meat samosas were delicious and Avijit took a second helping along with the thick and spicy mango chutney. He was just finishing his cup of tea when Ujjal arrived.

"Ah! Look who's here? I heard you left for Timbuktu!" Ujjal patted Avijit on the shoulder, after wishing the Ghoshs. "Let me give you the good news. Chandan has got a job as a singer. He performs every evening at one of the restaurants on Park Street." Ujjal wore a red shirt that was sure to invite a bull's wrath. "Chandan has invited both of us to the show one evening."

"Sure. I will certainly come."

Avijit was happy that Chandan had recovered from the blow the music company had dealt him. Mr Ghosh finally came and sat down with them.

"What kept you so long?" the host asked Ujjal, "Chandan is tied up but you should have come earlier. We couldn't start without you."

And with that, he brought out a bottle of whiskey.

"Yes! Now the evening looks brighter," Mr Sen joked.

Mrs Bhattacharya excused herself. She raised her eyebrows and looked at her husband before vanishing inside, a clear signal to her spouse not to go overboard with the drink.

"Well, with these political parties blocking roads and taking out processions at the drop of a hat, one can never be on time," Ujjal was piqued.

"What was it today?" Mr Sankaranarayan spoke for the first time.

"I don't know. Must have been the aftermath of some petty fight on the floor of the Assembly. After all, our politicians are no longer the suave educated servants of the nation. They are bullfighters in their own right and each party takes turns to play the bull. Only we, the common men bear the brunt of their charge," Ujjal exploded.

"Don't be upset. Just accept it as a part of our daily suffering. Cheers!" Mr Bhattacharya raised his glass and toasted, "our present day politicians. May they succeed in stripping themselves of the little shame they still have left. And may they display their lust for power shamelessly in front of a nation, which is already on its knees and will soon be on all fours."

Avijit could never understand how complete strangers became friends so quickly, once a bottle of whiskey was opened. He silently sipped on the glass of cold drink offered to him.

"But frankly, things are going from bad to worse," Mr Ghosh joined in, "when we were young, politicians were revered. Today even goons become ministers. Many of them do not have a proper education! So how can they take the country forward?"

"We had a classmate, Anirban. He dropped out of school," Ujjal had the attention of everyone in the room, "I met him at the Calcutta

Book Fair recently. When I asked him what he did for a living, he said he was in politics. He proudly told me that his monthly earnings were in five figures. Can you imagine a backbencher in school earning so much in any other profession?"

"That is precisely the problem," Mr Bhattacharya spoke, after finishing his glass, "the best students go for a career in engineering, medicine or commerce. The mediocre settle for small time jobs. But these backbenchers have no other option but to join politics. And you see the result all around. Our politicians should be made to sit for a basic test. They must qualify before being allowed to contest an election."

"Don't worry. They will rig the tests too!" Ujjal chipped in, making everyone laugh. "I think your generation was plain lucky," he addressed Mr Ghosh, "you did not have to face the population explosion that led to this chaos. You could live a plain and simple life and still be happy. The media had not invaded your homes. Today the lifestyles of the rich and famous are so frequently exhibited on television that an average man starts dreaming of a similar life. His desire for money and material goods multiplies every day. But then, the entire middle class cannot become super rich overnight. So there is corruption to fall back on. Why blame the politicians alone, don't we all look forward to making a quick buck? Frankly sir, I am fed up with life."

Avijit was surprised at Ujjal's outburst. His friend had always looked like one who was happy.

"But why didn't you join the army?" the sudden question from Mr Sankaranarayan set Avijit thinking.

"Am I eligible to join?" Ujjal questioned back.

"Of course you are. Any Indian, who is physically and mentally fit, can join the defence forces. There certainly is an age limit, but you can still join," Mr Sankaranarayan replied.

"Life is different in the army. I have felt it throughout my career. It is one of the few institutions in the country, where you get to do something worthwhile. I always find it surprising that today's youth shuns it as a bad career option," Mr Ghosh added.

"Yes. You get the best food and shelter for doing nothing," Mr Sen mocked.

"Why do you say that?" Mr Sankaranarayan looked closely at Mr Sen.

"Well, there has been no war since seventy one and I don't think there will be one in the future. After all, every one knows we have nuke capabilities and it would be foolish to attack us. So what does that leave for the army to do? Train everyday and be ready for nothing. I feel the defence budget should be cut drastically and the money used for building schools and hospitals instead," Mr Sen made a dismissive gesture. He got his glass refilled and settled back again.

"I beg to differ sir," Mr Sankaranarayan spoke coldly, "no country can afford to reduce its defence preparedness, just because the common man feels there is no threat of a war. It has to be based on hard intelligence. And you seem to be totally unaware that one of our neighbours is fighting a war with us for the past decade, a proxy war to be precise. They smuggle arms and supply it to the frustrated youth of today, ask them to wage a war, kill mercilessly. Some youths fall for the bait and you have seen the result – violence all over."

"Ah, there you are," Mr Sen smiled knowingly, "how can arms be smuggled in? What do you do? Sleep?"

"More than five thousand soldiers have died fighting insurgency. They didn't die in their sleep. The army is capable of stopping this nonsense. But it is not autonomous. The common man's government controls it. The army needs to be given full authority and resources. And I would be surprised if that ever happens," Mr Sankaranarayan concluded.

"But I'm still not convinced," Mr Sen had filled his glass for the third time, "you don't need an army of the size we maintain, to fight a few infiltrators."

"Yeah, we can as well lay the red carpet for the enemy to march in," Mr Ghosh was unable to hide his irritation, "what is your point? The defence forces are not important for a country like ours? If it was that simple, then every country would have bought an atom bomb and disbanded their defence forces. I think the whiskey is paralyzing your senses."

The last words had a disastrous effect. Mr Sen stood up and started shouting at the top of his voice.

"What the bloody hell have you people done for the country in the past decade? You have just enjoyed a peaceful life, all made possible by taxpayers like me. Think of the hardships we face everyday – crowded buses, long hours in office, power cuts - while you armymen only pump muscle and box the air," Mr Sen fell back on his chair exhausted.

He looked fit to be a politician, Avijit thought. There was still no sign of Sraboni. What the hell was she doing inside?

"Well, you spoke of hardships, sacrifices," Mr Ghosh now stood next to Mr Sankaranarayan and addressed Mr Sen, "do you think this is one?"

He suddenly bent down and lifted Mr Sankaranarayan's trousers over his right leg. Avijit couldn't help but stare. There was no leg! It was an artificial stump of wood. Mr Sankaranarayan looked terribly embarrassed and quickly pulled back his trousers.

"Please sir, calm down," he pleaded.

"How can I Sankar? These people label us traitors! We are redundant!" he was far from calm.

There was pin drop silence in the room and Avijit felt embarrassed too.

"He took four bullets during a forward patrol near the international border," Mr Ghosh came back and sat down in his chair, "killed six enemy soldiers who had cornered him and walked back almost two miles. I carried him all the way to the hospital but it was too late. They couldn't save his leg."

The host seemed pained at the memory. Silence in the room prevailed.

"I'm sorry sir," Mr Sankaranarayan told Mr Sen, "this is not to evoke sympathy. But I can never accept people talking ill of the army without knowing facts."

Avijit wondered whether he could talk in the same vein about his employer? He was curious to know more about the institution whose officers put their lives on the line for it. His thoughts were cut short by Sraboni, who came in to announce that dinner was ready. She gave him a quick glance before disappearing again.

All the guests trudged into the dinning room. Mr Sen took each step with caution. The alcohol fumes seemed to have found their way up from his stomach to the head. A big cake was placed at the centre of the table; the cream was crafted to proclaim the number of years the Ghoshs had shared their lives. The happy couple cut the cake amidst loud clapping and cheering. Everyone had a bite of the rich creamy cake and then they sat down for the main course. It was a glutton's delight. The tiger prawns cooked in coconut milk melted in the mouth. Sraboni stood by her mother, occasionally helping her heap a big spoonful of some delicacy onto an unsuspecting diner's plate. The protest was loud but the food still disappeared. Everyone except Mr Sen had a contented smile on the face after the feast was over. The latter seemed to be in a terrible dilemma. He rushed towards the toilet, when Sraboni was serving *paan.* The invitees took leave, all wishing the couple a hundred more years of togetherness. Avijit felt intrigued. The hot debate of the evening left him confused. He had to admit that he had enjoyed himself fully, even though he hardly got to talk to Sraboni.

"Bloody shit! I thought there would be fisticuffs!" Ujjal exclaimed.

"Mr Sen was unduly harsh," Avijit observed.

"But I thought he had a valid point. If there is no threat of a war, then why feed a huge army? Everyone believes we have the bomb. So would anyone be stupid enough to hail doomsday for mankind?"

"But look at the rise in insurgency in the country," Avijit in fact was bored reading about it in the papers everyday, "who will fight it if you don't have an army?"

"Not me for sure. Anyway, let's meet at least once a week," Ujjal said before parting for the night.

Avijit's mind wandered back and forth over the events of the evening. The artificial leg seemed to mock Mr Sen's idea that every armyman lived a safe and secure life. He wondered how much courage it took to face the enemy alone and kill six of them. A gram? A kilogram? Or a tonne? Maybe more. And he had initially thought of Mr Sankaranarayan as a timid person. The armyman's appearance hardly hinted at the brave and rigid core. For the first time in Avijit's life, something other than football fascinated him. He even had a fleeting desire to join the institution before falling asleep.

CHAPTER

Six

"Hey! What's the problem? Let us down."

"Sorry mates. There is an emergency and I have orders to take you back," the driver drove back the way they had come.

"What emergency?" Ghoton asked the driver.

"I don't know. Lieutenant Nanda had sent an SOS over his wireless set." The trainees were pale with fear.

"Bloody shit! What happens now?" Ravi asked.

"Look, whatever happens please don't tell him I did it," Ghoton pleaded, "I can die for all of you, but cannot face that Lieutenant in anger."

They all agreed to stand by Ghoton, though Avijit felt like kicking him. The hot bath looked a distant dream. The fear of finding the Lieutenant injured or even dead and a subsequent court-martial looked a reality. It was a steep road and the Lieutenant might not have noticed the flat tyres and met with an accident.

But the Lieutenant was safe. In fact, he was enjoying a mug of tea, his legs stretched across the bonnet of his jeep, which had not moved an inch from its place.

"I'm sorry. I'm in a spot of bother and need your help," he looked closely at the trainees, who stood still.

"What is it sir?" Avijit tried to sound his normal self.

"Oh, my rear wheels have leaked their air. There is only one spare wheel and I cannot risk going up in this state. So I thought you guys could help," the Lieutenant smiled.

"How sir?"

"Simple. You push the jeep to the nearest petrol pump. The truck can follow us. It is only six kilometres."

It took them more than an hour to reach the fuel station.

"That was fast! Maybe, I should ask them to have some hot water ready for you at the camp," the Lieutenant took out his wireless set and waved them off.

"Next time you want to test the bastard, let me know in advance. I won't be within a mile of you," Ravi hissed at Ghoton, once they were on the truck.

"And you massage my back tonight or else I will tell the Lieutenant it was you," Guri grimaced, as the truck bounced over the hilly road, "shit! My ass seems to have turned to stone."

Most of them were now adept in handling small arms, as also the light machine gun. Avijit could shoot an apple a hundred yards away with ease. Ghoton had accepted the fact that the Lieutenant was blessed with more grey cells than him. He obeyed the latter's commands silently and there was peace all around. The trainees looked forward to the day when they would be formally inducted into their regiment as soldiers and posted outside the training camp. They also harboured hopes of spending a few days with their families after this long exile. It was during breakfast one day that a loud whirring noise caught their attention. The sound grew louder and many peeped out of the canteen window to see what it was. A large green helicopter circled their camp a few times, before descending onto the football field. There was an uneasy silence, after the rotors stopped.

"Must be some seniors coming down to give us more lectures on but Avijit's mother would have none of it.

"You have come all the way from Rajpur. You must be hungry. Wait, I'll quickly cook you some food."

"Both of you must come to the court on Wednesday. You might be needed," the officer reminded Avijit again.

Avijit was eager to know the identities of those arrested. But the officer didn't oblige.

"Can you really book the culprits?"

"Well, we seized a consignment of cold rolled steel last week. It was being taken out as scrap. It should lead us to the head honchos in the racket," the officer sounded confident.

"You said a few have been arrested ...," Avijit couldn't hide his confusion.

"Have faith. I can't divulge more now," the officer smiled and patted his arm, "please don't inform anyone in Rajpur either. I want the advantage of a surprise."

Avijit's mother served them puris and fried brinjals. The officer ate with relish and wiped his mustache contentedly after the meal. Avijit saw him off at the bus stop. He was surprised by the visit. It seemed all was not lost as long as the Sankaranayans and Samaddars were around. His mother though was sceptical.

"I don't like this idea of not informing anyone in Rajpur. Why this hush-hush? We have not committed any crime," she sounded suspicious, "we must consult your uncle before going there."

Avijit could not think of any ulterior motive behind Mr Samaddar's visit. What could he gain by asking them to go to Rajpur? There was little doubt that he was from the police. He had shown his identity card. Could they be forged just like every other thing?

"I feel you must go. I have a friend in the city police. He can check Samaddar's antecedents," Avijit's uncle remarked, after hearing of the visit. And he called up later to confirm about the police officer.

Mr Dayaram listened patiently when Avijit asked for a day off on Wednesday.

"I've no problem, but this case won't be solved in a day," he said. "Don't expect too much too soon," Mr Dayaram cautioned, "it won't be easy to nail the culprits quickly. Go this time. But you need to decide whether you can afford a visit every time a hearing date is fixed."

Avijit hated his boss. Mr Samaddar had told him the case was as good as closed. The culprits would be punished. And his boss, the miser, was already calculating the number of holidays Avijit might demand.

"You can deduct my salary if you want, but please don't stop me," he blurted out in frustration.

Mr Dayaram stayed silent for sometime before he replied.

"You got me all wrong. It is true that I always run after money. But I'm also human. I'm only asking you to be practical. The accused might spend money and get a verdict in their favour. After all, money can get you anything in this great nation of ours."

And then Mr Dayaram did an unexpected thing. He opened his

They started their crawl, one at a time.

"If you drop, your hands should leave the rope last," the Lieutenant directed, "then you won't fall on your head."

It was extremely difficult. Avijit's arms were aching from the effort by the halfway mark. His legs slipped off and it took all the strength in his body to manoeuver them back over the rope.

"Move, move. Just don't give up," Lieutenant Nanda shouted all the time, "you let go and I will make you do a hundred pushups."

Avijit was sure his hands would come off, but he held on. The Lieutenant helped him down when he reached the end.

"Well done," he slapped Avijit on the back, "go back and take some rest. You will have to do it three more times, so conserve your energy."

Avijit felt like bursting into tears. Ghoton managed to move three quarters of the length, before his legs slipped off. He hung helplessly from the rope, after repeated attempts to put his legs back over it failed.

"Come on, move you idiot," the Lieutenant shouted.

"I can't sir," Ghoton shouted back, "my hands have gone numb. Please let me off. I will do the hundred pushups, but I cannot bear this any more."

"Who asked you to do pushups? You can let go, but then you won't be served lunch. Suit yourself."

Ghoton sat down next to Avijit, panting heavily after completing the full crawl.

"Bastard," he muttered, "just wait. I'll make him pay dearly for this."

"Better shut up. You will have to do it three more times before lunch," Avijit passed on the bad news.

No one spoke a word after dinner that night. Everyone was too tired to move a muscle. They crawled like snakes for the next five days, before being released for a day. Most decided to laze around in the camp and there were only twelve of them in the truck to town. Ghoton and Guri went to the town for fun. The former to taste the half burnt chicken *kebabs* at the restaurant, the latter to stand and gape at the few girls who passed by. That day was no different. Only no one was willing to stay back after lunch. They didn't know what new discipline awaited them the next day and their bodies ached from the exertions of the past week. Everyone wanted to rest and the truck was on its way back by the early afternoon. It was where the plain merged into the hills that they spotted Lieutenant Nanda. His jeep was parked and he was having tea at a roadside kiosk, which was possibly the last shop before the camp.

"Hey stop," Ghoton shouted to the driver, "we would like to have some tea."

They had had tea in the shop before and Avijit was not too fond of the warm liquid, which the owner offered. But it was a cold day and they all got down.

"Hello, sir. Thought we would have some tea," Ghoton beamed at the Lieutenant.

"Yeah, go ahead. Though I am not too sure whether he is serving last look at their papers before proceedings started. Avijit had not confided anything to Naluda about the officer's visit. Yet things fell in place after what their neighbour had told them. His father's killers would finally be punished. It was another ten minutes, before Mr Samaddar walked in with a small police contingent. They escorted two handcuffed men and sat down on the benches near the Judge's podium. Avijit looked at the men and wondered how they could kill his father. A silent rage was building up within him and it took his best effort not to get up and jump on them. The Judge came in shortly and the hearing started.

The businessman was the first to be put up. The man must have been in his late forties and the sweat glistened on his bald head. He looked nervous and repeatedly mopped his brow with a handkerchief.

"There is some mistake, sir," he pleaded, "I'm a pious businessman and have never broken the law. The police unnecessarily detained me."

"But a consignment of good material was being sold to you as scrap," the public prosecutor interjected.

"I don't know anything, sir. There must have been a goof up in the plant."

"But you had received such material in the past too. Haven't you?" the lawyer continued.

"Objection Your Honour," the defence counsel had jumped to his feet before the accused could reply, "my client is being accused of malpractices without any proof. Can my esteemed colleague prove what he is saying?"

"Objection sustained," the Judge spoke in a deep voice. He

requested the public prosecutor not to make sweeping statements unless there was supporting evidence.

"Sir, the police intercepted a truck carrying cold rolled steel to his warehouse. Only, the material was certified as scrap. Isn't that proof enough?" the public prosecutor protested.

He was middle aged and energetic, as compared to his counterpart. The deep lines on the latter's forehead and the still-brown eyes spoke of many years of life. He looked at his younger colleague with a sense of indulgence, just like a teacher who had met a new student.

"How can we be sure my client is not being framed? Maybe, someone knowingly planted good material in that consignment. Sir, my client has done no wrong and should be released immediately," the defence counsel concluded.

The Judge sat deep in thought. He ordered the police to send samples of the seized consignment to an independent laboratory for analysis and present the report to the court at the earliest. He then asked the public prosecutor to continue.

"Do you know Mr Roy?" the lawyer pointed towards the union leader.

"Yes."

"For how long?"

"A couple of years. He is a social worker and we work together to help improve the living conditions of the poor in our area."

"What role does he play in your dealings with the steel plant?"

"He has no role."

"Well, only a matter of fifteen days," Guri thumped Avijit on the back, "and don't come back with a wife. I don't want to lose out on the chance to see a Bengali marriage." "And you," he turned to Ghoton, "don't die for someone just because he smiled at you. I won't be able to share my escapades with anyone then."

And thus they parted, each for his home, rest and recreation. Ghoton had decided to make a brief visit to his uncle's place and spend the rest of his vacation with Avijit. He carried a big parcel other than his luggage – food packed from the army canteen.

"I had to tip the chef an extra ten bucks for the boiled eggs," he said.

He also bought whatever food he could lay his hands on at the station.

"You never know where the train might get stuck. So why take a chance?" he reasoned, when Avijit questioned the wisdom of buying twenty packets of biscuits for a twenty-hour journey.

Ghoton opened the food packet the moment they were on the train and threw away the leftovers, even before the train had picked up its full speed. The landscape rushed past, the dusty summer making the green look wilted all around. Avijit remembered his last train journey a half-year back. He had felt nervous and insecure. The training had changed all that. He now looked forward to every new dawn with hope and joy. His excitement grew at the thought of being able to meet Sraboni soon. He was not too sure he could keep Guri's request. If Sraboni agreed, they could marry that very month. He would throw a party at the regiment later, to pacify the *sardar*.

He looked at Ghoton, who was already snoring and debated whether to make him the best man at the wedding. The train stopped at a few stations and Ghoton immediately jumped up to buy more food.

"At this rate, you will be grossly overweight by the time you report back for duty. They will simply sack you," Avijit warned his friend.

"Would they dare?" Ghoton shrugged him off and continued on his eating spree.

"Objection, sir!" the defence counsel was visibly upset, "my colleague here is firing allegations at my client without a single piece of evidence. How does he know Mr Roy has wealth disproportionate to his income?"

"I can prove it sir. Please allow me to proceed."

"Objection overruled. Please proceed," the Judge remarked.

"What is your current monthly salary, Mr Roy?" the public prosecutor continued.

The union leader thought for a moment before replying.

"Eight thousand six hundred rupees."

"Are you sure?"

"Of course I am."

"Well, My Lord, this is interesting," the lawyer looked at the Judge, "Mr Roy is working for eight years in the steel plant and his salary is around rupees eight and a half thousand. In today's world, can such a salary ensure enough savings for Mr Roy to buy a flat near Calcutta for rupees eight hundred thousand?"

There was pin drop silence in the court and the accused glanced in desperation at the defence counsel. It seemed the revelation had hit him hard.

"Tell me Mr Roy, where did you get the money from?" the public prosecutor sounded triumphant.

"Objection sir," the defence counsel shouted, "my client is being subjected to too many leading questions."

"Objection overruled," the Judge directed his rival to proceed.

"So? Who gave you the money?"

"I took a loan from the bank," the accused replied.

"How much was it for?"

"Rupees six hundred thousand."

"How many years do you need to pay back the loan?"

"Ten."

"Is it by monthly or yearly instalment?"

"Monthly."

The public prosecutor took a break and brought out a calculator.

"Well, well, well. At the current bank lending rates, your monthly instalment works out to almost seven thousand rupees! How do you run your family then? You have only one and a half thousand rupees left from your salary."

"I manage."

"But I am told you live lavishly."

"Sir!" the defence counsel was up again, "my colleague is depending too much on conjectures."

"Don't interrupt," the Judge dismissed the plea.

"Who stays in your flat at Calcutta?"

"Why?" the accused shot back. He calmed down, after a glance at the defence counsel, and replied in a sober tone. "I stay whenever I go."

"So it is empty when you are in Rajpur?"

"Yes."

when a sudden gust of wind hit the helicopter, making it tilt. Jadav fell through the air, his shriek rising above the noise of the rotors, as the others watched helplessly. Everyone ran forward and crowded around the body that lay in a heap. It still seemed to have life left in it.

"Make way. Let me see him," the Lieutenant had jumped from the chopper with the rope.

Jadav was rushed to the hospital and their heli-jumping session aborted for the day.

"It was all because of Lieutenant Nanda," Ghoton fumed.

They were in their barracks after dinner. Even a glutton like Ghoton had not been able to eat, as news had come out that Jadav had died. "I don't agree with you," Avijit came up in defense of the Lieutenant, "its partly Jadav's fault too. He stood too near the door. It was also destiny. Who would have known such a strong gust of wind was going to hit the chopper? The Lieutenant is blaming himself and spoke of quitting."

"Your remark will hasten his decision and we will miss the guidance of one of the best trainers in the army," Guri added.

Major Chawla put in an unexpected appearance the next morning on the parade ground.

"In the army, you need to come to terms with death and injury. Yesterday's incident was unfortunate, but the training must go on. Once in a battlefield, you may lose many friends and colleagues. But you should not dither from your primary responsibility to safe guard the nation," the Major turned towards the Lieutenant, "Lieutenant

Nanda feels he has not been able to discharge his duties properly and wants to resign. I do not agree with him. But he persuaded me to take your opinion on whether you want him to continue or not. I'm not sure there is precedence, but I had to agree. So tell me what you want?"

"We want him to continue sir," Ravi shouted.

"Yes sir," all the others including Ghoton, joined in.

"So Lieutenant, you have your answer. I am sure you can train them to be some of the best soldiers in our army," the Major waved to them and departed.

They continued with heli-jumping for the next five days. Most of them did not need the lifeline by the third day.

Avijit felt he belonged to the real world again, a world where discipline, sincerity and humanity were more important than money and power. He occasionally felt homesick too, but cheered up when he received his mother's letter or spoke to her over the phone. She wrote at least two letters a week and looked forward to meeting her soldier-son. Khokon had consented to marrying a Calcutta girl. He was planning to come down that very month to finalize one from a long list of proposals. An engineer settled abroad was after all a prize catch. Avijit had spared his mother the ordeal. He wondered what Sraboni might be doing? They had not seen each other for four and a half months now and his feelings for her had only grown stronger.

Their entire training pattern was changed around the fifth month. It became a combination of all the disciplines they had practiced separately. Avijit particularly liked the mock fights. They would be

"Objection, sir. My client was in no way involved in any killing. Nor is he involved in any racket. These are all frivolous charges. Can I question the witness too?"

The Judge granted permission.

"Tell me Ma'am, did you ever meet Mr Roy before?"

"No."

"Then how are you sure he is the same man your husband spoke of? It could be someone else. There are quite a few Roys working in the steel plant."

Avijit's mother stayed silent.

"Did your husband say anything specific against Mr Roy? Like swindling the plant or issuing threats?"

"He asked me not to allow Mr Roy into the house."

"Yes, you have said so before. But did he say Mr Roy was intimidating him?"

"No."

"So it could be anything? Maybe they had a small tiff and that's why he was unwelcome."

"But my husband spoke of corruption in the plant."

"It doesn't prove anything," the defence counsel dismissed her reply all together and turned towards the Judge, "Sir, can we rely on such trivial information to conclude that my client is guilty?"

"I have two more witnesses. They heard Mr Roy threatening Mr Bannerjee," the public prosecutor added.

Avijit's mother came down from the witness box and sat quietly next to him. The public prosecutor called on the next witness. He was a familiar face; Avijit knew the young man used to work with his father.

"Your name?"

"Amulya Das?"

"Mr Das, where do you work in the steel plant?"

"In the blast furnace division."

"The same department where Mr Prasun Bannerjee worked?"

"Yes."

"What sort of man was he?"

"A very good man."

"Did he tell you anything about the scrap dealings in the steel plant?"

"No."

"But you told the police he had?" the public prosecutor looked surprised.

"No, sir. I know nothing," the man kept glancing furtively at the accused.

"Okay, tell me, did that man threaten Mr Bannerjee?"

"I don't know sir," the witness looked at his own feet.

"But you told the police Mr Roy threatened Mr Bannerjee of dire consequences, if the latter didn't keep his mouth shut," the lawyer looked perplexed.

"I don't remember any such episode, sir."

And it went on and on. The public prosecutor gave up and called on the second witness. Avijit had never seen the young man before. He also worked in the same department. And he too denied being a witness to any altercation between the accused and Avijit's father.

"So, what do we have now?" the defence counsel had a triumphant look, "a few allegations and no proof. Sir, my colleague is wasting our time. There is just no evidence. Please dismiss the case."

The accused, who had looked distraught, gradually got back his smile. The Judge finally adjourned proceedings and asked the police to collect evidence against the accused. The businessman and the union leader were released on bail and asked to appear before the court when summoned. Avijit was appalled! He had expected a verdict that day itself. But the police didn't have enough evidence. Then why the hell had Mr Samaddar called them? Just to hear what his father had told them. It was just a peripheral issue. A non-issue. Irrelevant.

"The witnesses let us down," Mr Samaddar put up his excuse, "they must have been threatened by Roy's goons. We will book the culprits. Don't worry."

There was nothing to worry about. Avijit's father was not coming back.

"I knew this," Naluda summed up, "those people are rich and powerful."

Avijit's mother was silent. She refused Naluda's invitation to have lunch at his house. She didn't even go to her own house and sat stoically on the wooden bench at the station. They boarded the evening train back to Calcutta.

CHAPTER Seven

"What happened?" Sraboni asked Avijit the next morning, when they met at the bus stop. "Well, do not give up hope. The police might come up with something in the next one month."

His uncle promised to call up his friend in the city police, to know what had gone wrong. Khokon felt the witnesses must have been paid off. Avijit had never thought of such an eventuality. Yes, anything was possible.

"I told you as much," Mr Dayaram seemed pleased that his prediction had come true, "never expect justice unless you have money power. You will realize as you grow up that money is the only solution to all our problems. So never give up on a chance to make money."

Avijit was intrigued. Everyone seemed to know what could happen next, though he didn't have a clue.

"All this can never bring your father back. Better forget it and get on with life," his mother told him in the night.

She seemed to appreciate the futility of expecting justice and didn't want her life to be dented further. But Avijit could not accept it so easily. His father's untimely death had not only robbed him of a normal adolescence, but also put his future in jeopardy.

Khokon's visit came to an end. There was a sombre silence in the house, when Avijit reached on the day of his departure. Khokon's parents sat in the drawing room, their faces betraying the emotion that ravaged their hearts. Avijit peeped into Khokon's room. The latter was relaxing on the bed, listening to music through earphones. The stark contrast in the mental state of the old and the young made Avijit flinch.

"Ah, here comes the busy young man," Khokon saw him and took off the earphones, "so how was the day?"

"What are you doing here?"

"Why? What am I supposed to do?" Khokon sounded surprised.

"At least sit with your parents. It seems the world has come to an end for them. Try and cheer them up."

"Look, they'll have to face my absence a few hours from now. They may as well get used to it."

Avijit knew it was useless to argue with his cousin and decided not to broach the subject further.

"So when are you coming down next?" he asked instead.

"If given an option, never. But then, I have to meet Dad and Mom. I will never understand why they want to stick to this god forsaken place. They can stay much more comfortably with me. But no! They have to force me back to my roots every year. To cleanse all the sins, they believe I commit abroad."

"It will be difficult adjusting to a new lifestyle at their age," Avijit reasoned, patting a plume of smoke from Khokon's cigarette away from his eyes.

"All bullshit! It's simple. They just won't let me live in peace," Khokon banged a fist on the bed, "but you tell me, what's your decision?"

"What decision?"

"Are you joining a software course or not?"

"No. I can't leave mother alone. Let things settle down a bit. Maybe we can discuss it the next time you come," Avijit explained.

"It might be too late by then. Look, aunty can come and stay here, while you go out to build your career. I think the three of them will be pretty safe together," Khokon suggested.

"No, no. Don't push me into anything now. Give me sometime to adjust," Avijit was firm.

They got into his uncle's car shortly, the devastated parents and their egocentric son, to make the journey to the airport. His uncle drove the car; his aunt occasionally sobbed into her saree, while Khokon stared stoically at the road ahead. Avijit helped in putting the luggage onto a trolley at the airport. His uncle suddenly embraced his son and burst into tears. Khokon touched his parents' feet and hugged them, before proceeding for the check-in. Avijit caught a glimpse of tearful eyes, before his guru turned and slowly disappeared from sight.

"Let's go up to the balcony," his uncle suggested, after they had sat silently for a full hour.

The balcony gave a clear view of the vast tarmac. Avijit had never seen a plane from close quarters and it was big beyond his imagination. There were three of them standing side by side and they could see passengers boarding one. They had to wait another half hour before the plane started with a roar, making them cover their ears. The plane slowly moved towards the runway at the far end. It looked like a path to heaven, brilliantly lit by a row of lights against the backdrop of the night sky. The plane halted at the start of the runway before racing down and out of their sight. His aunt pointed skywards a few moments later, where they could make out the blip of the plane's light.

"Come down with your mother whenever you can," his uncle requested.

"We feel very lonely at times and you are our only hope," his aunt blurted out, just before he got down from their car.

Avijit decided that night that he would never leave his mother alone. Ever. Little did he know that destiny would prove him wrong again.

His life continued in the same vein; meeting Sraboni at the bus stop; serving Mr Dayaram in the office, spending time with his mother or friends at home. Life was both demanding and frustrating. He went with Ujjal one night to the restaurant where Chandan performed. Chandan sang his heart out. But the diners were busy with their food and drink. Mr Dayaram increased the frequency of his outstation tours and Avijit was left to handle the office alone. He always felt nervous on such occasions, handling loads of cash, but luckily, nothing went against him.

"I'll be leaving for Patna tonight," his boss announced one morning, "so, look after the office."

Mr Dayaram gave his contact number as usual, but also left Avijit a gift he hated. Another rumpled 'chit' for two hundred thousand rupees.

"Collect the money by tomorrow and give it to my wife," was the simple directive.

Avijit dreaded such work and did not sleep well that night. The monsoon had descended, the rain announcing its arrival with rhythmic knocks on the windowpane. The trees rustled in delight, as they bathed in the rain after a long hot summer. The skies opened up the next day, just when Munna was driving him down to his rendezvous. They located the shop, another small and shabby one and the transaction was quickly completed. Avijit noted that the 'chit' this time was a receipt for two cases of apple. Disaster struck on their way back. Avijit always felt Munna drove recklessly and his plea to slow down only made the latter drive faster. Munna was driving down a narrow road at over sixty, when he spotted a huge pothole. He braked in time to ensure the front wheel teased its edge. The damage wouldn't have been much had not a speeding bus rammed into them from behind. The bus driver must have learnt driving from the same school as Munna and had applied the brakes a trifle late. Munna's head banged into the windscreen and his dark, cherubic face turned blood red in no time. Avijit was lucky to escape with a minor cut on his forearm, though the impact numbed his senses. They slowly got out from Mr Dayaram's prized car. Or whatever was left of it! The rear of the car looked as flat as his bedroom walls. The back seats were smashed in with the leather upholstery in tatters. A crowd from the nearby shops gathered round the car. Most seemed pleased that a rich guy had been creamed off.

"Idiot, can't you drive carefully?" Munna shouted at the driver of the bus, who had not bothered to climb down.

"Mind your language, you imbecile. Why did you stop suddenly?"

the driver shot back from the safe confines of his cabin.

"Can't you see my car fell into a pothole, you bitch's son," Munna had climbed halfway up to the cabin and was trying to drag the driver out.

A few passengers, irritated with the delay, had got down from the bus and they now joined in.

"How dare you hit the driver, you rascal? It was all your fault," a well-built passenger pulled Munna down and punched him full in the face. Munna, who had been spilling a lot of venom from his thin and frail frame, collapsed. He tried to get up, but the youth kicked him in the ribs. Avijit, who had been watching this madness silently, could not control himself any longer. He pushed past a few mute spectators and grabbed the youth, before the latter could hit Munna again. The youth, though shorter than him, was not short on stamina. He seemed ready to hit anyone who challenged him and punched Avijit in the chest. Avijit blocked the punch and twisted the youth's hand with all his strength. He followed it up with a straight upper cut to the youth's face and floored him. Munna still lay in a heap on the rain drenched road. A thin line of blood was trickling out of his nose. But before Avijit could pull Munna up, blows started raining on his body. The mute spectators had turned aggressors. Things could have been serious, had not a traffic sergeant arrived on the scene. The policeman's arrival made the crowd disperse immediately. The bus driver started his vehicle and prepared to leave.

"Thank you. Those people acted like beasts!" Avijit felt drained. His shirt was torn and blood still oozed from the cut in his forearm.

The policeman helped Munna to his feet. The latter had a deep cut under the left eye and blood all over his face. Avijit had to use his clean white handkerchief to stem the blood flow from Munna's nose.

"I'm fine. Let me see if I can start the car," Munna croaked, after a shopkeeper gave him a glass of water.

Thankfully, the engine started and the policeman waved them off, after noting the car number.

"We're back to the prehistoric age. It's a daily fight for survival," Munna observed.

Avijit had to agree. He still couldn't comprehend why the youth had hit Munna. Was it fun or sheer frustration?

Munna drove carefully for the rest of their journey. He knew Mr Dayaram would roast him alive, if the car got into another accident.

"You go in. I'll take the car to the garage," Munna dropped Avijit in front of the Dayarams' residence.

Avijit trudged down the lawn and rang the bell at the front door. It was well past four and he hoped the lady of the house was not taking an afternoon nap. Or was she in the gym? The same maid opened the door and asked him to wait. Mrs Dayaram appeared shortly at the head of the stairs and beckoned him up. Avijit followed her down the passage to a room on the left. It was the Dayarams' bedroom. The bed was like one from the sets of a movie. The polish dazzled on the wood and the flowers looked real on the colourful bedcover.

"What's happened to you? Oh God! Are you hurt?" Mrs Dayaram squinted at Avijit. She was wearing a saree and looked fresh and beautiful. "Maya, get me some hot water," she called out to the maid, once Avijit had narrated his tale. "You should never get into a fight with such anti-socials. I don't know what is happening to this city! It used to be such a lovely place even a few years back."

The maid reappeared with a tumbler of hot water. Avijit was surprised. Mrs Dayaram had neither counted the money that lay on the bed, nor enquired about the state of their car, which would cost a fortune in repairs. Instead, she poured antiseptic into the water and sponged the cut on his forearm. He was sure his boss would inflict a fresh wound, once he returned.

"Wait. Your shirt is torn. I will get you a new one," she got up and opened a wardrobe at one end of the room. "Here, I think this will fit you," she brought out a shirt and handed it over, "but wash yourself first. Come with me."

She opened the door to the bathroom and Avijit stepped into paradise. He saw himself all around the walls; they were all mirrored. The basin had an array of taps and Avijit fidgeted with all of them, till water started pouring out. He took off his torn shirt and wrapped a towel hanging from the rack on his upper torso, after washing himself clean. Mrs Dayaram would surely not mind. But it drew a squeal of laughter from the lady the moment he came out.

"Are you feeling shy?" she smiled, "don't worry. I've seen a lot more bare-chested males than you can think of."

Avijit didn't know what to make of the remark and stood shyly at one end. Mrs Dayaram came up to him and pulled the towel off.

"Oh my! You have a great body," she ran her eyes down Avijit's hairy chest. Many of his fellow footballers had appreciated his physique, but never a lady. "You must be a rage amongst the girls in your locality," she ran her fingers lightly through his hairy chest.

Avijit was not sure what the lady had in mind and stood like a dumb puppet, at the mercy of his master's wife. Mrs Dayaram continued to run her fingers over his chest and well-muscled shoulders and it felt soft and exciting. He could smell the sweetness of her perfume and feel the heat of her body. She was too close for comfort. He moved away from her and tried to pick up the shirt, which was lying on the bed.

"No, no. Wait. Let me spray some perfume," she went into the bathroom.

Avijit had noticed the bottles stacked up in a rack. He wondered how his boss smelled so bad, even after owning the best fragrances in the world. Or were they for someone else? He wrapped the towel around his upper torso again.

"Oh, you are so shy," the lady came out with a bottle in hand, "take off the towel now."

The spray came out in a fine mist and a spicy smell drowned his senses.

"Umm, it smells good on you," she brought her face close to his chest and inhaled deeply. Avijit took a step backwards.

"I must leave. It's getting late," he tried to put on the new shirt. But she put it back on the bed.

"What is your hurry? It seems you have never been with a woman before," she smiled slyly, "let me show you what a woman looks like."

She dropped her saree from the shoulders and quickly unbuttoned her blouse. Avijit was dumbfounded! He always thought of sex as the ultimate expression of love and never, ever imagined making love to someone else's wife. He wanted to run out of the room. But the evil in him coaxed him to stay put and enjoy this forbidden fruit.

"How do I look?" Mrs Dayaram was standing in front, with her saree draped around her waist.

Avijit couldn't help but stare at the heavy and heaving breasts that wanted to burst free from the low cut bra. She looked the modern day Eve and it was only the fear of his boss that made him resist the temptation building up between his legs.

"Come and kiss me," the lady commanded.

"Madam, please let me go. I will lose my job if your husband comes to know of this," he pleaded.

"He won't know," the lady smiled.

She came near him and forced his hand onto her left breast. It was the first time he had touched a woman there. It felt hot and soft and his senses turned to jelly.

"Do you find me unattractive? Then what is stopping you?"

"But you are married!" Avijit pulled his hand back.

"What marriage are you talking of?" Mrs Dayaram took a step back and shouted, "I'm only married to this wealth and am sick and tired. I have a husband who is obsessed with making money and has forgotten everything else. I couldn't even have a kid. He got our first child aborted, since it was likely to be a baby girl! Don't talk of marriage. Just satisfy me."

She came closer and unhooked the last stitch of cloth that covered her breasts. Avijit knew he was at a defining moment in life. He picked up his soiled shirt from the floor and rushed towards the door.

"I'm sorry. Please do not misunderstand me," he told the lady, before rushing down the stairs.

He snatched up his shoes from near the door and kept running, till he reached the road. Passersby looked at him strangely, as he put on his shoes and pulled the torn shirt over his bare torso. He decided not to go back to his office and boarded a bus for home instead. It was crowded and the passengers looked suspiciously at the strange commuter, who smelled like fresh flowers, but wore a torn and soiled shirt.

"You fought again!" his mother exclaimed, the moment he set foot in his house, "you will end up in hospital at this rate."

Avijit hastily narrated the car accident to pacify her.

"Oh God! What sin did I commit that you inflict this daily punishment on me?" she sighed, "let's go back to Rajpur. This is not the right place for you."

He couldn't sleep for most of the night. The image of Mrs Dayaram, standing bare within touching distance haunted him. He took a bath in the middle of the night to cool his senses, but the events of the evening didn't leave him. He wondered what Khokon would have done in a similar situation. The realization only increased his discomfort. He finally fell back on his trusted hand to bring him relief from the stiffness, which had permanently set in between his legs. The next morning brought a new worry. Mrs Dayaram was surely not happy and might seek her revenge. Avijit was not sure how she might extract it though. What if she called him home again and forcibly had sex? Or was it just a passing fancy for her? She might have already forgotten him and latched onto someone else. He reached office torn between such thoughts and jumped whenever the phone rang, fearing it might be the lady in heat. But she didn't call. He regained confidence by lunchtime and could concentrate on his job, though a nagging worry continued to bother him.

He decided to spend the evening with his friends. Chandan was not available, as he was singing at the hotel. Ujjal was alone in his house and welcomed Avijit with open arms.

"Hi foot-baller! I thought you had gone into hibernation again," he called Avijit into his room. "Good you came. I have a big surprise," Ujjal said, once they had settled on his cot, "the best whiskey in town and the hottest movie in the universe."

Avijit noticed that a video cassette player and a TV adorned Ujjal's room. A large bottle of whiskey and a half-full glass stood on a table.

"My folks have gone to Puri on a vacation. I am the king for the next few days," Ujjal exulted, "let me initiate you into the pleasures of drinking." He wouldn't listen to Avijit's protest and poured out a small measure in a second glass, topping it off with cold water. "Just try it and you will forget all your woes."

His friend looked back at the TV screen, where a couple fornicated in front of the camera.

"Ufooof! Look at her boobs!" Ujjal's eyes were riveted to the screen.

Avijit looked and immediately regretted it. It brought back memories of the last evening.

"Can one really forget one's woes by drinking this?" he asked his friend hesitantly.

"Try and see for yourself."

It tasted bitter and Avijit sipped carefully. He felt nothing and sipped a little more. He soon finished the full glass, but still felt nothing. It made him confident and he asked his friend to pour him another shot.

"Hey, relax. Don't rush into anything. I'll be hanged if you get drunk."

"Don't worry. I know my limits."

But he didn't, after downing two more glasses. His head started spinning and the room seemed to revolve all around him. He found it difficult to focus his eyes and fell on Ujjal's bed, holding his head with both hands.

"Get up and come with me," Ujjal's voice seemed to float down from oblivion. His friend helped him reach the bathroom. "Put your fingers into your throat and try to vomit," he commanded.

Avijit didn't need to raise his fingers an inch. The vomit rushed out on its own. He tried to clean the bathroom after the deed was done, but felt too weak to do so.

"Forget it now. I'll get it done by the maid," his friend pushed him back into the bedroom. He brought something in a cup and asked him to drink it.

"No, no. Not any more," Avijit warded it off.

"Stupid! This is not whiskey. Its lime juice. Drink it and you will feel better."

It worked and he felt a lot better after a few minutes.

"Now tell me about your woes that made you gulp down those pegs so fast," his friend sat down in front of him on the bed, "is it a heart break?"

Avijit knew he had to confide in someone, share his burden and who better than Ujjal? He narrated the previous day's incident.

"Holy cow! You got a chance and didn't do it!" his friend jumped up. "Has your boss returned?" he asked as an afterthought.

"No."

"Then give me her address," Ujjal demanded.

"But why?"

"Hell! To finish off your unfinished job!"

"What?"

"Bloody fool. The whole city is teeming with unsatiated males like me, who can only have sex by either visiting a brothel or getting married. We end up masturbating everyday, as we can afford neither. And you let go of an opportunity, which had come for free!" his friend seemed peeved. "Look, I'll treat you at the best place in town. Just introduce me to her," Ujjal pleaded.

Avijit was shocked into silence. Ujjal made him feel stupid. He started doubting his decision to run away from his boss's wife. Was he wrong? Were taking bribes and sleeping with a married lady the new codes of existence? He was confused.

"But why did you want to drink yourself to death?" his friend reined in his excitement.

"I'm afraid she might seek revenge," Avijit could finally speak of his real worry.

"But what will she gain? You wouldn't poke her, even if she bared all and stood within sniffing distance!"

"What if she sacks me?"

"On what grounds? You could spill the beans to her husband. Would she risk it?"

Ujjal sounded logical. Avijit was nothing special for Mrs Dayaram to risk exposure.

"But I can show you the shortest route to a promotion," Ujjal was talking in riddles again.

"Which one?"

"Introducing me to her – I the greatest lover east of the Ganges."

Ujjal escorted him home. Avijit made him promise not to discuss the incident with anyone. His mother looked worried, as it was close to midnight.

"Where had you been?" she demanded.

"Sorry Mom. I was watching a movie with Ujjal. Did you have your dinner?"

She as usual, was waiting for her son. Mother and son sat down and had the frugal meal.

"There are certain things in life, which are best avoided. They can cause you a lot of pain, if you make them a habit," she told him, once he finished his food, "and next time you want to drink, sit in the house and do so. At least I won't be scared to death thinking of your whereabouts."

Avijit wondered whether mothers' could read minds.

"Forgive me this time. It will never happen again," he told his mother the next morning, before leaving for office.

Avijit felt nervous the moment he entered his office. His boss had still not returned and he sat alone, his anxiety increasing with the hour. Would Mrs Dayaram pardon him? Should he call her up to beg forgiveness? But she could have forgotten him. He decided not to disturb her. Mr Dayaram called up in the afternoon and said he was boarding the night train and would be in office the next day. He took details of the daily transactions and disconnected the phone. Relief flooded Avijit. His boss didn't even raise the incident of the car accident. It meant Mrs Dayaram had not told him anything. There was no news of Munna either. Avijit hoped he was fine. Munna was likely to face the worst time of his life, once Mr Dayaram saw the car.

Mr Dayaram arrived the next day. Avijit was having lunch.

"Come into my room after you finish," his boss smiled at him.

Avijit quickly gobbled down the dry parathas and potato curry his mother had packed for him. He drank two glasses of water and ventured into his boss's chamber. His boss was speaking on the phone and asked him to sit down. Avijit waited patiently. Everything looked normal about Mr Dayaram's behaviour.

"Why did you do it?" the sudden question broke his spell.

"What, sir?" he mumbled. Mrs Dayaram would surely not mention the episode to her husband. She was the guilty party.

"Bastard! You are asking me?" his boss exploded.

A cold shiver ran down Avijit's spine. It seemed his worst fears were coming true.

"I didn't do it sir," he replied lamely.

"Then where is the money?"

"What money?" Avijit was relieved. It was not what he had feared. His boss often lost track of his finances and immediately flared up. He only calmed down, after Avijit showed him the missing link.

"The money you were to give to my wife."

"But I had given it to her," Avijit's fear returned.

"Yeah, but it had ten thousand rupees less. Where is it?"

Avijit suddenly realized what must have happened. Mrs Dayaram proved to be a bitch all right.

"Sir, believe me. I gave the entire money to her. I swear on my father's name," he pleaded.

"You mean to say my wife is lying!"

"Yes."

"Get the hell out of here," Mr Dayaram was red in the face. "You steal my money and then call my wife a liar! You need not come from tomorrow. You cease to be an employee of this company."

"Sir, please hear me out. Believe me. I didn't take any money. You can ask Munna. He was with me all the while," Avijit didn't know how to clear the air.

"Oh! So he was an accomplice," his boss seemed to be beyond reason. "I employed you only because of Mr Bannerjee's recommendation. You could have asked for the money and I would have given it. But you steal! You thought I wouldn't notice, ah?" Mr Dayaram paused for breath. "Just get out before I call the police. One bastard ruins my car and the other steals my money. Oh God! What has this world come to?"

Avijit came out of the chamber and sat on the sofa. He hoped his boss would calm down. But that was not to be. Mr Dayaram came charging down and pushed him out of the office. He then closed the door to the hellhole. Avijit had never felt so demeaned in life. He felt lost. No one would believe him. He decided to go back home and talk to his mother. She was the only person who would understand.

He wandered aimlessly down the road for some time before catching a bus home. The bus was half full and Avijit was sitting alone staring sullenly out of the window, when someone tapped him on the shoulder.

"So, you have bunked office?" Sraboni was returning home. "Is something wrong?" she asked, after giving him a close look.

"Yeah, I just lost my job," Avijit managed a thin smile.

"Are you joking? But why?"

"I'm supposed to have stolen money," he looked her in the eyes.

"Come with me," Sraboni got up and pulled him along.

They got down at the next stop. Avijit followed her silently, as she hailed a cab and got in.

"Lake," she told the driver.

Avijit had heard that the lake was a rendezvous for lovers. He wondered what Sraboni had in mind. They reached shortly and Sraboni paid the cab. She took his hand and walked down the road, till they found an empty bench near the edge of the lake.

"Now tell me, what is it?" Sraboni asked.

"I told you. I just lost my job."

"How?"

So Avijit told her. She couldn't believe it.

"What? The witch abused you and you didn't say a thing? And today, when her impotent husband sacks you, you leave! You must protest," she was firm.

"My boss believes his wife. He won't listen to me."

"But how can he ignore your service and loyalty for the past many months? You could have stolen much more money had you wished. Go and explain to him tomorrow. I am sure he will understand."

"Okay. I will try if you say so," Avijit got up to leave. "I want to go home and think out my options," he told Sraboni, who followed reluctantly.

"Don't worry. I know everything will be fine," she tried to cheer him up before they parted.

CHAPTER Eight

His mother was surprised to see him back so early. She sensed something was amiss, once he avoided her queries and collapsed on his bed.

"What is it today?" she asked cautiously.

Avijit had tears in the eye when he looked up. His mother immediately pulled him towards her and ran her hands through his hair. Avijit knew this was the one shelter that would never desert him.

"Tell me, what is wrong?" she asked again.

"I lost my job."

"How could you?" she was stunned.

"My boss thinks I stole his money."

"My son can never steal," she was firm in her conviction.

"But he wouldn't listen to me and pushed me out of the office. I don't know what to do now."

"You must talk to your uncle. I'm sure he can convince your boss," his mother sounded confident.

She did not pursue the topic further and dismissed it as a petty misunderstanding.

Avijit reflected on this new dimension that night. Both Sraboni and his mother were confident that Mr Dayaram would see reason and take him back. But then Sraboni was a young girl and knew little about life. His mother too knew half the story. He could not speak freely with his uncle. Everything was topsy-turvy. And all because of an over-sexed woman! He mused whether he should beg her forgiveness? But what if she took him to bed? He imagined ravishing her shapely body, before finally falling asleep.

"I can't believe this," his uncle was shocked. "Surprisingly, he did not call me up to complain," he picked up the phone and called Mr Dayaram.

"Dayaram? What is this I hear from my nephew? Have you sacked him from the job?"

His uncle listened silently for the next few minutes, his bushy eyebrows curled up.

"I think there is a mistake somewhere. He is a good boy and I have full faith in him. I would request you to reconsider," he said after a while.

Avijit's nerves were on edge and he waited with bated breath to hear the final verdict.

"I remind you, he is my nephew. You are not being fair. How can you dump someone unceremoniously, after he served you satisfactorily for the past many months? I'm sure you will give him one more chance," his uncle pleaded.

He listened for some more time and his face seemed to contort in a silent rage.

"Fair enough. I think he is capable of getting a better job. It was my mistake that I sent him to a goon like you," he shouted and slammed the phone down.

Both sat quietly, not knowing what to say. Avijit knew Mr

Dayaram's door was closed to him for ever. It meant a new struggle for existence.

"Give me a few days. I'll find something for you. But don't lose heart and do something silly," his uncle warned, "everything will be fine."

Avijit had long given up the hope of a fine life.

He spent the next few days at home with his mother. She wanted to go back to Rajpur.

"I'm sure you will get a job in the steel plant. After all it's a small town and we know people there."

"But if I draw a blank in a big city like Calcutta, how do you expect me to get a job in Rajpur?"

His uncle came down to their house one afternoon.

"I might be able to help you. There is a vacancy in this company," he handed over a visiting card, "go and meet him. The world does have a few devious men like your previous employer. This should be better."

It certainly was. The office was located on the fifth floor and a well maintained lift took him up in no time. A young lady at the reception listened to him patiently and asked him to wait. Avijit sat on the plush sofa for a full hour, before a peon directed him to the owner's chamber.

"Come in and sit down," a voice floated out, after he had knocked on the door.

The owner, who looked to be pushing forty, sat behind a large table. He was smartly dressed in a blue safari suit and wore gold-rimmed spectacles. Avijit sat silently for the next five minutes, as the man stared at a computer screen on his table. Avijit found no files or papers strewn across the table, as used to be the case in his previous office. They were stacked neatly in two trays marked 'IN' and 'OUT'. The man looked up shortly and frowned.

"So you are the one," he started, "okay, tell me something about yourself."

The man lowered his glasses a little down his nose and looked at him over it. Avijit thought for a moment before he started. He spoke of his life in Rajpur, but the owner interrupted him.

"I don't have time for your life history. Tell me about your education," the man sounded rude.

Avijit told him.

"Why did you give up your studies midway?"

"I had some financial problems at home, sir."

"What financial problems?"

"My father died, sir."

"How?"

"He was murdered, sir."

"By whom?"

"I don't know, sir. The police are still investigating."

"I see."

Avijit was not sure what the man saw and waited for the next question.

"Tell me, what is the capital city of Uganda?"

The question baffled Avijit. He had read of Uganda as a nation in Africa, but could not recall the name of its capital city. He kept quiet.

"I see. You are poor in geography. Tell me, when was Hitler born?"

Avijit didn't know and remained silent.

"I see. You are poor in history too. Tell me, how do you calculate compound interest?"

Avijit noticed the man had a habit of pulling on his hair before every question. He wondered whether the query depended on which strand the man pulled? He answered the last question correctly.

"I see. That was simple enough for a schoolboy to answer. Tell me, who was the first Indian to win a Nobel?

"Tagore."

"No."

"Yes, sir."

"I said no. Why are you arguing?"

"Only because Tagore was the first Indian to win the Nobel!"

"You are wrong. Aryabhatta was the first Indian to win the Nobel," the owner replied firmly.

"But Aryabhatta died much before Sir Alfred Nobel was born sir!"

"So what? It must have been given posthumously," the owner gave a wry smile.

Avijit was appalled and decided not to argue. After all, what relevance did such questions have to his job? It might be the job of a peon or a clerk and neither Aryabhatta nor Tagore could do much to change his destiny.

"Have you worked anywhere before?"

The question put Avijit in a dilemma. He initially wanted to avoid talking of his stint at Dayaram & Company. But his uncle might have told the man opposite him about his last job. He decided to play fair and spoke about his previous job.

"Give me the number of your last employer," the owner demanded.

Avijit knew the consequence, but waited till he was asked to leave. The owner got through and started talking. He listened intently for a few minutes, before putting down the phone.

"He said you stole his money. Did you?"

"No. That's why I came to you for a job. Otherwise, I would have opened a school with the money and given people like you a crash course in general knowledge," Avijit got up from the chair, smiled and left.

He knew he had nowhere to go. The Dayarams had labelled him a thief and it would be difficult to wipe off the stigma. He called his uncle from a public booth to give him the bad news. His uncle sounded more dismayed than him.

"Don't give up. I will definitely get you something. Just be patient."

But Avijit had no hope. He knew his mother was right; it would be prudent to go back to Rajpur. At least Dayaram would not be able to sour his chances there. He decided to go home and plan their return. His mother looked disappointed when she opened the door and didn't even ask him about the interview. Naluda was sitting in his room. His presence made Avijit uneasy. What could have gone wrong again?

"I came to buy clothes for my family ahead of the festive season. Thought I would drop by," Naluda smiled.

Avijit suddenly remembered that *Durga Puja*, the annual Bengali festival, was round the corner. Everyone wore new clothes during the festivities. People in small towns like Rajpur came down to Calcutta to shop for the latest designs. His father had always bought him new clothes and a pair of shoes. There would be no festivity for him this time though.

"Mr Samaddar has been transferred," his mother broke the news.

"What?"

"Yes," Naluda replied, "they had connections with the higher ups. A man like Samaddar was not one to compromise. He would have booked the culprits. So they pulled all the strings and got him transferred to North Bengal."

"But his successor can start from where he left," Avijit tried to reason with his father's colleague.

"Doesn't seem likely. They will force him to look the other way."

"This means my husband's killer will never be punished," his mother's voice quivered in disbelief.

"That's how the world is," Naluda replied sadly.

Avijit decided they were wasting time discussing the improbable.

"Ma, its better to think of survival than justice. It's good that Naluda has come here. I feel we should go back to Rajpur, instead of me running around here in search of a job. Tell me Naluda, what are my chances of getting a job in the steel plant?"

"But what of your job here?" Naluda sounded confused.

Avijit told him.

"As far as I know, the sanction is still stuck at the head office," Naluda replied, after regaining his composure, "our plant has been doing badly for the past few years and the management wants to cut costs. The first step would be retrenchment and half the workers may be offered voluntary retirement. So fresh recruitment is farthest from their mind."

It was a few weeks later that Avijit decided to pay Mr Ghosh a visit. It was more to break the monotony than anything else. But it opened up a new chapter in his life. Mr Ghosh was sitting alone in the drawing room, watching a cricket match, when Avijit knocked on his door.

"Oh! What a surprise," Mr Ghosh seemed pleased to see him, "I thought you had forgotten this old war horse."

Avijit sat down in the drawing room.

"Just give me a few minutes. We are in the final over of our innings and Sourav is still playing," the armyman stared at the television.

They watched with increasing excitement, as the batsman hit the remaining four balls for fourteen runs.

"I think we will win today," Mr Ghosh remarked, before switching off the TV. "Where had you been? I have not seen you on the football field for quite some time."

"I was busy," Avijit didn't know where to begin.

"Well, young man, a job is not the sole priority of life. You should give equal attention to family, sports and recreation. We managed a little bit of everything in our time."

"Your time was different. Your job was secure and people were happy with a simple life."

"Maybe you are right. Staying simple is no longer easy. So, how are you doing in the office?"

Avijit weighed his words before replying.

"I've lost my job."

"What?" Mr Ghosh fell silent. Thankfully, he did not ask for the details.

"I'm in a terrible dilemma sir. I don't know whether to stick to Calcutta or go back to Rajpur. I've come to you to seek guidance. Please help me."

His plea seemed to touch a soft spot. Mr Ghosh came around and put his hands on Avijit's shoulder.

"You are just like my son. Tell me what you want me to do?"

"I don't know sir. Can you get me into a football team? I might still make a living out of it."

"Look, you can't support your family unless you get into the best team. You get your focus right and try for a job. Calcutta would definitely be a better bet than Rajpur. Football can come later," the armyman sat down again. "Has anyone offered you a job?"

"No."

"Fine. Would you be interested in joining the army?"

"Will they take me?"

"First tell me whether you are interested. It will be a tough life. But the rewards can be high. You will be respected and the chance to do something good will present itself regularly," Mr Ghosh looked at him closely, "it will also mean staying alone, away from your mother."

The last words put Avijit in a quandary. How could he leave his mother all by herself? That was unthinkable.

"But my mother can adjust to the tough conditions. Can't she stay with me?"

"No. The army doesn't give family posting to a fresher. She can stay with you, once you get it after two-three years. She has to live alone till then."

Avijit didn't know what to say. He desperately needed a job. But could he sacrifice his mother's company for it? He was not sure.

"Take your time and discuss it with your mother. Though you will be separated from her, you will earn much more to provide her a better life."

Their conversation was cut short, as Mrs Ghosh came in with a tray full of vegetable pakoras. Sraboni followed with a bowlful of puffed rice.

"I'm sure you are hungry. Eat it while I make some tea," Mrs

Ghosh departed, after putting down the food on the table. Sraboni sat down next to her father.

"I think you have met my daughter before," Mr Ghosh looked at Avijit, "I'm really worried about her."

"Why?"

"Oh, her exams are nearing, but she has given up on her studies. I don't know what she will do."

"Marry her off," Avijit joked.

"Yeah, that's a great suggestion," Sraboni narrowed her eyes and looked at him, "that will solve all your problems, Dad."

"But it's not a bad idea either. A girl has to be married off after all," Mr Ghosh agreed with Avijit.

"This is the problem with the males of the world. They always think a girl cannot survive without marriage. That's crazy! Times have changed. We can fend for ourselves now," Sraboni retorted.

"But how will you fend if you do not study?"

"Dad. Your ideas are obsolete now. You don't need to study sixteen hours a day to score high marks. Wait till my results are out. I'll penalize you dearly for doubting my ability. And I would like to be a journalist. So don't listen to people and marry me off!"

"Okay, okay. Don't get angry. I was just joking," Mr Ghosh raised his hands in surrender, "how can I live without my dear little *Magpie*?"

"Yes, or who else will help you dye your hair every week and hide your grey hairs?" Sraboni mocked.

"Stop! Stop! You are letting out my darkest secrets. This is not fair," Mr Ghosh covered his hair with both hands.

Mrs Ghosh came in shortly and joined the fun. They looked a close-knit family. Avijit remembered similar evenings in his own family, when his father was alive. It all seemed a distant dream now. He decided to go home as it was getting late; his mother would be worrying.

"Remember to discuss with her. I don't think she will stop you. It will be good for both," Mr Ghosh told him.

It was almost nine by the time he reached home. He found his uncle's car parked near the house.

"Where had you been?" his mother sounded upset, "your uncle is waiting for more than an hour."

"Its all right. He's not to blame. How could he know I would come?" his uncle reasoned.

"I'm sorry. Mr Ghosh had asked me several times to spend an evening with him. I went there today."

"That's good. You should always take some time out and mix with people. It will help you relax," his uncle tried to cheer him up.

They spent the next few minutes in chitchat, till his uncle got down to business.

"Forget about the last interview. It will be difficult for you to get a job immediately, as your future employer will definitely refer back to Dayaram," his uncle paused, "I suggest you join my office."

"But how is that possible? Don't burden yourself just to help us out," Avijit's mother was aghast, "you already have sufficient people in your office. What will he do there?"

"Then what will he do now?" his uncle seemed annoyed.

"I would like to join the army," Avijit announced calmly.

There was an uneasy silence in the room, broken only by the whirring of the old ceiling fan. His uncle spoke finally.

"But is there any recruitment on?"

"Mr Ghosh has assured me, he will get me a job in the army, if I agree."

"Ha! It's easier said than done. Don't get into this confusion. Simply report for work at my office tomorrow," his uncle got up to leave.

"No Uncle. Let me try this. I will have to face many more Dayarams, if I join you. I am sick and tired of such people. So don't be angry. Allow me to try my luck."

"Okay. Fair enough. But keep me posted on the developments. And as I said, my office door is always open for you."

Avijit went with his uncle to the car. His uncle turned before getting into it.

"I'm happy you want to try something on your own," he patted Avijit on the back, "best of luck."

Avijit and his mother had a quiet dinner of their staple roti and potato curry that night. He sat with his mother in her room later.

"Is it okay if I join the army?" he asked tentatively.

"It should be good if you can get it. Your father always believed in a disciplined life. I hear army life is a disciplined one. Will you get it?"

Avijit somehow had a lot of faith in Mr Ghosh. His only worry was his mother.

"You might have to stay alone for the next few years, if I get the job," he spoke softly, as if to cushion the shock.

"I will, if I have to. If I could bear the pain of you in my belly for nine months and your father's dead body in my arms, then anything is bearable. At least you can eke out a living. That will drown all my sorrow," his mother cried silently. Avijit watched helplessly, as a thin stream of tears dripped down her face.

He called on Mr Ghosh the next morning.

"Oh, good to see you again. See, I told you we would win the match. We did."

Avijit was not in the frame of mind to indulge in the luxury of watching a cricket match. He had his own match to win and there was very little time. He was in the slog overs. Getting slogged all over life. Beyond boundaries he had built up in his mind.

"We can talk freely today as no one is home," Mr Ghosh poured out a cup of tea for him from a thermos.

"Why, where are the others?" Avijit asked, though he knew Sraboni was in college. They had met in the morning for a few minutes.

"Well, my daughter must be roaming around with her boyfriends, while my wife is on a puja shopping spree with her girlfriends," Mr Ghosh laughed out aloud. "So? What is your decision?"

"Yes sir. I would like to join the army. My mother is willing to stay alone."

"You have your tea, while I make a call."

Mr Ghosh walked down to the phone, which stood on a raised stool at one corner of the room. He dialled a number and asked for Mr Sankaranarayan. The armyman spoke softly for the next few minutes, while Avijit sipped on the tea.

"He still believes it was I who saved his life. Tell me, can I change destiny? He was to survive and he did – a true soldier. Still fighting life with one leg." Mr Ghosh marvelled at his colleague's courage. "He'll call back within fifteen minutes. So let's relax and watch TV."

The phone rang after ten minutes. Mr Ghosh listened intently to what the caller had to say. He thanked him profusely and put down the receiver.

"For a change, I have some good news for you," the armyman's remark sent Avijit's pulse racing, "the army is planning to recruit just after the *Durga Puja*. So you have a few weeks to prepare yourself. Sankar said they have already advertised in the papers. You need to fill up the application form immediately. Sankar should send it to me by tomorrow. Come down tomorrow with all documents."

"But how do I prepare myself?"

"Just stay fit. They might ask you to do a hundred push-ups and run a thousand metres. I think you should practice everyday with the football team."

"I'll do that sir."

A hundred push-ups and a thousand metres. Avijit was ready to do ten times that if it ensured a living.

"And brush up your general knowledge. They normally have a one hour objective test."

Avijit watched TV for sometime, before he decided to leave. He felt relaxed and determined. He almost bumped into Mrs Ghosh near the door. She was returning from her shopping and was half bent under the weight of the gift packets she held with both hands. Avijit helped her put down the packets in the drawing room.

"This yearly ritual!" she exclaimed, "the markets are swarming with people. Thank God, I'm almost done. Maybe another day for the shoes."

She sat down on a chair and mopped her brow.

Avijit knew *Durga Puja* was just round the corner. Everyone seemed to have completed their shopping, though he didn't know when to start and what to buy. His mother always bought her quota of sarees for the full year during the pujas. But this year would be different. She had stopped wearing coloured sarees after his father's death and had settled for the cheap white ones worn by widows. So there was nothing he could buy her.

He spent the next few weeks practicing football for four to five hours each day. He knew on the very first day that an office job had robbed him of the fitness, which was his pride. He panted for breath after running a few laps, when he could easily run fifteen laps earlier without stopping. He toiled hard to regain his lost form. His mother was busy again. She had agreed to sing along with the other ladies in their locality, during the *Durga Puja,* and they had regular rehearsals. His uncle visited them just before the festivities.

"Do you like this?" his uncle had bought a shirt and trousers for him, "see if it fits you."

It fit perfectly. Avijit was thrilled. "Thank you."

There was also a saree for his mother, but she refused to accept it.

"My dreams and desires are lost. What will I do with such a colourful saree?"

Durga Puja was the celebration of the victory of Goddess *Durga* over *Asura*, the evil one. Everything but fun was secondary during the festival. Each locality had its own celebrations; huge pandals brilliantly lit, the images of Goddess *Durga* and her children crafted out of clay by the best craftsmen, people in colourful clothes hopping from pandal to pandal. The entire city got transformed in to a glittering paradise.

Avijit woke up on the first day at the rhythmic sound of the *Dhak*. But it did not rouse the same excitement as it used to. Though there were fewer pujas in Rajpur, the ambience was the same. His father had always been in the organizing committee of their local puja and the entire family would spend most of the day at the pandal. Lunch was a community affair, with everyone in the locality sitting together at the pandal and gulping down the khichuri and payesh. There was a great sense of bonhomie. But the entire thrill was now lost. His mother, who used to be a lively soul during the pujas, was strangely subdued.

"Wear the new *Punjabi-pajama* I have left for you on the bed," she told Avijit, after he had come out of the bathroom.

He was pleasantly surprised. In spite of her state, she had not forgotten to buy him something. It would be difficult to live away from her, he mused. He put on the new clothes and went to the puja pandal. He met Ujjal and Chandan there.

"Well, you had told me not to give up. I didn't. But neither should you," Chandan remarked, after hearing of his misfortune.

Avijit spotted Sraboni sitting and chatting animatedly with a few other girls. Everyone around him looked happy. He could hear young and old alike, planning for a night of pandal hopping and revelry. He felt out of place and went back home. His mother didn't talk much, till Sraboni dropped in to wish her.

"Aunty, you must come with us tonight," she requested.

"Where?"

"Oh, we will visit the major pandals. You must come."

"No dear. I would rather stay at home."

"But why don't you go?" Avijit insisted.

"Then what will you do, all alone in the house?"

"Why? He is also coming with us. Dad asked me to invite both of you. Be ready by eight. We will come and pick you up," and Sraboni left, as quickly as she had come

They came around nine. Mr Ghosh was at the wheel of the car.

The ladies got into the back, while Avijit sat next to Mr Ghosh. It started off well with Mr Ghosh driving fast till they saw a pandal. All of them got down to see the decorated images and the lighting. Then they drove down to the next one. There was a constant chatter amongst the ladies, as to which was the best pandal they had seen. They invariably changed their decision, after every new visit. Avijit got bored of the ritual soon. The roads were jammed with cars and progress was slow. The traffic policemen sweated and shouted to bring the unruly traffic under control. The pujas didn't seem to hold much thrill for them either. It was a long queue to each pandal and Avijit felt tired. But the ladies wouldn't give up and his ordeal continued till the early morning. The Ghoshs dropped them home when the dark sky was turning a light purple, heralding a new dawn.

CHAPTER Nine

A telegram arrived a few weeks later, asking him to report at Fort William the day after. Fort William was the military headquarters of the Eastern Command in the Indian Army. It was adjacent to the Maidan, the vast green playground of Calcutta. Avijit found a big crowd in front of the gate when he reached. Most of the aspirants seemed to have come from the outskirts of Calcutta.

"Fall in a line," a command was issued shortly.

Avijit stood in the middle of a long queue. They were asked to follow an armyman into the main compound. Everyone followed silently, their steps a little tentative. The registration started within five minutes. Each aspirant's chest, weight and height were measured. A few were directed to go and sit behind the queue after their names were registered, while most were asked to leave. It seemed they were either overweight or didn't qualify in the height and chest measurements. Avijit prayed that the excess food he had gobbled down during the past few days wouldn't prove to be his bane.

"Good morning, sir," he greeted the officer when his turn came.

"Yes, good morning," the man looked up, a trifle surprised. It seemed no one else had bothered to greet him so far.

"Please step on the weighing machine," the officer directed.

Avijit stood on his toes, trying hard not to put his full weight on the machine.

"Relax and stand," an assistant standing near the machine, directed.

Avijit obeyed and his weight was noted.

"Take a deep breath and push out your chest," the assistant quickly wrapped a tape round his air filled torso and noted the circumference.

"Okay, now breathe out," he again measured the centimetres.

"Done. Stand here with your chin touching the scale," he indicated the height-measuring machine.

Avijit felt a soft press of the pointer on his head. He waited with bated breath. The assistant looked shorter than him. It meant he would qualify on the height. But he was not sure of his weight. He swore he would stop eating if he got disqualified.

"Your name?" the officer's query eased his tension.

He had crossed the first hurdle. The officer jotted down his address and educational qualifications in the register. He was then asked to sit behind the queue and wait. Avijit suddenly felt hungry. He had hardly eaten the rice and dal his mother had prepared for him in the morning. He spotted a nut seller outside the gate and bought a big packet.

"So? You are through?" the gangly youth sitting next to him asked.

"Yes," Avijit tore open the packet and popped a few peanuts into his mouth. There was too much salt in it.

"Where are you from?" the youth asked again.

"Calcutta," Avijit was too tense to get into a conversation and chewed the nuts silently.

"Well, I'm from Munsui in Midnapore district. I'm Ghoton."

Avijit had never heard of the place. The gangly youth had extended his hand, and Avijit looked around quickly before touching it, afraid that the gesture might disqualify him.

"What are you eating?" the youth pointed to the packet in his hand.

"Peanuts. Want some?" Avijit had finished about half the contents and extended the pack.

The youth seemed to consider the offer for a moment, before snatching the pack from him. Avijit watched helplessly as the entire peanuts vanished in one go.

"Thank you. That was good."

Avijit felt disgusted and sat silently.

"So you want to join the army?" the youth continued.

"No. I've come here to cut grass."

"Come on. I know you are joking. You want to join the army."

Avijit was saved a reply, as an armyman approached them.

"Get up and stand straight," he ordered.

The first round was over and the people who had qualified were asked to follow the man. They were taken to a big playground and an officer addressed them.

"Your fitness will be tested in this round. You need to run sixteen hundred metres under six minutes. It means four laps on this ground. Now break up into groups of ten each."

Avijit tried to measure up the competition. He decided to stand in the queue nearest to him.

"Hi, so we meet again," it was the tall gangly youth again, "can you run fast? I can."

Their group was fourth in the line. The playground was big and looked well maintained. Trees surrounded it and the leaves rustled, as a pleasant breeze blew across. Three guys each from the first two groups qualified with ease, the others either dropping out or lagging behind. Avijit's heart raced faster by the time the third group entered the last lap.

"Are you sure you want to join the army?" the gangly youth, who was in their group, asked again.

Avijit stared at the stupid guy. He couldn't hide the contempt in his eyes, before nodding his head. The third group finished and it was their turn. They took position next to each other.

"Okay. On your marks, get set."

Bang! The pistol sounded and they were off. Avijit knew he needed to preserve energy for a final burst in the last lap. He decided to take the lead and control the pace of the race. But try as he might, he couldn't overtake the gangly youth, who seemed to maintain the lead effortlessly. The others in the group looked equally strong. As a result, everyone started running at a very fast pace from the first lap itself. Two youths, who were running just ahead of Avijit, started to look tired by the third lap. They blocked his path and he couldn't overtake them. He was sure to be disqualified if he ran at that pace. They were almost in the last half of the final lap when the gangly youth, who was still ahead of the pack, did a strange thing. He reduced his pace and dropped back, till he was just in front of the two youths who were blocking Avijit's path. He suddenly stretched a leg backwards and tripped one of them! The guy next to the one who was tripped did not notice it and fell on the body of the first runner.

Avijit swiftly averted the cursing bodies and ran as fast as he could. The gangly youth maintained his lead till the end and Avijit touched home just before the six-minute was up. He was sure the guy from Midnapore would be disqualified, but to his surprise the latter's name was registered. It seemed the tripping incident had not been noticed, as it had taken place at the far end of the ground. The two youths, who had been felled, came charging down. Instead of complaining to the officer, they attacked the youth from Midnapore. Two armymen rushed up and separated them immediately. They were asked to leave.

"Why did you trip him?" Avijit asked, the moment he had got back his breath.

"Otherwise, you wouldn't have qualified."

The realization made Avijit start! He looked closely at this sudden acquaintance whom he had ignored for the last hour. The guy was tall, with large protruding eyes and long curling hair. His egg shaped head looked bigger than the rest of his body. His long hands hung loosely from his square shoulders, as if they were pasted to his undernourished frame. But the strange looking fellow, for some mysterious reason, had just given Avijit a new lease of life.

"I'm Avijit. Thank you. You risked your own chance."

"Well, you must have forgotten my name," the young man smiled. Avijit indeed had, but felt embarrassed to admit it.

"I'm Ghoton. I like you because you spoke to me earlier and offered me those peanuts. If I like someone, I can die for him."

Avijit looked at this strange looking lad in amazement.

"You think I am crazy? Should I die and show you?"

"No, no! You don't have to die for me," Avijit jumped up.

"Maybe we can die together for this country, if the army selects us today," Ghoton beamed.

Avijit didn't like this discussion of death. It seemed his new friend did not value life. Their chat was broken by the army officer's command.

"Follow me."

They were taken into an office building and asked to wait in the hall. There were fifty of them; fifty who had survived from the few hundred who had started off. The officer returned shortly with an assistant.

"Go with him and have your lunch. You have exactly fifteen minutes," he ordered.

Avijit suddenly realized it was well past noon and his stomach was churning. They were led into what looked like a canteen. Armymen were sitting around tables spread all over the hall, having lunch. They were led to the counter, where a lunch tray was handed over to each of them. They sat together and had a hearty meal of rice, dal, vegetable curry and plain curd. The assistant escorted them back, once they had finished.

"Oh! What a lunch that was," Ghoton sounded happy.

"Yeah, it was okay," Avijit responded.

"You say okay! It was simply great. I can't remember when I last had a meal like that."

They had a general knowledge test after lunch.

"We will have an objective test now. I'll take back your papers exactly after an hour," an officer distributed the sheets.

There was an audible sigh from Ghoton.

"Shit. I have always been poor in studies. I don't stand a chance. Maybe I should quit before I lose face," he almost got up from his seat.

"Sit quietly," Avijit pulled him back, "I will help you."

And so he did, evading the sharp eyes of the invigilators. The questions were simple enough and Avijit had done his homework. Both he and Ghoton had satisfied smiles on their faces after submitting the papers. The former for having answered most of the questions correctly; the latter for having managed to put ink on paper.

"Thank you gentlemen. That is all for today. You have to report back tomorrow at ten a.m. A board will interview those short-listed. You will then be put through a medical test, if selected. So be here on time," the officer picked up all the papers and left the room.

Avijit felt deflated. He had hoped to bag the job after the written test, but now he had to face an interview. What if they referred to Mr Dayaram? Ghoton too seemed pensive.

"See you tomorrow," Avijit waved, before moving away. He spent an agonizing night, turning and tossing on the bed. His mother smiled when he spoke of Ghoton. "He looks like the devil but has the heart of a saint. And I was angry with him for having eaten my peanuts!"

He reached the venue well in time the next day. Ghoton stood near the gate, wearing the same dress that looked rumpled. They waited eagerly for the clock to strike ten and strode with purpose towards the administrative building. Thirty names were displayed on a notice board. Avijit started looking from the bottom of the list, but his friend seemed more confident. He started right at the top. Both their names were in the middle of the list.

"We've done it," Ghoton hugged him. It seemed he had not even brushed his teeth and Avijit turned his face away to escape the smell.

"Hold on. There's still the interview," Avijit reminded him.

"Will they ask tough questions?"

"How would I know?"

The interview started. Avijit was tenth in the queue after Ghoton.

"Will you swap seats with me?" the latter whispered suddenly.

"Why?"

"Well, you can tell me what they asked, if you go in ahead of me. Will you?"

"But you will have to go in after me. So how do I tell you?"

It set the youth thinking. It was when the sixth interviewee had gone in that Avijit felt a nudge.

"I will say I need to go to the toilet. Then we can meet there."

"But I don't know where the toilet is. There may be quite a few in this building."

"Then what do I do?" Ghoton croaked.

"Just relax and go in on your turn," Avijit was once again feeling irritated. There was silence till Ghoton's turn came. He mopped his brow with his shirt sleeve and closed his eyes for a moment before getting up.

"Let's hope I pass. All the best," and he went in.

Avijit suddenly felt lonely and nervous. He realized Ghoton had kept him occupied. All his worries returned. What would they ask inside? Would they ask about his last job? It seemed Ghoton was taking a lot longer than the others. Had he tripped someone inside? The back of Avijit's shirt grew wet from his sweat. But he didn't have to wait for long, as Ghoton came out shortly. He took a few deep breaths and walked towards the door. Ghoton tapped him on his shoulder, but he was too tense to respond.

"May I come in sir?" he asked, before parting the deep green curtain.

"Come in please."

He entered. Three men sat behind a large table. He recognized one of them as the young officer who had been present during the physical tests. The other two were older.

"Come and sit down," the man in the centre indicated a chair.

"Thank you sir."

Avijit had to repeat his name, family background and educational qualifications.

"What does your father do?"

"He used to work in a steel plant, sir."

"What does he do now?" the young officer asked.

"He died sir," Avijit paused, "he was killed by unknown assailants near the steel plant."

"I'm sorry to hear that son," the man in the centre remarked. He wore a lot of ribbons and coloured straps on his uniform, and looked senior.

"Show me your mark-sheets."

Avijit handed them over. The three men glanced through them, one by one. Avijit waited till the papers were returned to him. He could only hear the sound of his heartbeat, which seemed to be on overdrive. The senior man spoke again.

"We are recruiting for the position of sepoys today. This is a junior position in the army. With your score, you could have joined the National Defence Academy and graduated as an officer. Are you sure you want to join as a sepoy?"

"Yes sir."

"But life can be very tough."

"I have lived a tough life sir."

"I understand," the senior nodded towards his colleagues.

"How long have you known your friend?" the young officer asked.

"Who sir?" Avijit was puzzled.

"The chap who came in before you. He asked us to give you priority over him, if there is a crunch."

Avijit's amazement grew.

"Since yesterday morning sir."

"What?"

"Yes sir. We met here for the first time. I think he is from a remote area and needs the job more than I do. If it is a standoff between him and me, then I would like to opt out," Avijit rattled out under a single breath.

"And what would you do then?" the man in the centre looked at him closely.

"I can try something else. Play football for a big club maybe."

"You play football well?"

"I've represented my district team sir."

"You can play in the army as well. Okay. I'm pleased with you. You were ready to sacrifice the job for an acquaintance of a day. That takes a tough mind and a big heart. That's what our army is all about," the senior man smiled.

"There is one last formality. Go with this form to our medical unit on the second floor," the young officer handed over a blue sheet, "you will find your friend there too."

"Thank you sir. Thank you very much."

Avijit fought back his tears. The first light of a new dawn seemed to beckon him. But he still had to pass the medical test. He jogged up the staircase and reached the medical unit. Ghoton was nowhere in sight. Avijit wanted to thank him for everything.

"Take off your clothes," the doctor ordered, after browsing through the form.

Avijit took off his shirt and placed it on a chair.

"The rest of your clothing please," the doctor looked impatiently at his watch.

Avijit felt embarrassed, but took off his trousers too. He stood awkwardly in his underwear.

"You are delaying the whole process. Are you feeling shy?"

"No sir," Avijit was worried he might be disqualified, if he spoke his mind. He looked around and reluctantly lowered the last cover.

"Follow me," the doctor walked towards the door.

Avijit was aghast! Was the man planning to parade him naked down the corridor? He had not bargained for this. Thankfully, the doctor did not go out but locked the door instead. Then he went to the far end of the room and waited for his guinea pig. He checked Avijit thoroughly for the next fifteen minutes. Avijit dressed quickly, once it was over and waited for the verdict.

"You know, this is the irony of life," the doctor stretched on his chair and spoke, "I often get to examine bullet ridden bodies of young men, whom I once certified as fit. Sometimes I wonder whether I should declare everyone unfit and stop this madness."

The doctor started scribbling on the form. Avijit hoped the man was not carrying out his wish. If he didn't get the job today, then poverty would kill him faster than a bullet.

"There you are!" the doctor handed over the form, "you're fully fit. Go and meet the officer who sent you here. Good luck." The doctor shook his hand firmly. "And don't get killed," he added as an afterthought.

"You just saved my life," Avijit smiled back.

Avijit went back to the hall outside the interview chamber. He found Ghoton seated at one corner and joined him.

"I'm sorry. I was harsh in the morning," Avijit shook the extended hand, "I'm thankful for everything you did."

They sat silently for the next half hour, both trying to fathom what the future had in store for them. Ghoton was finally called in.

"You must wait till I come out," Avijit said, when the latter came out and it was his turn to go in.

The same three men sat behind the table, no stoop in their postures since Avijit had last seen them. The young officer quickly went through his medical report and nodded to the other two.

"Congratulations," the man in the middle remarked and shook his hand, "you have been selected to join one of the prestigious regiments of our army, as sepoy in the infantry division. Your joining letter will reach you shortly. But let me tell you, enjoy life for the next ten days. You will be off for a six-month training after that."

"Thank you sirs."

Avijit and Ghoton came out of Fort William together.

"Let's go and sit in the Maidan," Avijit suggested. He needed some time to collect his thoughts.

It was afternoon and the sun beat down on the green in all its ferocity. They sat under the shade of a large tree. A vendor selling peanuts approached them and Avijit bought two small packs. They didn't speak till Ghoton finished eating.

"So? What will you do these ten days?" Ghoton asked him.

"Spend time with my mother. She will be lonely after I leave. What about you?"

"Oh, I will try to stay in Calcutta itself."

"But won't you inform your parents?"

"They know already," was the short reply.

Avijit felt his friend was talking in riddles.

"Have they come with you?"

"Yes."

"Where are they? I didn't see them," Avijit looked all around.

"You can't see them in the daylight," Ghoton spoke, looking up at the sky, "they became stars when I was ten. They dazzle only in the night. But they are always with me."

They stayed silent for the next few minutes, Avijit unable to decide what to say.

"Where will you stay here?" he finally asked.

"I'm not sure. I can find a place. It is only a matter of ten days."

"But don't you have anyone in Midnapore?"

"Oh yes, my uncle and aunt. They stay in my father's house, but treat me like their servant. Who wants to listen to their grumbling again? I'm better off alone."

"But do they know you have come here?"

"No."

"Then they might worry if you don't return," Avijit tried to reason with his friend. "You must go back and tell them you are joining the army. What if they report to the police that you are missing? And what about your appointment letter? It will be posted to your home address."

Ghoton supported his chin with both hands and thought for a moment.

"You feel I should go back, ah?"

Avijit nodded.

"But it's late today. I will not get a bus to my village by the time I reach our railway station," Ghoton consulted Avijit's watch. It was half past three. "Well, I can always sleep on the bench near the main road, like last night."

Avijit was appalled! It explained why Ghoton smelled like a dungeon.

"You stay at my place tonight."

Ghoton protested before agreeing in the end.

"You said you stay with your mother. What about your father?" he asked, once they were on their way.

"He is also up there with your parents," Avijit sighed.

They had egg rolls at a street kiosk, as the rumbling in their stomach was too much to bear.

His mother opened the door and looked at him in anticipation.

"What happened?"

"I got the job," he touched her feet before replying.

"Thank you," his mother closed her eyes and looked skywards, offering a silent prayer.

Ghoton followed them into the house. His mother noticed the intruder and looked questioningly at Avijit.

"Oh, this is Ghoton. Remember, I spoke about him yesterday. He is also joining my regiment and will stay the night with us."

"Please come in," his mother remarked, after Ghoton too had touched her feet to show respect. "We have a small house," she continued, "I hope it won't be too uncomfortable for you."

"Hah! I am used to sleeping with the cows in our house. At least, I will have human company."

Avijit went to have a bath, while Ghoton sat with his mother.

"I'm very fond of eating. I also cook well. I can cook you a delicious potato brinjal curry, if you cook some chicken for me," Ghoton's simplicity made Avijit's mother smile. "I've not had chicken curry for ages. My uncle and aunt had it a month back, but didn't serve me any. They said it was costly and I should not be pampered till I start earning."

Avijit decided to go to the market and buy some chicken, after he heard of Ghoton's request. He showed his friend the way to their bathroom and also offered him a spare set of clothes, so that his smell would be washed away by the time he returned. He decided to first pay the Ghoshs a visit. Sraboni opened the door.

"What happened?" she asked in a whisper.

"I've come to thank your father. I got the job."

"Come on in. He is having a bath."

She looked like a goddess with her hair untied, falling in waves over her shoulder. Avijit felt a great urge to kiss her, but decided not to stir her up again. It was only a matter of a few more days. He had always reasoned that once he had a decent job, he could propose to Sraboni and talk of marriage.

"I want to talk to you regarding something important," he spoke in a low tone, once they had settled down on the sofa.

"Father will take some more time and mother is not at home. So tell me," Sraboni moved her face closer to his and smiled.

"No, not now," Avijit wanted to prepare himself. He was no great orator and did not want to spoil this momentous event by stammering.

"Why not? Nobody can hear us now," Sraboni seemed eager.

"I can't. Can we meet at the lake tomorrow?"

Sraboni seemed lost in thought. Avijit was worried she would refuse. She finally looked up and nodded.

"Fine. Let's meet. I'll wait near the entrance around three. Don't be late. It isn't safe for a young girl to wait alone there."

Mr Ghosh came in shortly, looking fresh in his white kurta-pyjama. Avijit touched his feet and gave him the good news.

"Tell me what happened there. This calls for a celebration!"

So Avijit told him. The story of his tension and exhilaration. He didn't forget to mention the role Ghoton had played.

"We need more boys like him for this country to prosper," Mr Ghosh remarked.

Avijit took his leave with a promise to come down again, once his appointment letter arrived. He was worried Ghoton might leave their house in search of food, if he didn't get back soon enough. He took a full kilo of chicken, rather than half the quantity he had initially thought of. He had seen Ghoton eat the previous day at the army canteen and knew a glutton when he saw one.

"What took you so long?" his mother sounded upset, "the poor boy went to sleep in your room."

Avijit peeped in to find Ghoton curled up on his bed, fast asleep. He thankfully had put on the clothes Avijit left for him.

"Why have you brought so much? You know I don't eat this," his mother pointed at the chicken.

"Ma, your poor boy might find it too little," Avijit mocked. He told her how much Ghoton had eaten the previous day. "A few more Ghotons in our regiment and there might be a stock out!"

"Don't talk like that about anyone's food habits," his mother scolded him, "he comes from a very poor family. What is wrong if he overeats one day? He may not have two square meals a day for the next ten days."

Ghoton got up only around dinnertime.

"Wow! I can smell the chicken. It must be delicious. Let's eat," he nudged Avijit.

They started off with the potato-brinjal curry Ghoton had cooked. Avijit choked the moment he pushed in the first mouthful. It was terribly hot and salty.

"So how do I cook?"

"The best I ever had," Avijit somehow managed.

Ghoton was too involved with his own food to notice that both Avijit and his mother avoided the great dish. He ate ten rotis, a large portion of his curry and all but two pieces of the chicken Avijit had brought. He had been kind enough to offer those two to his friend at the outset. He concluded the meal with a full plate of home made sweets.

"Oh! I will remember this day for ever," Ghoton spoke, after finishing the last bit of food on his plate, "a job and a grand feast. Pity, I'll have to go back tomorrow. It would have been great to stay here for the next ten days. But God doesn't want it."

Avijit thanked God for this one good gesture. Ten more days of Ghoton and he would have been bankrupt!

"You cook just like my mother," Ghoton said, after washing his hands, "you also resemble her in many ways. God knows why she left me so early."

Avijit and Ghoton squeezed into the small bed that night. Ghoton started snoring the moment Avijit put off the lights, but sleep was difficult for the latter. He could look back at the day with satisfaction after a very long time. But how would he stay away from his mother? He also thought of Sraboni and what he would tell her.

"Thank you for bearing with me," Ghoton told Avijit's mother the next morning. He had just completed a breakfast of fifteen puris with a full bowl of fried potatoes and was preparing to leave. "Don't worry about your son," he said, "I will look after him well in the army."

Avijit saw him off at the bus stop.

"Tell me, what is the bus fare from here to Howrah station," Ghoton asked him.

"It should be four and a half rupees. Why? You need any money?"

"No, no. I must have the right tickets then."

Avijit watched in amazement, as Ghoton brought out a bunch of tickets from his pocket.

"There, four rupees fifty paise," he selected two tickets from the bunch and put them back in his pocket, while throwing away the rest. "Now I need not buy tickets. I had collected these from the interviewees yesterday. The conductor won't notice the number in the crowd."

Avijit sat with his mother after returning home. He could sense her helplessness and repeatedly asked her whether he should refuse the job. But his mother stood her ground.

"This is your only chance to do something worthwhile in life. Initially it might be tough, but I will manage. So don't even think of giving up."

His uncle dropped in around noon.

"Congratulations young man," he hugged Avijit. He seemed lost in thought for a while though, after Avijit told him that he was joining the infantry. "Being in the infantry, you will be the first to face the enemy, if there is a war. But don't worry. There won't be a war in the next hundred years. We are all civilized now," he tried to allay his own fears, "go right ahead."

They chatted for a few more minutes, before his uncle suggested what Avijit was hoping he would.

"So, when are you leaving this house?" his uncle asked his mother.

"But I cannot go back to Rajpur. Our tenants are still occupying the flat," she replied, a trifle surprised.

"No, you are not going to Rajpur. You are going to my place," his uncle was matter of fact.

His mother continued to protest, but his uncle had his way. Avijit felt relief flood him. His mother was safe as long as she stayed with his uncle and aunt. They also had a phone and he could at least speak to her from his training camp.

Avijit had a quick lunch, as he had to meet Sraboni. He put on his best T-shirt and jeans, and the sneakers Khokon had given him. He looked at himself in the mirror and felt confident. The cab dropped him at his rendezvous well in time, but Sraboni had still not arrived. He stood next to the entrance and waited.

"Wow! The original hero!"

"Don't wait for her. We can be better."

A group of young girls remarked and squealed in delight. They looked in their early teens and were probably still in school. He felt stupid standing in the heat. It was another ten minutes before Sraboni arrived.

"What happened? You are late," Avijit was flustered.

"I made sure you were here before me," she smiled, "its irritating to wait for someone."

They walked along the side of the lake. It was teeming with young revellers and they had to walk to the far end before getting an empty bench.

"Now tell me?" Sraboni looked at him and waited.

Avijit never expected such a direct approach and forgot his well-rehearsed dialogues.

"Let's have some popcorn first," he tried to sound cool.

"Tell me what you have to say," those dark liquid eyes never left him. "I'm getting late and father might worry."

"I got the job," Avijit stammered.

"I know that, silly. You told me yesterday. Is that all or there is something more?" Sraboni mocked.

"I have decided to get married," Avijit felt embarrassed after completing the sentence.

"Oh my God! Congratulations! That's pretty fast. A job yesterday and a marriage today! So, who's the lucky girl?"

Avijit was ready to deliver the well-rehearsed dialogue, when a tramp came and sat next to Sraboni.

"Hey! What do you want?"

Avijit wanted to hit the man. He was ready to deliver the all important line, but the stupid rogue spoiled it.

"Why are you disturbing us?" Sraboni couldn't hide her anger.

"Okay. Pay me five rupees and I will go."

"What for?"

"It's the *lovers* tax."

Avijit moved threateningly towards the tramp, hoping to drive away the meddler. But he only left after Sraboni handed over a two-rupee coin.

"What a way to earn a livelihood," Sraboni sighed. She focused on him again. "So you are getting married and want me to tell your mother. Are you worried she won't approve?"

"No, no. You are getting it all wrong. I don't want you to tell her anything."

"What?" Sraboni looked closely at him, "you are marrying without informing your mother! This is outrageous."

Avijit felt the situation was going out of hand and decided to speak out.

"I want to marry you."

Sraboni stared at him blankly for sometime and then covered her face with both hands. Avijit thought she would cry. Did he say something bad? But his worry was short lived. Sraboni burst out laughing.

"That's the silliest thing I've heard in my life," she said.

Avijit was confused. Was he being refused?

"You don't like me?" he asked, his voice wavering.

He knew it would be the end for him, if Sraboni rejected his love.

"I'm not saying that," Sraboni's answer made him breathe easy.

"Then what is it?"

"I'm just not ready for marriage now. I've never thought about it, my career is most important now. I want to become a journalist and an early marriage can come in the way."

"I promise you, I won't stop you in any way."

"That's okay. But now is too early," Sraboni was firm.

"Then what happens to our relationship?" Avijit's frustration was reflected in his voice. It was not lost on Sraboni.

"Look, don't be emotional. It is not that I don't like you. But marriage is out of the question now. Imagine our age! It's too early to marry. Why don't we enjoy each other's company for some more time before taking that ultimate step? You can settle down in life by then."

Avijit was amazed to hear Sraboni speak so maturely. He knew she was the right girl for him.

"Fine. But I want a commitment before I leave."

"Commitments are made to be broken," Sraboni took his hand and smiled, "have faith in God. If we are destined to marry, we will."

It was getting late and they got up. Avijit was happy that Sraboni had finally endorsed his love.

The next few days went by quietly, with mother and son trying to enjoy the little time of togetherness, which was left. Chandan and Ujjal came down to congratulate him. They parted with a promise that Avijit would treat them to dinner, the day he returned. His appointment letter arrived and drove out the last nagging worry from his mind. His salary was three times higher than what he had earned all these months. His landlord was delighted, when Avijit told him they would vacate the house soon. It ensured him a few hundred rupees more as rent from the next tenant. The Ghoshs came over one evening. They were surprised to hear that Avijit's mother would be staying at Salt Lake.

"But you wouldn't feel lonely here. Not with the social workshops we are planning from the ladies club," Mrs Ghosh quipped.

"We will certainly be in touch," Mr Ghosh noted down his uncle's address and phone number.

Avijit's uncle arrived on Saturday afternoon with a small van in tow. They had little to shift. It took them a little over an hour to put everything onto it and hand over the keys to the landlord. He felt sad to leave the house, but it was a new way of life for Avijit now.

Khokon called up the next day.

"Bloody fool, you want to be a martyr!" he sounded upset, "you still have time to change your decision. A soft guy like you will be a complete misfit in the army. Listen to my advice and join a software course. I will make sure you get a job here."

"But I told you, I don't like computers. Joining the army is a matter of pride," Avijit defended his decision.

"Idiot. It's risky as well. What will aunty do if you get killed?"

"But there is little chance of a war. Don't worry, I won't get killed."

"You don't need an official war. Thousands of our soldiers are killed every year because of insurgency. Why take a risk?"

Khokon continued sharing his wisdom for some more time, before he disconnected suddenly. He must have realized that the phone bill would be a waste, as Avijit wouldn't change his mind. However, Avijit had no ready answer to the doubts Khokon had raised. His mother and aunt cooked him one of the best dinners of his life. He enjoyed every dish, not quite sure when he could have a similar meal again.

The day finally arrived. Avijit packed a light luggage of casual wear. His mother suggested he carry his woollens but he refused.

"The army will provide everything."

He did not forget to take his most precious possession though, a photo of his father. The smiling face seemed to cheer him up, each time he looked at it. He was sure his father was watching his every move and would caution him in some way if danger lurked nearby. They got into his uncle's car.

"Call back the moment you reach the army camp," his uncle reminded him.

"I will, if there is a phone," was his stoic reply.

They reached Fort William and Avijit took out his luggage from the car. He touched the feet of the elders and was about to leave, when he felt his mother's hand on his shoulder.

"Take this," she handed an envelope.

"What is it?"

"Just some money. You might need it. Bye son."

His mother covered her face with her white saree and turned away. Avijit felt a lump swell up in his throat and started walking towards the office building before he lost control. He paused near the gate and turned back one last time. The three of them stood together, waving at him. They looked marooned on a lonely island, their near ones far far away. He waved back.

CHAPTER
Ten

Avijit sat silently in a hall, along with a few others, awaiting departure. His thoughts were broken by the excited voice of what looked like a new recruit.

"Hi, how are you?" the question was directed at Avijit.

It took him sometime to recognize the bald headed young man, standing in front of him, as Ghoton.

"Why did you shave off your hair?" Avijit asked incredulously.

"I had promised to offer God something, if I got the job. What better than the hair on one's head?" He carried a tin suitcase that could only be seen in old movies. "Tell me, how is aunty?" Ghoton asked after settling down on a chair.

"She's fine."

"Did she cook something good for me today?"

"Don't worry. She has given me a very heavy packet. It must be half the weight of my luggage."

"Well, I can help in reducing its weight," Ghoton looked eagerly at his friend.

"Wait till the train."

An officer walked in with an aide at five p.m. sharp.

"This is Subedar Ranjan. He will accompany you to the camp."

Each one of them was given a hundred rupees, as allowance for lunch and dinner on the train.

"Are you sure there is enough food for the two of us?" Ghoton asked again.

"I hope so."

"Good. It means we can save at least half the allowance."

"I'm not too sure about your part," Avijit chuckled.

"What do you mean?" Ghoton looked closely at him.

"You need to have breakfast and lunch tomorrow. I think the allowance is too little for you."

"Oh, don't worry. I'll take the balance from you."

A surprise awaited Avijit at Howrah station. They had been asked to wait on the platform, as their train had not yet come in. He was glancing through a sports magazine, when someone tapped him on the shoulder. It was Sraboni! Avijit couldn't believe his eyes.

"What are you doing here?" he stammered.

"I'm catching the train with you," her reply startled him. Had she run away from home? How could he take her with him?

"But why?"

"Why? You wanted to marry me and here I am."

Avijit cast a quick glance at the others. Ghoton was watching Sraboni with a lot of interest, though he was not within earshot. Avijit had already started sweating.

"How can I marry you here?" he threw up his arms.

His gesture attracted the attention of his colleagues and all eyes were now focused on them.

"Just relax. I was joking, silly," Sraboni seemed unnerved by the stares, "I hope you are not this dumb after the training."

"But you have come here alone. How will you go back?"

"Don't be silly. I've come with Dad and Mom. They are waiting for you."

Avijit was overwhelmed. It seemed Mr Ghosh had taken a particular liking to him. He was confident the armyman wouldn't object to his marrying Sraboni.

"How did you know I would be leaving by this train?"

"Dad got the information from Mr Sankaranarayan. Now will you come and meet them, or I go back and say I could not find you?"

Avijit took permission from Subedar Ranjan and walked towards the gate with Sraboni.

"Thank you," he blurted out.

"For what?" Sraboni asked, after narrowly avoiding being elbowed in the chest by an old man.

The station was over crowded and it was extremely difficult to hear each other's voice over the din.

"For supporting a silly person."

"I'm not supporting anyone. It's just that Dad wanted to meet you. Mother and I came along, as it would mean a free car ride. So don't get ideas," Sraboni smiled sweetly.

"You only came for a free ride?" Avijit suddenly stopped in his tracks.

"Oh, you can be so sentimental. Silly, I was joking. Now hurry up or you will miss your train."

"Thank you sir," he told Mr Ghosh and bent down to touch his feet. The armyman stopped him midway and hugged him instead.

"May you succeed in your new career."

Mrs Ghosh handed him a large packet.

"What is this?"

"Nothing much. Just some fruits and sweets."

Avijit thanked her too. Ghoton was now assured of some savings. He looked back one last time. Those dark eyes and the smile left him spellbound. He was not sure when he would see her again. There was not even a photo of her. But her image was etched permanently in his mind.

The train came in shortly and they boarded the coach reserved for the military. The bright lights of the city rushed past as the train picked up speed and was soon replaced by an all-pervasive darkness. Only the dim lights of the train glowed to keep them connected to the modern world.

"Open the food packet," Ghoton wasted no time.

They had still not been acquainted with the other members of the team and everyone quietly ate whatever they had brought.

"Oh, that was great," Ghoton stretched in satisfaction after the meal, "I'm already feeling sleepy. Good night."

Avijit was relieved to have some time to himself, but it was short-lived. The train reached its first halt after about an hour. There was loud banging on the door and a few of them, including Ghoton, got up to investigate. It was a group of young boys.

"We're going for a trek in the Himalayas. We have no reserved seats and the other compartments are full. Will you kindly allow us in?"

The polite tone made the Subedar open the door. There were six of them. They occupied the empty berths and chatted up the new recruits, who were planning to call it a day.

"Can we offer you a drink sir?" one of them asked the Subedar.

"I would rather sleep. You may offer it to the others."

It opened the floodgates. Almost all the recruits except Avijit joined in. Suddenly, there was mirth in the air. The recruits clapped and danced for the better part of the night, while the Subedar slept soundly. The rhythm of his snoring added a strange dimension to the high notes of enjoyment. Ghoton gulped down each drink as if he was in a great hurry. The idea of the others finishing off the bottle seemed to play on his mind. He fell down on the floor after his fifth glass. It took four of them to lift him onto his berth. This didn't deter the others though, and the merriment continued. It was difficult to sleep amidst the noise and the rumbling of the train, but tiredness finally caught up with Avijit.

Avijit woke up when the first rays of the sun caressed the earth. He had not slept well at all. The wooden berth was extremely uncomfortable and added to that was the swaying of the train. He looked out of the window at the bright sky and the green paddy fields. They seemed to extend for an eternity. Occasionally, scattered amongst the green, were a few mud huts. Rice was the staple diet of the nation, but the farmers who ensured its supply, lived in medieval conditions. Most of his colleagues were still asleep, as he went up to the toilet to wash his face. Subedar Ranjan beckoned to him from his seat.

"Would you like to have some tea?"

"Yes sir," Avijit felt parched.

The Subedar poured out some from a thermos into a plastic cup.

"It might be a trifle cold. Have it for now. You can get more at the next station."

"When shall we reach the camp?" Avijit asked after the first sip.

"Not before the evening. The train should reach the station around four p.m. It will take another one and a half hours by road."

Ghoton got up only around noon.

"How are you?" he asked Avijit.

"Very drunk."

"Did you drink too much? That's bad. You should have known your limits like me."

"Yeah, then who would have carried you all the way from the floor to your berth! Go and freshen up. I've still not had breakfast."

The last word had a magic effect. His friend shot up from the berth and was sitting next to Avijit within the next few minutes. In between, he had rushed to the toilet and back.

"Why did you drink so fast?" one of the new recruits asked Ghoton.

"Oh, that's how I enjoy my drink," was the emphatic reply.

Avijit opened the food packet given by Mrs Ghosh. It had apples, oranges and a box of *sandesh*. He decided to share it with everyone in their row of berths. Ghoton watched stoically till all had a share. He simply picked up whatever was left and gobbled it down.

"Do you drink often?" Avijit asked Ghoton, when they had alighted for a cup of tea at a small station.

"Never tasted it till yesterday. I will go a little slow next time," Ghoton confided, "and don't think I was drunk. Only my head was spinning a little."

They reached their destination an hour behind schedule. Subedar Ranjan directed them to the army office at the far end of the railway station. The sky had turned pink and night was round the corner. The air felt chilly, ahead of the approaching winter and Avijit regretted having dismissed his mother's suggestion to carry his woollens. He pulled up the collar of his shirt and followed the others towards the office.

"Fall in a line," an immaculately dressed army officer addressed them.

It took almost a half hour for the formalities and they finally boarded the truck to 'Camp Zero', the code name for their training camp. The truck travelled through plain land for the next forty minutes, before taking a circuitous route through a hilly terrain. They could vaguely make out the shape of the trees, which stood like spears on the uneven landscape. The truck had to negotiate hairpin bends every few minutes and the excessive turning and rolling made them dizzy. There were no signs of any human habitation.

"This looks like a journey to hell," Ghoton observed, "I hope they have a masseur at the camp. A good massage and a full day's rest should see us fighting fit."

They finally reached the camp, a dimly illuminated plain land.

One could make out a few dark buildings at the centre and a row of long semicircular structures all along the perimeter. They were ushered into a large, brightly lit hall. Pictures of soldiers adorned the walls and a small dais stood at the front of a row of chairs.

"Welcome gentlemen," a stout middle aged man addressed them, "I am Major Chawla and am in charge of this camp. I am proud to note that all of you have decided to serve the motherland. There is no better way to enjoy life. As you will see, our sense of achievement and pride is second to none. Our motherland is resourceful, prosperous and home to almost a billion people of various castes and creeds. Our strength is unity in diversity. Our enemies want to break this harmony for their own vile gains. Hence, our motherland needs to be protected. Over the next six months, you will be trained to combat that threat in every form. But remember one thing. Be a good human being. Never accept a wrong, but neither undo a right. I now introduce you to Lieutenant Nanda, who, along with his team, is in charge of your day-to-day training. I would expect you to cooperate fully with him. I once again welcome you here and wish you the very best for your training."

Lieutenant Nanda was tall, clean-shaven and had piercing eyes. A scar on his chin added a handsome ruggedness to his face.

"You will be shown to your barracks. Go there and have a wash. Report back here sharp at twenty hundred hours for dinner," he said.

They were taken to one of the long semicircular structures. It had two rows of coir beds arranged from one end to the other. The space between the two rows acted as a passage. A small locker was placed at the head of each bed. There was a row of toilets just outside the barracks and they took turns for a wash. Avijit was famished by the time he had taken the cold-water bath. He waited for Ghoton, who took a long time to get ready. They reported to the main hall to find the others waiting. Lieutenant Nanda approached them the moment they entered.

"Why are you late?" he asked in a soft voice.

"Oh, I was having a bath," Ghoton answered casually.

"And what about you?" he looked at Avijit.

"I was waiting for him sir."

The Lieutenant seemed to weigh their answers for sometime, before he turned and addressed the others. He did not speak in a soft voice anymore; he barked!

"Discipline is a way of life here and punctuality needs to be maintained without fail. If you do not turn up for a meal on time, you won't be served a meal."

Avijit could hear Ghoton curse.

"I will pardon you as this is your first day. But make sure you maintain time in future."

They walked into an adjacent building, which housed the canteen. The smell of hot food whetted their appetite. They were served a meal of rice, roti, dal, potato curry and meat. It felt delicious after the long and tiring journey.

"You can rest in the barracks now. Wake up call will be given at five hundred hours. Report to me at the parade ground at six hundred hours sharp. Good night," and the Lieutenant walked away.

They trudged back to their barracks. Avijit made up his bed and put his belongings in the locker. Ghoton, whose bed was next to Avijit's, didn't waste much time and went off to sleep.

"I shouldn't be late again," he said, "imagine if the madcap had refused us food tonight!"

Avijit counted twenty beds in their barracks and only ten were occupied. It meant there would be another group. The lights went out at half past nine and he had no other option but to get into his bed. His last thoughts were of his mother before sleep overcame him.

Ghoton shook him awake the next morning.

"Wake up. Its already a half past five."

Avijit shot up immediately, the fear of a reprimand gripping him. Most of the others had already woken up. He quickly went through his morning rituals and was ready just as the clock struck six. An armyman led them to the centre of the camp. A few more groups had already assembled. The camp was in a valley, surrounded by small hills on all sides, the green row of trees effortlessly blending into the pale blue sky. The air felt fresh and the breath condensed into a fine mist, every time one opened one's mouth. Avijit could count ten barracks along the perimeter of the camp and a line of brick buildings in the centre, all painted in a mazy green and brown. He would come to know later that it was to camouflage their presence, in case an enemy plane flew over. Major Chawla addressed them stressing the importance of discipline within the camp. They were then led to the store, housed in one of the brick buildings. Each recruit was issued army uniforms, underwear, woollens, boots and slippers.

"You have ten minutes to dress," Lieutenant Nanda said, "I want to see everyone in their uniform."

They ran back to their barracks and changed as fast as possible. Avijit's uniform was a size too large for him and he had to fold back his trouser legs. The boots felt heavy and were uncomfortable to walk in.

"Shit! What do I do now?" Ghoton shouted in frustration.

His trousers were too tight and the fly had come undone under the forceful tug. The trousers were short as well. But time was ticking away and Ghoton ran back with the others, his fly open.

"Let it be," he reasoned, "I will be late, if I try to put on the other one. Then I might be offered only flies for breakfast."

They were put through a light drill for the next half hour. The Lieutenant watched from a distance, while his two assistants warned them if they paraded out of tune.

"I don't want you to move like a pregnant woman," one of the assistants thundered, "stomp on the ground and bring out the petrol from it."

Avijit felt very hungry by the time the drill had ended.

"You will get uniforms stitched to your sizes shortly," the assistant, a Junior Commissioned Officer, assured them as they had a breakfast of puris and vegetable curry.

They were taken to the hair-cutting saloon after breakfast. It was a row of four chairs under the shade of a tree, behind the administrative building. One could hear the screeching of birds along with the swish of the razor. No mirrors were needed to check the cut, as the barbers expertly removed every trace of hair, making their heads glisten in the sunlight. It was noon by the time everyone finished.

They were taken around the camp after lunch. Other than the brick buildings that housed the stores, canteen, hospital and classrooms, it had a gymnasium, a basketball court and a lush green football field. Avijit's heart soared at its sight. He felt life there would have been complete, if only his mother were at his side. He suddenly remembered his promise to call her the moment he reached the camp.

"Sir, can I make a phone call from here?" he asked the Lieutenant.

"Where to?"

"To my mother. She must be worrying."

"Why should she worry? You are in the army. We can take good care of our people," Lieutenant Nanda turned away.

"But sir, I had promised to call her," Avijit pleaded.

"Where the hell do you think you are?" the sudden outburst made everyone turn towards them, "do you think you are on a picnic and can call anyone and everyone! This is the army. Our only mission is to serve our motherland. You need to focus on the training. You can leave if you feel otherwise."

Avijit felt terribly embarrassed. He had seen telephone wires leading into the main office building. It was surely not an unknown technology in this god-forsaken place. So what was the big deal? He would have paid for the call. It meant he wouldn't be able to talk to his mother, till he completed the training. That was unthinkable! His mother would go mad, if she didn't hear from him within the week. Maybe he should leave immediately. He had enough money to buy the train ticket. It was not going to work out.

"Don't do anything stupid," Ghoton whispered to him, making sure the Lieutenant was out of earshot, "just relax. Take a few deep breaths and you will feel better."

But nothing helped. Avijit felt lost in this distant land and his heart yearned to hear his mother's voice. They had a class in the afternoon, in which more people lectured about discipline and the need to accept orders without a doubt.

"Always remember, a soldier never gives up till death."

They were allowed to go to their barracks in the evening. Most collapsed on their beds having nothing else to do. A few chatted amongst themselves, trying to shed the skin of strangers. Avijit sat sullenly on his bed. He wanted to scream and run away, back to the frugal comfort and uncertainty of his home. He couldn't face this exile much longer.

"Try it for a few more days before giving up," Ghoton came and sat next to him, "after all, you get good food and a decent salary. I'm sure the Lieutenant will cool down and allow you to call aunty tomorrow."

A new group arrived just before dinner and the ten vacant beds were soon occupied. One of them was a tall and handsome *sardar*, his hair covered in a bright blue turban.

"Hi, I'm Gurinder. You may call me Guri," he had met everyone and now stood in front of Avijit. "Nice cozy place, huh," the *sardar* wanted to strike up a conversation, but Avijit was not listening. The new arrival stood awkwardly for some time, before moving away.

Avijit ate silently, when they were called for dinner and retired to bed. They again reported to the Lieutenant at six a.m. the next morning and had to parade in those heavy boots for a full hour, before being allowed to rest. Most paraded in tune, while those who erred adjusted fast, as an error called for a hundred push-ups.

"We will begin with physical exercises to strengthen the body and increase your stamina. You will then be put through all the intricacies of self-defence. It will be followed by armed combat, rock climbing, trap setting, heli-jumping and much more. You will be a true soldier by the time you complete the training," Lieutenant Nanda addressed the full group. "We will start the day with a run. Pick a sand bag from that pit. You will have to run with the bag on your back. No one can stop till I order you to do so."

The bag felt heavy and Avijit had to hold it with both hands over his shoulder. Ghoton seemed to take an inordinately long time in picking up his bag and the entire group was held up.

"What the hell is your problem?" one of the officers barked.

"There is sand on the bag sir. It will spoil my uniform."

"Well, you are not joining a dance party," the trainer mocked, "you better get used to grime and dirt. A battlefield is never clean."

They were off, the entire group. Lieutenant Nanda ran in the front and the recruits followed with the bags on their backs. The assistants brought up the rear. It didn't feel bad to run under the comforting warmth of the sun, though the weight of the bag and the heaviness of the boots made it difficult to keep pace with the Lieutenant. They raced along a narrow path till they reached the main road outside the camp. It spiralled along the serene hillside. The trainees were out of breath by the time the road started meandering up the hills. They came across a few residential quarters, the home for the permanent members of the camp. Avijit felt thirsty and wanted to halt for a glass of water. But the Lieutenant kept shouting at them to run faster. Most had slowed down and a few even collapsed. Avijit could hear an assistant shouting to the fallen comrades to get up and run. He didn't look back to see whether the order was obeyed.

"Try to breathe normally," Ghoton whispered to him.

The glutton seemed least affected and ran comfortably. He fell back to cheer Avijit and again increased his pace effortlessly. The latter would have accepted him as Superman, had not his eyes suddenly locked onto the bag on Ghoton's back. Avijit increased his pace to have a closer look. He was appalled! The bag didn't seem to have much sand in it.

"Okay. Put down your bags and rest for ten minutes," the Lieutenant's order came as manna from heaven.

Most collapsed on the carpet of grass by the road.

"How did you manage to get an empty bag?" Avijit asked Ghoton in a whisper, after he got back his breath.

"Oh, I punched a hole in it with my fingers. Most of the sand drained out within the first hundred metres. Should I dig a hole in yours too?"

"No, no. What if I get caught?"

"Suit yourself. You can never gain anything without taking a risk."

They started their run back to the camp exactly after ten minutes. They were not allowed any water till they reached it.

"We disperse for lunch. You report for your classes at fourteen hundred hours," the Lieutenant ordered.

"See, nobody could catch me," Ghoton beamed proudly.

They were issued the ugly looking rifles after lunch. An officer showed them how to dismantle and assemble one, and Avijit's hands were a dirty black with the oil from its barrel, by the time the session ended.

"Love it like your girlfriend," the officer told them, "it is the only lifeline for a soldier."

They reported to the sports trainer in the evening.

"You have to participate in at least one sports discipline. The choice is yours."

It didn't take Avijit much time to choose his, while Ghoton opted for volleyball. They had to play barefoot, as the football boots had to be ordered after checking the player's size. Most in his group played like novices. Pure lusty shooting dominated the proceedings, except for the odd moment when Avijit dazzled with his footwork. But that was rare, as his mind was not on the game. He had still not been able to call his mother and hoped she had not panicked.

"Try and concentrate on the game. You can play better," the instructor told him later.

Avijit found some solace in the evening, when an assistant came to their barracks and distributed postage paid envelopes.

"The army will provide you three envelopes every week. Your relations just need to mention your name and regiment on their replies. It will reach you."

Everyone got busy writing whatever they could. Avijit wanted to write about his miseries, but decided against it. It would only increase his mother's worry. Instead, he wrote about the picturesque valley, the sense of discipline in the army and Ghoton's eternal quest for food.

"Write down your address on this envelope," Ghoton requested him, "I have nobody to write to. So I wrote to your mother."

"Let's hope it reaches her," Avijit sighed.

They paraded for an hour before breakfast the next day and prepared for the run after it.

"Pick up the bags and get ready," the Lieutenant ordered.

Everyone obeyed. Ghoton winked at Avijit. They stood in a line awaiting the next directive. The Lieutenant came down the line and stopped in front of Ghoton.

"You! Fall out of line and put the bag down," he barked. "Naik Jung Bahadur, come here," the Lieutenant hailed a short and stout assistant, and turned to Ghoton, "you run with him on your back today. See if you can punch a hole in him too. That should make him lighter. Now move."

The assistant jumped onto Ghoton's back and the latter almost fell down under his weight. No one dared to mess with the sand bags and they ran the entire stretch silently. There were fewer dropouts, though it was extremely difficult to balance the heavy bag on the back and maintain a steady pace. They took the same path and rested at the same spot for ten minutes. Avijit squinted down the winding road, but there was no sign of the prankster or his rider. They saw Ghoton almost half way back to the camp. He puffed and panted his way up, though Jung Bahadur seemed to be enjoying the ride and waved at them.

Ghoton was back only after lunch. He threw up his hands in despair and almost wept, when he was refused food at the canteen, as he was late.

"Its not my fault," he protested, "he is very heavy and I couldn't even walk at my normal pace. That's why I'm late."

"Neither is it my fault," the Lieutenant replied, "you dug out all the sand from the bag. I'm sure you would have poked a finger into a solid iron pipe and melted it down too. So I had to risk it with Jung Bahadur. I'm glad he is safe. Now go and join the class."

"Don't do anything stupid," Avijit whispered to a very agitated and hungry Ghoton, "just relax. Take a few deep breaths and you will feel better."

"Here, take this," the lanky *sardar* handed an apple to Ghoton, "go behind the toilet and eat it quickly."

"Thank you. I can die for you now," Ghoton snatched the apple away. His reply left the *sardar* a trifle confused.

Ghoton reported for dinner a half hour in advance and put up a splendid show. He called it a day only when Guri spoke of Jung Bahadur on the back and the Lieutenant on the head for the run as punishment for overeating.

"I can't continue any longer. I'm quitting," Ghoton exploded, once they were back in the barracks.

"Me too. This is inhuman," a recruit named Ravi joined in.

Ravi had fallen down twice during the run and had complained of acute back pain. He had been ordered to report to the doctor.

"You can't believe what happened. The Doc made me take off my shirt and asked me to lie face down on a bed. Then he put a very hot bag on my back! Shit, I can still feel it. Said he would put it on my ass, if I had a recurrence. I am out of this for sure."

Ghoton and Ravi soon had a few more sympathisers.

"We will all go and meet the Major and tell him we are quitting," they decided before retiring for the night.

They reported to the Lieutenant on time the next morning and went through the parade without a hitch. Ravi and Ghoton approached Lieutenant Nanda, after they had been dismissed for breakfast.

"We need to talk to the Major, sir," Ravi took the lead.

"What for?"

"We want to quit," Ghoton replied in a wavering voice.

"Why?"

"We cannot stand this inhuman torture."

"I see," the Lieutenant turned towards the rest of the group, "those who want to quit, step out and stand on the left."

More than half the group stepped out. Avijit wanted to follow suit, but decided to give it one last try. He stood his ground.

"That's good," the Lieutenant now addressed the group, which had decided to risk a stay, "I don't need pussyfooters here. This is no place for the chicken hearted, who run away from the call of their motherland. I am proud of you. Now go and have your breakfast. We will start our daily run after that."

The Lieutenant turned and marched away without bothering to look at the group, which had thrown in the towel.

"This is not fair. He called us chicken hearted," Ghoton fumed at the breakfast table.

"He also called us pussyfooters!" Ravi retorted.

"Well guys, prove him wrong. He might call you much more if you don't," Guri remarked.

The entire group reported for the run.

"Are you ready?" the Lieutenant barked.

"Yes sir," the group roared back.

"Then let's go."

A new determination echoed in everyone's step and there were no dropouts. All of them finished the run together.

"I am proud of you my boys," the Lieutenant spoke in a soft

voice, "never give up till you have tried your best."

The rest of the day was spent in the same routine. Firearms training followed by sports, an evening stroll followed by dinner. There was a great sense of achievement amongst them that night.

"Lets prove him wrong everyday," Ghoton referred to the Lieutenant's earlier remarks. It seemed he had taken them to heart.

Avijit continued to worry about his mother. His mind also wandered back to his last meeting with Sraboni. She had really shaken him up. He was desperate to get back to his earlier world.

"You will have a day off today after breakfast. Those interested in visiting the town can apply for an out-pass and avail of the army truck that leaves sharp at nine hundred hours," the Lieutenant's announcement a few days later, made the group parade with increased fervour. Nobody had expected a day off from this living hell.

"I'm going to the town. Are you coming with me?" Ghoton asked Avijit.

"No," the latter's melancholic strain had resurfaced.

"We are all going. So what will you do alone? Get dressed and come with us," Guri persisted.

"Okay."

They filed into the back of the truck, while the Lieutenant and an officer sat alongside the driver. The road meandered along the hillside like a thin line caught between the hills and the ridges. The camp soon vanished from sight and it was only the rows of cedars, deodars and the bright blue sky that greeted the eyes. Sparse habitation could be seen, once they reached the plains. The driver pushed on the pedal after a struggle with the gears and they hurtled towards the town.

It was a small town, smaller than even Rajpur and the truck halted at the central market place. There were a cluster of small shops and a restaurant down the road. Most went around in small groups but Avijit stood alone next to the truck, unable to decide what to do. He suddenly felt a hand on his shoulder. Lieutenant Nanda stood behind him.

"Do you have money on you?"

"No sir," Avijit had forgotten to bring his purse. But why was the Lieutenant asking for money?

"Take this," he held a hundred rupee note towards Avijit, "walk down the road and turn right. You will get a telephone booth. Call your mother from there."

Avijit's heart soared. But he did not want to take the money from the Lieutenant. What if he asked for a favour later? He wanted to kick himself for having forgotten his purse.

"What happened? Take the money and return it to me at the camp. And don't stand like a stupid fool. The others might get there before you."

Avijit took the money and ran. Luckily, the booth was empty and he got through quickly.

"Hello?"

"Uncle, how are you?" Avijit couldn't hide the excitement in his voice.

"Oh, we are fine. What took you so long to call?"

"Sorry, but we have to drive down to the town to phone. This is the first day I got to come here."

"Okay. Talk to your mother."

Avijit waited with bated breath, till he heard his mother's voice. She sounded like a young girl.

"How are you my son?"

"I feel very lonely Ma. Life is very tough and I often think of quitting."

"Don't even dream of it. When others can bear it why can't you? And I'm fine with your uncle and aunt. Tell Ghoton that I am replying to his letter."

Avijit was surprised. They had posted their letters only four days back. Mail from Rajpur to Calcutta took eight days to reach its recipient. But their letters had travelled possibly ten times the distance within half the time. It only spoke of the swiftness of the army. Avijit glanced at the meter to find that the call had already cost him forty rupees. He wanted to keep on talking, but it would be on borrowed money. So he decided to be careful.

"Ma, I need to disconnect now. I will call you whenever I come to the town. Take care."

Avijit felt relieved. His mother was safe and that removed his worries. It was also an eye opener. The Lieutenant was one of the most decent human beings he had ever met. Though he had refused Avijit earlier, he made up at the first available opportunity. Avijit soon caught up with Ghoton, Guri and the others in his group. Ghoton was delighted to hear that he could finally speak to his mother. A few others wanted to call up their parents too and moved towards the booth. Ghoton suddenly pulled Avijit aside and whispered in his ears.

"Can you spare me some money?"

"Yes. Would you like to make a call?"

"No, no. I'm feeling hungry ever since I went through the menu in the restaurant. Lets go."

Avijit was not too sure the money he had would ensure a satisfying lunch in the restaurant.

"Look, have a simple meal today. We can have a sumptuous lunch the next time we come."

Ghoton sulked at Avijit's words, but the craving in his stomach made him follow his friend to a cheap roadside eatery. They watched a movie in the afternoon and returned to the camp by late evening.

Everyone looked fresh, when they reported for their morning drill the next day. Their life fell into a routine. With each passing day, running with the sand bag became easier.

"The human body can endure a lot. Its only a question of mental willingness," the Lieutenant would tell them.

The evenings became a lot brighter with movies screened twice a week in the camp. The freshers could also use the information room for the latest news, as also the library, which had a vast collection of books on a range of topics. And Ghoton and Guri were always up to some prank or the other to ensure a few lighter moments. Ravi had grown a beard and was extremely proud of it.

"I look so handsome," he would look at himself in the small mirror and comment, "I'm sure she won't be able to refuse me, the next time I meet her."

The she, according to Ravi was a very beautiful girl, whom he had met at a family function. He didn't know her name, but was madly in love.

"Well, it was love at first sight," he would recollect, "she kept looking at me in a dazed way."

Avijit noticed a bottle of hair remover, after coming back from the town one evening. It was half concealed under Ghoton's pillow.

"What the hell are you doing with this?" he asked Ghoton.

"Oh, nothing," the latter seemed to shrug off the question.

"You will know tomorrow," Guri had a knowing smile, "but please, not a word to anyone."

Avijit had to clean his rifle for the inspection drill and didn't give it another thought. The inmates were jolted out of sleep by a loud howl the next morning. Ravi was shouting at the top of his voice.

"What is it?" Avijit jumped out of the bed and rushed to his aid.

"Look what has happened!" Ravi pointed to his right cheek. It seemed someone had cruelly plucked away a part of his beard. "Oh my beard! What do I do now?"

He ultimately had to shave it off, without an inkling as to how it had happened.

"You must eat more protein," Guri suggested, "this is dangerous. You may lose all your body hair, if you are not careful. Report it to Lieutenant Nanda."

Avijit was sure Ravi could grow a new beard and kept quiet.

"Let him grow a new one. The bottle is still half full," Ghoton joked, once they were alone.

"Tell me, did Miss No Name see you with a bald head and a beard?" Guri asked Ravi in the evening.

"No."

"Then how would she recognize a well dressed ape? Have faith in God. Whatever happens, happens for the best."

Ravi nodded his head in deep understanding.

It was two days later. The twenty young soldiers took turns at the ten toilets and baths everyday. It was five thirty and Avijit was still waiting his turn at the toilet. The winter had set in and it was very cold. A shout from one of the toilets followed by loud curses made him move towards the source of the commotion. The toilets were arranged side by side and had walls on three sides and the door on the fourth; the top was open. The cursing continued and the voice sounded like Guri's.

"What's up? Are you okay?" Avijit shouted.

The *sardar* opened the door and came out shortly.

"Who was it?"

He had wrapped his towel around him and looked drenched from head to toe.

"What happened?" Avijit tried to calm down a very agitated Guri.

"Bastard! Someone poured a bucketful of cold water from the top. Can you imagine! I was only half way through and now I am stuck."

Avijit understood his plight.

"This is serious. Don't eat breakfast today. What if nature calls during the run? Report it to Lieutenant Nanda," Ravi seemed concerned, "anyway, have faith in God. Whatever happens, happens for the best."

Their training pattern was changed from time to time to build up new skills. Only the run every morning and the weapon inspection in the afternoon were mandatory. They were made to jump from a fifteen-foot high platform onto an adjacent one twenty feet away, with the help of a rope, which was tied to a pole between the two. It looked innocuous enough, till a few of them banged against the side of the landing platform and winced in pain. Avijit always feared heights and was nervous. Failing the jump would mean doing a hundred pushups and the choice was clear. He clutched the rope with both hands and prepared for the jump. But he made the mistake of looking down and instantly felt dazed.

"What the hell, jump," the Lieutenant ordered.

But Avijit couldn't.

"What's your problem? You are holding back the others. Do you want to do the pushups instead?"

"No sir, I'll jump."

He jumped without a warning and bumped with a lot of force into an assistant on the landing platform. The impact made the man fall straight down to the ground and he was badly injured. He had to be carried to the hospital and Avijit met him there in the evening.

"I'm sorry. I didn't mean to bang into you," he told the injured man.

"Hey, that's okay. I've just cracked a rib. It should heat in a couple of weeks. It was great fun working with you guys," the man smiled, "don't worry. I will be up and about in a couple of days."

Avijit wondered how these people could be so simple and forgiving. Back in the cities, one had to hear a lot of abuse if one accidentally brushed against someone on a crowded bus or street. He was beginning to like the place.

The afternoons were dominated by firearms training. The camp had a shooting range behind one of the hills. Avijit initially had problems adjusting to the recoil, but settled down soon. The bullets hissed out harmlessly from the barrel and thudded into the targets, giving little impression of their lethal effect on a living creature. The trainees enjoyed it as clean good fun, seemingly oblivious of the fact that they might have to shoot at human beings any time in the future. But the time which Avijit enjoyed the most was the late afternoon, when they played football. Avijit always got to play full time as he was considered a very good prospect. The army had provided them the best sporting gear and the only thing that Avijit missed was a packed gallery.

"You sure stand a good chance of making it to the Army eleven," the coach confided in him one day, "but first finish your training. I'll do whatever I can to push you into the team. You can then play in all the big tournaments in the country."

Avijit had stopped dreaming. He only hoped he would qualify the army training at the first attempt.

He often thought of Sraboni and wanted to call her, whenever he went to the town. But his heart sank at the last moment. What if her parents picked up the phone? How would he ask for Sraboni then? Her parents knew nothing about their relationship. Such thoughts made him stop dialling after the area code. He would call his mother instead. She sounded a lot more relaxed in the company of his uncle and aunt, and would speak softly till Avijit spoke of finishing the call. She would become emotional, repeatedly asking him when he would return. Avijit would disconnect midway, unable to bear it any longer. He would sit all by himself in the evening, till his friends coaxed him to join them for dinner. He then wrote to his mother asking her not to cry the next time he called, as it made him uneasy and homesick. She would promise not to do so in her reply, but would again lose control over the phone.

Their training progressed satisfactorily. Avijit felt a lot more fit. Now, their entire group could run five miles at a stretch with those heavy rifles slung across their backs. Ghoton ran with Jung Bahadur on his shoulder one morning. It was not a punishment, but a self-test of his stamina. He took only fifteen more minutes to complete the run. Avijit's body had become wiry and taut; his muscles tough yet supple. He had never felt so full of energy before.

"We will try out a new exercise today," the Lieutenant informed them one day, "follow me."

They reached a clearing behind the camp. Ten volunteers dug a pit a foot deep and three feet wide, which was then filled with wood chips and saw dust.

"You need to jump over the pit," the Lieutenant announced. Avijit couldn't comprehend why they had been brought to this secluded place for such a simple exercise. Each of them was asked to jump thrice and they completed their part successfully.

"Okay, that's good. You should now be able to jump over the pit with your eyes closed," the Lieutenant smiled, "well, lets try it a different way. Lets jump over the burning pit."

The Lieutenant set fire to the wood shavings. There was a lot of smoke and the fumes shot up almost a foot in the air. Avijit, who had cleared the pit easily each time he had jumped before, was no longer confident. He always hated flames, as they reminded him of his father's pyre. The others seemed equally hesitant and everyone waited for a lead.

"In the battlefield, you may face such pits at every corner. What will you do then? Jump over it without fear or wait stupidly for the enemy's bullet? Come on, follow me," the Lieutenant bellowed.

He ran for a few yards, before jumping over the fiercely burning pit. He jumped so well that he landed a clear two feet on the other side.

"Look. I'm safe. Come on, act like a soldier and jump," the Lieutenant ordered.

Avijit decided to take the first leap. He started his run a good twenty yards away and increased his speed as he approached the pit. But he mistimed his jump and was in the air a foot away from it. He could feel the heat waves and closed his eyes in panic. He landed on the edge and was on the verge of falling back, when two strong arms hauled him away from certain disaster.

"You can do better," the Lieutenant released him, "go back and await your turn."

And it went on and on. Fresh wood and sawdust was poured into the pit to keep the flames alive. Each trainee was made to jump ten times. None fell into the pit, everyone trying their best not to get burnt. Avijit felt relieved at the end of his final jump. He sat down in exhaustion and had lowered his head to get his breath back, when the accident occurred. He suddenly heard the Lieutenant shout.

"Get him out!"

Avijit looked up to find that everyone had rushed towards the pit. He too got up and ran. Someone had fallen into the burning bed and the Lieutenant and an officer had jumped in and hauled him out. It was Ghoton!

"Are you all right?" the Lieutenant cradled Ghoton's head in his lap and shook him. But Ghoton didn't respond.

Two assistants appeared with a stretcher and Ghoton was taken to the hospital.

"Are you okay, sir?" Avijit noted the Lieutenant's uniform was burnt near the elbows and the knees.

"Don't worry. I'm fine. You are dismissed for now. Report for lunch at the usual time."

The Lieutenant seemed to suppress a lot of pain, as he raced towards the hospital followed by the others.

"Don't crowd around here. Go back to the barracks," he ordered, before disappearing into the building.

The others obeyed, but Avijit and Guri waited silently.

"Was it fatal?" Avijit asked the *sardar.*

"Oh, he should be fine. They hauled him up within seconds. His face looked all right to me," the latter tried to sound confident.

It was almost an hour before the Lieutenant came out. His shirt was off and his left elbow bandaged in thin gauze.

"He's fine. Another few seconds and it could have been disastrous," he told them, "but why are you standing here? It is lunchtime and you should be in the canteen."

They went to meet Ghoton in the evening. The hospital smelled of antiseptic and they found their friend reclining on the bed. Only his left palm was slightly burnt.

"So? How do you feel now?" Guri asked.

"On top of the world. The doctor has advised me rest till my palm heals. So no hard work till then," Ghoton sounded jubilant.

"But you ran straight into the pit! Why didn't you jump over it?" Guri's statement surprised Avijit. He had not seen it happen.

"Oh, I wanted to see whether they could save me. They test our mobility and fitness everyday. I always wondered whether they would be as agile as we are in an emergency," Ghoton added nonchalantly.

"This is crazy. What if they didn't react so fast?" Avijit couldn't hide the anger in his voice.

"I would have died. Maybe, I could reach my parents then," Ghoton reflected in a sad voice.

"Look you idiot," Guri raised a finger at Ghoton and spoke in a cold voice, "I've had enough of this. We all die someday. But it doesn't mean you stop living."

"And you should thank the Lieutenant for saving your life," Avijit's respect for the man increased with every passing day.

"You would have had your pecker burnt if he was not fit!" Guri summed up.

CHAPTER Eleven

Ghoton recovered and joined the training within a week. The trainees had become friendly and often chatted for an hour after dinner. The discussions varied from Lieutenant Nanda to sports and politics. The most popular and talked-of topic though was the fairer sex.

"She kept on glancing in my direction. We maintained eye contact for a full minute," Ravi would often remember his dream girl, "I know its love."

"But you never spoke a word. Nor are you good looking. She might have forgotten you the moment you lost eye contact," Ghoton suggested innocently.

"Shut up, you idiot," Ravi was upset, "what would a village bloke like you know of love?"

"Why, don't people fall in love in villages?" Guri came to Ghoton's rescue.

"But this dumb fellow doesn't know what love is. Its all in the heart and mind. You don't have to be good looking to fall in love."

"I never understand how you guys can only talk of falling in love," Guri interjected, "how about some action? Unless you bed a girl, you can't taste the real thing."

"You maniac, you have a dirty mind," Ravi objected, "love is divine while sex is perverse."

"I see," Guri pouted, "well, Mr Divine, you would not have been here but for a perverse act. And what will you do, if the girl touches you and your one-eyed-monster rears up its ugly head? Will you read out poems to her? I can assure you, she will be in someone else's arms in no time."

"What would you do?" Ghoton asked Guri, his eyes wide in excitement, an eager pupil ready to delve into the unknown.

"What do you mean what I would do! I have done it many times," Guri proudly declared.

Ghoton and the others would then press for the details, which the *sardar* joyously narrated. Ravi would curse and leave the barracks, while Avijit settled down to write a letter to his mother. In spite of repeated proddings, Avijit never spoke of Sraboni. But he thought of her more often with each passing day. He would re-live their first few meetings again and again. Those memories were a sublime refuge for a lonely and overworked soldier. But memories alone couldn't sustain him much longer and he decided to call her one day, when they had gone to the town.

"Hello," a female voice answered the call.

Avijit was sure it was Sraboni and his heartbeat increased.

"How are you? I miss you so much," he blurted out.

"Who are you?" the voice asked hesitantly.

"Its me," he continued in a low pitch, as a few people stood behind him in the queue, "I dream of you in my arms everyday, but when will this wait be over?"

"As soon as the police can catch you. We have complained to the local police station and they should have tracked your number by now. I hope they can teach you how to talk to a lady of your mother's age," the voice paused before spitting more venom, "in case the police fail, my husband can teach you a trick or two, as he is a retired army officer. You will soon know the consequence of making regular crank calls."

The line was disconnected.

Avijit stood dumbfounded. He wanted to kick himself for not having identified Mrs Ghosh's voice. Now a new fear gripped him. What if the police tracked the number and lodged a case against him? Would he be court-martialled for indecency? It could also end his relationship with Sraboni. He didn't know what to do. He had already called his mother and trudged back to the centre of the town, his mind heavy with worry. He wondered why everything with him had to go wrong. There was surely something called an exception. He decided to write a letter to Sraboni and clear up the misunderstanding. He finished writing a full page that evening, before tearing it up. What if it fell into her mother's hands? He would rather wait till his training was over. Then he could go back to Calcutta and explain to her in person.

Their training continued with its rigour increasing every week. Emphasis was on close quarter battle. The soldiers were made to charge with their bayonets and stab violently into sand bags. Avijit hoped he would only split sand bags with his bayonet and never a man.

"The enemy must be killed," the officers repeated everyday, "without fear, without pity, without remorse."

They were initiated into the art of rope crawling one day. It was at the same place, where they had jumped like monkeys from one platform to the other. The platforms were still there; only a thick nylon rope was tied tautly across them and it created a ropeway between the two. Each trainee was to cling to the rope and traverse the entire distance. Letting go would mean a drop of almost fifteen feet and likely injury. Guri volunteered for the first attempt. He clutched the rope with both hands and tried to move towards the opposite direction, continuing with increasing strain, till he finally gave up around halfway. Luckily, he landed on his legs and was not injured.

"Hah! And you call him the strongest," Ghoton teased, "let me show you who really is the strongest."

He followed the same technique and didn't even reach halfway. He landed on his back and limped his way back to where the others were standing.

"Oh! I think I'm hurt. I must report to the hospital."

"Don't do that," Ravi whispered, "the Doc will put a very hot bag on your ass and you won't be able to shit for the next seven days!"

"Follow my technique," the Lieutenant shouted.

He caught the rope with both hands and crossed his legs over the rope, so that his body was parallel to it. Then he advanced with his hands and pushed with his legs on the rope, crawling like a squirrel. He was across in no time.

"I know it can be difficult initially, but practice makes you perfect. Just do it, "the Lieutenant raised his thumb.

They started their crawl, one at a time.

"If you drop, your hands should leave the rope last," the Lieutenant directed, "then you won't fall on your head."

It was extremely difficult. Avijit's arms were aching from the effort by the halfway mark. His legs slipped off and it took all the strength in his body to manoeuver them back over the rope.

"Move, move. Just don't give up," Lieutenant Nanda shouted all the time, "you let go and I will make you do a hundred pushups."

Avijit was sure his hands would come off, but he held on. The Lieutenant helped him down when he reached the end.

"Well done," he slapped Avijit on the back, "go back and take some rest. You will have to do it three more times, so conserve your energy."

Avijit felt like bursting into tears. Ghoton managed to move three quarters of the length, before his legs slipped off. He hung helplessly from the rope, after repeated attempts to put his legs back over it failed.

"Come on, move you idiot," the Lieutenant shouted.

"I can't sir," Ghoton shouted back, "my hands have gone numb. Please let me off. I will do the hundred pushups, but I cannot bear this any more."

"Who asked you to do pushups? You can let go, but then you won't be served lunch. Suit yourself."

Ghoton sat down next to Avijit, panting heavily after completing the full crawl.

"Bastard," he muttered, "just wait. I'll make him pay dearly for this."

"Better shut up. You will have to do it three more times before lunch," Avijit passed on the bad news.

No one spoke a word after dinner that night. Everyone was too tired to move a muscle. They crawled like snakes for the next five days, before being released for a day. Most decided to laze around in the camp and there were only twelve of them in the truck to town. Ghoton and Guri went to the town for fun. The former to taste the half burnt chicken *kebabs* at the restaurant, the latter to stand and gape at the few girls who passed by. That day was no different. Only no one was willing to stay back after lunch. They didn't know what new discipline awaited them the next day and their bodies ached from the exertions of the past week. Everyone wanted to rest and the truck was on its way back by the early afternoon. It was where the plain merged into the hills that they spotted Lieutenant Nanda. His jeep was parked and he was having tea at a roadside kiosk, which was possibly the last shop before the camp.

"Hey stop," Ghoton shouted to the driver, "we would like to have some tea."

They had had tea in the shop before and Avijit was not too fond of the warm liquid, which the owner offered. But it was a cold day and they all got down.

"Hello, sir. Thought we would have some tea," Ghoton beamed at the Lieutenant.

"Yeah, go ahead. Though I am not too sure whether he is serving tea or cow's piss," the Lieutenant laughed out aloud and they joined in.

The Lieutenant seemed to be in a good mood and they chatted freely.

"So how are things? Any urge to quit and go back home?" he asked Ravi.

"No sir. None at all. I'll complete the training, come what may," Ravi replied emphatically.

"Ah, that's good," he patted Ravi on the back and turned towards Avijit, "and what about you? How's your mother?"

"She is fine sir. She would like to see her son a true soldier," Avijit was touched to note the Lieutenant still remembered his mother.

"I'm sure she would."

The tea was served. Ghoton raised his index finger and vanished behind the Lieutenant's jeep to relieve himself. The Lieutenant paid for their tea and waved them off.

"I've done it," Ghoton shouted jubilantly, after their truck had taken the first bend on the hilly road.

"What have you done? Screwed someone?" Guri joked.

Ghoton raised one hand like a priest, requesting for silence and brought forward the palm of the other. There were two tiny metallic objects, which he displayed proudly.

"What are these?" Avijit asked, bewildered.

"Guess," Ghoton wanted to sustain the suspense.

"I know what they are," Ravi remarked, "tyre air-valve covers."

"Yeah!" Ghoton shouted, but immediately stopped.

He looked towards the driver's cabin and lowered his tone.

"This is not fair," Avijit was appalled.

"Why not? The bastard treats us like slaves everyday. Let him face the music."

Ghoton had taken out the air from the two rear wheels of the Lieutenant's jeep. There was no way the latter could inflate the tyres. Avijit had noticed only one spare wheel at the rear of the jeep and the Lieutenant would without doubt, be stranded. The shop was almost fifteen kilometres from their camp and there was hardly any traffic on the road, as it was a Sunday.

"We must go and pick him up," Avijit announced and was about to talk to the driver, when two strong hands pulled him back. They argued for the next few minutes in whispers. Only Ravi and Avijit felt the need to go back. Avijit would have had his way, had Guri not explained the odds.

"What will you tell the Lieutenant when you reach him? How do you know he is stranded unless you are aware that the air has been taken out of the wheels? He will surely be pleased and make us all crawl on the bloody rope for the next seven nights."

They continued quietly towards the camp. Avijit felt tired and looked forward to a hot bath, though it would mean lighting a fire and heating the ice cold water. Their truck reached the camp and stopped near the gate. The sentry spoke urgently to the driver. The passengers were too exhausted to bother, but jumped up in alarm when the driver started reversing the truck.

"Hey! What's the problem? Let us down."

"Sorry mates. There is an emergency and I have orders to take you back," the driver drove back the way they had come.

"What emergency?" Ghoton asked the driver.

"I don't know. Lieutenant Nanda had sent an SOS over his wireless set." The trainees were pale with fear.

"Bloody shit! What happens now?" Ravi asked.

"Look, whatever happens please don't tell him I did it," Ghoton pleaded, "I can die for all of you, but cannot face that Lieutenant in anger."

They all agreed to stand by Ghoton, though Avijit felt like kicking him. The hot bath looked a distant dream. The fear of finding the Lieutenant injured or even dead and a subsequent court-martial looked a reality. It was a steep road and the Lieutenant might not have noticed the flat tyres and met with an accident.

But the Lieutenant was safe. In fact, he was enjoying a mug of tea, his legs stretched across the bonnet of his jeep, which had not moved an inch from its place.

"I'm sorry. I'm in a spot of bother and need your help," he looked closely at the trainees, who stood still.

"What is it sir?" Avijit tried to sound his normal self.

"Oh, my rear wheels have leaked their air. There is only one spare wheel and I cannot risk going up in this state. So I thought you guys could help," the Lieutenant smiled.

"How sir?"

"Simple. You push the jeep to the nearest petrol pump. The truck can follow us. It is only six kilometres."

It took them more than an hour to reach the fuel station.

"That was fast! Maybe, I should ask them to have some hot water ready for you at the camp," the Lieutenant took out his wireless set and waved them off.

"Next time you want to test the bastard, let me know in advance. I won't be within a mile of you," Ravi hissed at Ghoton, once they were on the truck.

"And you massage my back tonight or else I will tell the Lieutenant it was you," Guri grimaced, as the truck bounced over the hilly road, "shit! My ass seems to have turned to stone."

Most of them were now adept in handling small arms, as also the light machine gun. Avijit could shoot an apple a hundred yards away with ease. Ghoton had accepted the fact that the Lieutenant was blessed with more grey cells than him. He obeyed the latter's commands silently and there was peace all around. The trainees looked forward to the day when they would be formally inducted into their regiment as soldiers and posted outside the training camp. They also harboured hopes of spending a few days with their families after this long exile. It was during breakfast one day that a loud whirring noise caught their attention. The sound grew louder and many peeped out of the canteen window to see what it was. A large green helicopter circled their camp a few times, before descending onto the football field. There was an uneasy silence, after the rotors stopped.

"Must be some seniors coming down to give us more lectures on discipline," Ghoton concentrated again on his food.

Avijit was not so sure. They had been climbing rock faces for the past one-week and his fear of heights made him look forward to manoeuvres on plain land. But that was not to be. The Lieutenant addressed them, once they had gathered at the centre of the camp.

"We will train in heli-jumping today. Armies the world over try and surprise the enemy by heli-dropping troops behind the enemy lines. That way, the enemy is sandwiched from both sides. It also helps in rushing troops to forward positions quickly. So this is mandatory for everyone. Any questions?"

There were none. It looked perfectly simple the way the Lieutenant explained it. They would initially make the jump from fifty feet and would have to slide down a thick rope from the helicopter. A lifeline would be attached to each jumper, in case one lost his grip over the rope. They followed the Lieutenant to the football field, where the chopper stood. It was big enough to accommodate eight of them, the Lieutenant and two of his assistants.

"Put on the safety line," the Lieutenant ordered.

Avijit took the lead and drew the rope from a payoff. He tied it expertly around his body. He now understood why the Lieutenant had insisted everyone learn to tie a lifeline and slide down a rope from a twenty foot high platform, for the past week.

"Release the safety line when you reach the ground," the Lieutenant reminded him again.

The helicopter started with a roar and lifted off slowly from the ground, its rotors cutting the air, making the lush green grass on the field quiver. The chopper stood still, once it reached its desired height. Avijit caught the sliding rope and moved towards the door, but his legs started shaking the moment he looked out. The height made him dizzy and he could vaguely make out that one end of the rope was touching the ground.

"Are you ready?" the Lieutenant shouted above the noise of the flying machine.

"I'm not sure I can do it sir," Avijit tried to swallow hard, but his throat was absolutely dry.

"Why? What's your problem? Okay, let me show you how simple it is," the Lieutenant took the rope from Avijit and jumped out. He slid down the rope all the way, without even a lifeline.

The pilot had to take the chopper down to pick up the Lieutenant.

"Do it now," he ordered, the moment they were up again.

"Give me sometime, sir," Avijit pleaded.

"Why, you are frightened! You should have stayed at home. You leave the camp today and join the football team. I don't want sissies to graduate from this camp. Who's next?"

The Lieutenant's words had the desired effect. Avijit took a deep breath and jumped. It was as if the world had come to an end. He felt weightless and closed his eyes in panic, but gripped the rope firmly. He slid down the thick coil easily and hit the ground with a thud. He suddenly felt free. He had done it.

The session continued smoothly till the mishap. A trainee named Jadav was standing near the door of the chopper, waiting his turn, when a sudden gust of wind hit the helicopter, making it tilt. Jadav fell through the air, his shriek rising above the noise of the rotors, as the others watched helplessly. Everyone ran forward and crowded around the body that lay in a heap. It still seemed to have life left in it.

"Make way. Let me see him," the Lieutenant had jumped from the chopper with the rope.

Jadav was rushed to the hospital and their heli-jumping session aborted for the day.

"It was all because of Lieutenant Nanda," Ghoton fumed.

They were in their barracks after dinner. Even a glutton like Ghoton had not been able to eat, as news had come out that Jadav had died. "I don't agree with you," Avijit came up in defense of the Lieutenant, "its partly Jadav's fault too. He stood too near the door. It was also destiny. Who would have known such a strong gust of wind was going to hit the chopper? The Lieutenant is blaming himself and spoke of quitting."

"Your remark will hasten his decision and we will miss the guidance of one of the best trainers in the army," Guri added.

Major Chawla put in an unexpected appearance the next morning on the parade ground.

"In the army, you need to come to terms with death and injury. Yesterday's incident was unfortunate, but the training must go on. Once in a battlefield, you may lose many friends and colleagues. But you should not dither from your primary responsibility to safe guard the nation," the Major turned towards the Lieutenant, "Lieutenant

Nanda feels he has not been able to discharge his duties properly and wants to resign. I do not agree with him. But he persuaded me to take your opinion on whether you want him to continue or not. I'm not sure there is precedence, but I had to agree. So tell me what you want?"

"We want him to continue sir," Ravi shouted.

"Yes sir," all the others including Ghoton, joined in.

"So Lieutenant, you have your answer. I am sure you can train them to be some of the best soldiers in our army," the Major waved to them and departed.

They continued with heli-jumping for the next five days. Most of them did not need the lifeline by the third day.

Avijit felt he belonged to the real world again, a world where discipline, sincerity and humanity were more important than money and power. He occasionally felt homesick too, but cheered up when he received his mother's letter or spoke to her over the phone. She wrote at least two letters a week and looked forward to meeting her soldier-son. Khokon had consented to marrying a Calcutta girl. He was planning to come down that very month to finalize one from a long list of proposals. An engineer settled abroad was after all a prize catch. Avijit had spared his mother the ordeal. He wondered what Sraboni might be doing? They had not seen each other for four and a half months now and his feelings for her had only grown stronger.

Their entire training pattern was changed around the fifth month. It became a combination of all the disciplines they had practiced separately. Avijit particularly liked the mock fights. They would be heli-dropped on a hilly terrain in groups of ten. There would be cardboard cutouts of the enemy hidden in the dense forest. The group had to search them out and shoot into them, within a specific timeframe. They would cut through the forest, jump over crevasses and often climb up steep rock-faces to reach the end point. They had to fire from the rifles at certain targets and hurl grenades at others. Lieutenant Nanda and his assistants watched every step and later suggested measures to improve their performance.

The day of their passing out parade finally arrived. They ironed their uniforms, till the creases stood out. Their boots shone like mirrors. The entire group assembled at the centre of the camp to be formally inducted into their regiment. Major Chawla stood on a platform and administered the oath. Each one of them shouted it out word by word, pledging their lives for the good of their motherland. The guests clapped loudly, once it was over. Lieutenant Nanda personally clipped the badge on each of their uniforms. He also conveyed the good news to them; each of them had earned two weeks leave before they were to join their regiment. They could leave the very next day. Avijit had a drink in the evening to celebrate the occasion. Booze flowed freely at the party and Lieutenant Nanda also joined in the fun. Avijit watched in awe, as the man who could take on any hazardous assignment, guzzled down a dozen whiskeys with equal ease. He even cracked a few jokes.

"Thank you boss, you were simply great," Ghoton remarked.

"Did you call me *boss*, son?" the sudden question caught everyone off guard. "Do you know there was a fight between the various organs, when God created man?" the Lieutenant seemed to enjoy the confusion amongst the juniors. "Everyone wanted to be the *boss*. The brain felt it was the boss, as it ran all the other organs. The eyes didn't agree and said that if they did not see, the brain couldn't work. The hands and the legs put in their nominations and the debate gained momentum. Suddenly, the tiny rectum stated it was the boss! The others laughed out so loud that the poor chap closed down in shame. It was born shy and never showed itself in public. The laughter made it feel humiliated and it didn't open up for the next seven days. And guess what happened? The brain got foggy, the eyes couldn't focus, the hands and legs couldn't move. And God got his answer. So what is the moral of the story?"

"Never mess with the ass," Ghoton replied emphatically.

"Is it, to be a boss you need to be an ass?" Ravi asked cautiously.

"No. The moral of the story is you can call me anything, but never call me the boss!" the Lieutenant boomed.

The fun continued till late in the night. It was a tearful moment the next day, when the time came to take their leave from Lieutenant Nanda. The Lieutenant hugged each one of them.

"Always behave like a true soldier. Don't be afraid of anything in life. God is always with you," he told them, before bidding good-bye.

Avijit looked back at the receding figure from the army truck, grateful for the confidence the man had instilled in him. He hoped they would meet **again some** day. It felt bad to be separated from their batch mates, as most had become fast friends.

"Well, only a matter of fifteen days," Guri thumped Avijit on the back, "and don't come back with a wife. I don't want to lose out on the chance to see a Bengali marriage." "And you," he turned to Ghoton, "don't die for someone just because he smiled at you. I won't be able to share my escapades with anyone then."

And thus they parted, each for his home, rest and recreation. Ghoton had decided to make a brief visit to his uncle's place and spend the rest of his vacation with Avijit. He carried a big parcel other than his luggage – food packed from the army canteen.

"I had to tip the chef an extra ten bucks for the boiled eggs," he said.

He also bought whatever food he could lay his hands on at the station.

"You never know where the train might get stuck. So why take a chance?" he reasoned, when Avijit questioned the wisdom of buying twenty packets of biscuits for a twenty-hour journey.

Ghoton opened the food packet the moment they were on the train and threw away the leftovers, even before the train had picked up its full speed. The landscape rushed past, the dusty summer making the green look wilted all around. Avijit remembered his last train journey a half-year back. He had felt nervous and insecure. The training had changed all that. He now looked forward to every new dawn with hope and joy. His excitement grew at the thought of being able to meet Sraboni soon. He was not too sure he could keep Guri's request. If Sraboni agreed, they could marry that very month. He would throw a party at the regiment later, to pacify the *sardar*.

He looked at Ghoton, who was already snoring and debated whether to make him the best man at the wedding. The train stopped at a few stations and Ghoton immediately jumped up to buy more food.

"At this rate, you will be grossly overweight by the time you report back for duty. They will simply sack you," Avijit warned his friend.

"Would they dare?" Ghoton shrugged him off and continued on his eating spree.

CHAPTER Twelve

The train was delayed and they reached Howrah station only around midnight the next day. The city had gone to sleep and buses were not available.

"Lets take a cab," Ghoton suggested.

They reached the cab bay to find around a dozen cabs waiting. But it was too few for the hundred odd families, who had alighted from the train.

"Need a cab?" a young man asked them.

"Yes, we want to go to Salt Lake," Avijit replied.

"Two hundred rupees each," the man indicated a cab, which already had three people in it.

Avijit was appalled! The normal fare from the station to his uncle's residence would be a maximum of fifty rupees. He tried to bargain, but the man would have none of it.

"Be on the platform for the night. You should get a bus at five thirty in the morning. Pay three bucks and you will be home," the man mocked.

Avijit didn't like the way he dismissed them and watched helplessly, as two other passengers boarded the cab without an argument. They had been taught to be patient during their training and it got tested that night.

"Do you want a girl?" an unshaven and dirty man approached them. They had been sitting morosely on their luggage for the last half hour and Avijit had almost dozed off. The station was full of sleeping bodies, who didn't look like train passengers. Avijit and

Ghoton had somehow managed to get a small space near a kiosk and waited for dawn.

"Don't disturb us," Ghoton said sternly, but it didn't deter the man.

"Very young and very good looking girl sir. Just come with me and you will never forget the night," the man persisted.

"Go before I hit you."

Avijit had dozed off again, when he suddenly felt a hand shaking him.

"Hey, give us your watch and purse," a dark, well built man, bare-chested and wearing only a *lungi* stood in front of them.

There were three other ugly looking characters with the man. Ghoton kept on snoring in spite of their nudges.

"Why should I?" Avijit tried to sound cool.

"See this?" the man brought out a blunt looking dagger and dangled it in front of Avijit. "Come, come, give it. Don't hold us back," he sounded impatient.

Ghoton's right leg suddenly kicked into the man's groin. The latter simply doubled over, dropping the dagger in the process. What followed was a nightmare for the two others, who tried to come to their leader's rescue. The third man was prudent enough to abandon his comrades. Avijit was sure Lieutenant Nanda would have appreciated the strength and swiftness his wards exhibited. A few sleeping bodies woke up, only to scamper away or simply turn over and go back to slumber.

"Bastards! You will pay for this with your life," the leader spat venom at them, unable to get up from his prone position. Ghoton's right leg kept him pinned to the ground, while Avijit held the other two firmly by their shirt collars.

"What's going on?" two policemen appeared from nowhere.

"These people tried to rob us," Avijit indicated the fugitives.

"But how can you take the law into your own hands?" one of them shouted.

"Because the law was not around."

"You must come with us," the policeman pulled Avijit by the arm, "they are not robbers. I know them. How do I know you were not robbing them?"

Avijit felt his welcome to the unreal world was complete. They were not in their army uniforms and he vowed not to undertake another journey, without being in his uniform. Being a common man was a curse in this great nation. Danger lurked at every corner for him. The three fugitives had found a new voice. They now stood behind the policemen and bayed for revenge.

"They beat us up," the leader complained, "arrest them."

"We are in the army and would like to meet your officer in-charge," Avijit spoke with unmistakable authority and took out his identity card.

The three fugitives vanished. The policemen saluted and stood undecided. They looked old and overweight, and Avijit wondered how they were expected to protect passengers.

"You should have told us before," one of them grinned anxiously.

"Are you aware what goes on in this station at night?" Avijit asked, "trains get delayed and there are no cabs to take the tired passengers home. You need to pay a fortune to reach home. You have unauthorized people sleeping in the waiting rooms, pimps and robbers having a free run of the station. So, what does the common man do?"

"Survive," the policeman replied, "come with me. I will get you a cab."

They reached home by two a.m.

"Who is it?" his uncle's voice sounded sleepy, as he peeped through the keyhole. Avijit had been ringing the doorbell for the past five minutes.

"It's me, Avijit."

His uncle squinted his eyes and looked closely at the two bald headed men after opening the door. It was almost a minute before he decided it was indeed his nephew and hugged Avijit. They stepped into the house. What followed was an emotional reunion, peppered with concerns and sermons on travelling in the middle of the night.

"You shouldn't have come in the night. You could have been robbed," his uncle observed.

"Well, if soldiers get robbed, then there won't be much hope left for this country," Ghoton reasoned.

"You think we are so weak! No Uncle. We can face the might of any army in this world. How can a few hoodlums threaten us?"

Avijit felt a lump in his throat, when he first saw his mother. She looked at him strangely and her eyes welled up with tears. She wept on his chest and only stopped, when Ghoton spoke of another son waiting for the mother's blessing.

"My God, you look stupid in the hair cut," she observed, after the initial euphoria had died down.

"You must be hungry," his aunt suddenly seemed to realize.

Avijit wanted to say they had dinner at the station, but Ghoton had already jumped up.

"Oh, we are famished Aunty! Imagine travelling for two days without any food," he winked at Avijit.

The ladies of the house got together and served them a meal of rice and fish curry within fifteen minutes. It tasted delicious. Later, Avijit sat with his mother in her room and shared his experience of the past months. The eastern sky had turned a light pink by the time mother and son fell asleep.

"Get up, it's getting late for breakfast," Ghoton shook him awake.

It was already nine o'clock, but Avijit wanted to laze around a little more. Ghoton though would have none of it, as his body, heart and mind yearned for food.

"How long is your leave?" Avijit's aunt asked him at the breakfast table.

"It's only for two weeks," Ghoton spoke through a mouthful of homemade sweets.

"But then you will miss Khokon's marriage," she looked

concerned, "he will be upset. Can't you postpone your date of joining?"

"Oh, don't worry, we will fix up something," Ghoton spoke as if it was no big deal.

Avijit wondered whether his own marriage could be arranged on the same date? He had to meet Mr Ghosh and Sraboni to know their mind.

"So? How many girls did Khokon meet before deciding on his match?" he asked his aunt.

He was sure it would be in double digits. Khokon was very particular about things personal.

"Thankfully, it was not like last time," his aunt sounded relieved, "in fact, we were very lucky. Khokon met her here. She or her family had no inkling that we were looking for a suitable girl for Khokon. They say marriages are made in heaven."

"Yeah, and celebrated on earth," Ghoton quickly reminded. It seemed he was already dreaming of the grand feast at Khokon's wedding.

"Anyway, your brother can never hold us responsible, if he has a fight with his wife," his uncle joked, "she was his choice."

"But how did they meet?" Avijit felt it was even more romantic than his own affair.

"Well, she had actually come to meet me," his mother replied, "I don't know whether you remember her – Sraboni, Mr Ghosh's daughter."

Avijit couldn't believe what he heard!

"*Who*?" he asked incredulously.

"Sraboni, the girl in our old locality. Her father helped you get into the army. How can you forget them so soon?" his mother sounded surprised.

Avijit wanted to shout and tell her that he had not forgotten Sraboni for a single minute during the past months. The world came to a sudden stop for him. The bright daylight seemed lost and a grey mist enveloped him. He started sweating. It couldn't be true! It surely couldn't be true! There must be some mistake somewhere. He got up from the table and went into his mother's room. He locked the door from inside, before sitting down on the bed. He had to think with a cool head. A part of him wanted to shout out in rage, while another wanted to let go of his emotions in a torrent of tears. He reined in both. He had to meet Sraboni immediately. She might have been forced into this. Yes, that must be it. She was too subdued and fragile to fight her parents. And neither his mother, nor her parents knew of their relationship. He felt stupid. He should have at least confided to his mother. Then it wouldn't have happened. Luckily, there was still time. He was sure Khokon wouldn't mind. There were plenty of beautiful girls in Calcutta. The Ghoshs would relent, once Sraboni told them about Avijit. Avijit was in the same profession as Mr Ghosh and the latter would surely stand by a junior. He put on a T-shirt over his jeans. He hoped Sraboni would be in college as it was a weekday. He would talk to her and get things right.

"Hey! Where are you going?" Ghoton asked, when he saw Avijit dressed.

"To meet some friends."

"Can I come with you?"

"No. You better stay at home and keep an eye on the kitchen. After all, this is our first lunch at home after a long long time."

Avijit's words seemed to hit a delicate nerve and Ghoton moved towards the kitchen. Avijit hailed a cab and reached Sraboni's college. A few girls stood near the gate. He approached one of them.

"Hello," he tried to draw her attention.

The girl turned towards him and seemed to stare. She suddenly started laughing and moved away towards the other girls.

"Oh, my! What a figure and what a hair cut!"

"Ask him, is he bald all over!"

Avijit was flustered. He was not there to listen to such silly comments. He had to find Sraboni quickly.

"Look I need to find someone. Could you help me please?" he requested a girl who was standing all by herself.

"I'm not that someone. So don't disturb me," she turned away.

"Please, I need to find a girl named Sraboni," he pleaded with her.

"There are a lot of Srabonis here. You have to tell me her full name and batch," the girl replied.

Avijit gave her the details.

"You mean Sraboni Ghosh? But she is no longer with this college."

"Are you sure?" Avijit found it hard to believe.

"Oh, yes. She is senior to me by a year and was very popular in college for her singing. I have not seen her after her part one results. She must have taken admission in some other college."

Avijit thanked the girl and moved on. He had only one option left. He decided to call her at her residence. But would she be at home? He wanted to chance his luck and dialled her number.

"I would like to speak to Sraboni," he mentioned firmly, the moment he heard a female voice on the other side.

"Who is this?" the voice sounded cautious.

"I'm Avijit."

There was silence for a few moments, before the same voice spoke again.

"How are you, my silly soldier?" it was she.

She sounded her old self. She had not changed. Avijit felt a strange sense of relief on hearing her voice and forgot his woes for sometime.

"I need to meet you," he finally said.

"When?"

"As soon as possible. I have a lot to discuss."

"Okay. Be in front of the lake tomorrow at three p.m.," she replied, after a pause.

"No. I have to meet you today. Now if possible," Avijit pressed hard.

There was a long silence and Avijit thought she had disconnected the line. But she finally spoke and agreed to meet him by noon.

It was another long wait near the entrance to the lake, before she made her appearance. Avijit found it difficult to breathe. Sraboni had put on a little weight and looked beautiful.

"My God, you look so rough," she took in his well-muscled body and hair cut, all in one furtive glance.

"Not rough but tough," Avijit tried to laugh.

She seemed hesitant and nervous and did not speak, till they had sat down on an empty bench.

"So? How are you?" Avijit didn't know where to begin.

"Okay."

There was an uneasy silence and Avijit decided to speak his mind.

"What is this I hear of you marrying Khokon? Is this true?"

"Yes."

"But did they force you?" Avijit knew they had, but wanted to hear it from her.

"No," it sounded like a slap.

Avijit couldn't believe his ears!

"You mean you agreed to it?" he was still not sure.

"Yes," Sraboni replied, her eyes downcast.

Avijit felt as if a car had hit him at full speed. He sat in a bewildered silence for sometime.

"But how could you? Didn't you remember your promise?" Avijit looked closely at her.

"I couldn't help it," Sraboni seemed to be talking in riddles.

Avijit sat stunned. He wanted to try one final time and gathered his thoughts before speaking.

"Look, we all make mistakes. I can still correct this. Just say yes. Everything will be fine again," he looked at her full of hope.

"No," Sraboni was firm.

"But why?" Avijit almost shouted.

"Because you cannot give me the life that Khokon can," Sraboni spoke calmly, "I have seen mother suffer all through her life. Father often got posted in sensitive areas and she had to fend for herself. Yes, the army was always there and she had no material needs unfulfilled. But she fought loneliness every minute. And the burden of rearing a child all by herself." Sraboni paused to catch her breath, before she continued. "He would often vanish for months and there would be no news of his whereabouts. Then, he would suddenly call for five minutes and wouldn't even give us his address for security reasons. My mother is a strong lady and could survive it in the name of sacrifice for the motherland. But I am more practical. I cannot let go of my life for a nation, which has lost all sense of purpose. You expect me to make sacrifices for this land, where a student, who worked sincerely for her college exams is awarded one, two and three marks in her main subjects! The examiner must have marvelled at the harmony of those three single digits on my marks sheet, little realizing the devastation it can heap on it's recipient."

Sraboni cried silently. Avijit was shocked! He knew Sraboni was a good student and even the devil would think twice, before giving her such marks.

"But why don't you fight it? Get your papers rechecked?"

"What for? You submit the fees and wait for six months. Even if justice is done, I will miss out one year, as admission to the current batch is already over. Do I need to lose one year of my life, just because the examiner felt bored while correcting my papers, or he had some friends to attend to! I had lost the zeal to live. I could not communicate with my parents. Neither were you around. Khokon was able to show me a new light. He told me I could easily pursue a career abroad."

She looked at Avijit and softened the hard look on her face. She held his hand and sat silently.

"I know I am sounding terribly selfish, but I have no other option. I cannot be a housewife as I would feel stifled. You can never be happy with me and both our lives would be wasted," she gave a sad smile, "you can always get a good wife and lead a happy life."

"You believe it's easy to forget love?"

"You can, if you try," Sraboni smiled again.

"And what do you know of Khokon?" Avijit asked as an afterthought.

"Not much, I agree. But then it doesn't really matter. I have already lived my death here. All my dreams are shattered. I just want to escape this shame," Sraboni added.

Avijit knew it was the end for him. It was difficult to believe that the little dream he had built up of sharing his life with the vibrant and bubbly girl sitting next to him, now lay shattered. She wouldn't hold his hand lovingly again, like she had for the past few moments. He slowly withdrew his hand, not willing to prolong the agony.

"I'm sorry, I bothered you today. I will never disturb you again," Avijit managed a thin smile, "I'm sure you'll be happy with Khokon."

He looked at his watch. It was well past one in the afternoon. His mother must be waiting, as he had promised to come back before lunch. He got up to leave.

"Let me drop you home," he suggested.

"No. I'll go alone."

Avijit hailed a cab. He couldn't control himself any longer and the tears flowed freely; a tired soldier, unable to brave the emotional blizzard of life. He had to wipe his eyes and behave normally, once the cabbie started glancing at him through the rear view mirror.

"What took you so long?" it was Ghoton, who opened the door, the moment he rang the bell, "I'm hungry as hell and you vanish!"

Avijit was surprised that Ghoton had waited for him. He had ceased to expect such gestures any longer.

"I'm sorry, my friends held me back."

He had a quick bath and joined the others for lunch. It was a feast, but he had no appetite. There was his favourite tiger prawn malaikari, but he didn't seem to notice it, till his mother forced a large piece onto his plate. Ghoton decided to have a nap after lunch and Avijit sat alone in his mother's room.

"What is wrong with you?" his mother's sudden query took him by surprise. He had not heard her come in.

"No, nothing," he mumbled.

"Tell me. I know something is wrong," his mother turned his face towards her with both hands and asked firmly. "You are my only hope. I live only for you. Tell me what it is."

He knew he could never fool his mother. So he told her. He wept into her shoulder, once he had finished. She was too stunned to react.

"Don't cry," she sounded firm, "how can you defend the nation if you are so weak? That girl went through hell after her results. So forgive her and look ahead."

Avijit knew his mother was correct, but the hurt was terrible.

They had a surprise visitor the next day. Mr Ghosh came down to meet his uncle.

"So, how was your training?" he asked Avijit.

His uncle had to leave for office and Ghoton was busy with the ladies in the kitchen.

"It was great, sir," he felt a little clumsy for not having met Mr Ghosh earlier.

"I've come here to apologize," Mr Ghosh looked around and whispered.

"Why?" Avijit couldn't think of a plausible reason.

"For my daughter's conduct," Avijit was dumbfounded, "look son, I knew you were close to my daughter. But her exams shattered her. She changed. She might have done something silly. But your cousin understood her problem. She suddenly started dreaming about life again. I couldn't stop her, for fear of upsetting her balance. I couldn't sacrifice my daughter's happiness. Your cousin doesn't know anything about the two of you. I've come today to request you not to tell him anything."

Avijit didn't know what to say. Everyone wanted to ensure their share of the pie.

"Uncle, I am indebted for whatever you did. How could you imagine I would spoil your daughter's future? Don't worry."

Khokon called a day later.

"Hi buddy! I'll be there in three weeks time," he sounded cheerful. "I finally gave in," Khokon continued, "those dark eyes and the smile drove me mad."

Avijit listened silently. He was happy, his vacillating cousin was finally settling down in life.

"And how's life with you? Why don't you get married too? Anyway, we'll speak once I reach. Bye."

Avijit didn't want to stir up Khokon by stating that he would be far away at the time of the wedding.

"Nothing is indispensable in life," his mother told him, "if I can adjust to your father's absence, why should you be bothered with an acquaintance of a few months? Time is the best healer. I will find a better girl for you."

Avijit told her he was in no hurry to marry and wanted to

concentrate on his job. His mother raised the subject of her going back to Rajpur.

"Our tenants are moving out next month. I want to go back there. That house has a lot of memories for me. I would rather stay there re-living them, than getting stifled here."

Avijit didn't comment. His mother had seen enough of life to decide what was best for her. Ghoton decided to visit his native place after staying for a week with Avijit.

"Let me go and see what has happened to my father's property," he mused, "who knows, my uncle might have already sold it off. I should be back in a couple of days. So don't leave without me."

Chandan and Ujjal came down on Sunday.

"We came to know from Mr Ghosh that you are in town. It seems you have conveniently forgotten your promise to treat us, the day you returned. So here we are."

It was good to meet his old friends.

"Hey, you look real tough!" Chandan patted his arm in admiration.

"Well, I must give you the good news," Ujjal paused for effect, "first, Chandan has made it big in life. And I have got married."

Chandan had been able to sign a deal with a new music company. This time, he had made sure the contract was in order, before singing a single verse. The songs were a sure hit and he was a busy artist nowadays.

"Life is good to people who are good to life," Chandan added philosophically.

"Exceptions prove the rule," Avijit smiled sadly.

"We hear Sraboni is marrying your cousin. What are you doing?" the sudden question from Ujjal caught him unawares.

"Look, everyone in our locality knew about the two of you," Chandan's statement shocked Avijit. He always thought it was a well-kept secret.

"Whatever happens, happens for the best," Avijit felt uncomfortable discussing the topic, "tell me, how did you get married?"

"It was a plain and simple arranged match," Ujjal was candid, "we didn't even know each other before the wedding, but are having torrid sex ever since!"

Ujjal went on sharing the details, little caring that it was his wife he was disrobing in front of his friends. Chandan stopped Ujjal midway and presented Avijit his cassette. The three friends babbled till lunchtime. Chandan sang a few of his new creations in honour of his old friend. It calmed Avijit somewhat.

Ghoton arrived with only a day left for their departure.

"I had a swell time," he told Avijit after completing a late lunch, "my uncle and aunt had never been so sweet to me in my life. They became sweeter after I signed the papers they had made out for me. I literally lived the life of a king."

"What papers?" Avijit was confused.

"I signed a document disowning the property owned by my father, of which I am the legal heir. It will now be transferred to my aunt."

"What? Are you crazy!" Avijit couldn't believe his friend, "where will you go after retiring from the army?"

"Oh, don't worry. I won't live that long," Ghoton smiled. "The army provides all that I need. So what will I do with a small property? Now I am assured of a grand reception whenever I visit my uncle."

Ghoton continued to amaze Avijit. He himself had cried, sulked and shouted for the past few days over things which were elusive; things, which he thought were his birthright. And his dear friend had gifted away his only possession, without a whimper! Avijit hoped there could be more Ghotons in this world. It would then be a very different place to live in. They decided to leave as per schedule in spite of the elders' persuasion.

"Khokon will be furious. He might even postpone the marriage," his aunt was apprehensive.

"You know him better than us. He would be very hurt, if you are not there," his uncle pleaded.

But Avijit stood his ground. His mother understood and did not push him either. He had expected pressure from Ghoton, but his friend was strangely silent.

"Write to me regularly," his mother reminded him, "and live life with your head held high."

The elders came to the station to see them off. Avijit suddenly realized he had wasted a major part of his vacation thinking of unreal situations. He had spent very little time with the person who mattered most. He promised not to repeat his folly and waved back at the frail and short lady in white, as the train moved out of the station.

CHAPTER Thirteen

They had to report to their regiment head quarters in the northern tip of the country. Though sweat poured out of the body in Calcutta, the weather in the new city was cold, as it was close to the Himalayas. They reported to the army office at the railway station and were asked to wait in a truck outside, as a few more people were expected.

"Hey, who are you?" one of the two soldiers, who sat on the truck, pointed a light machine gun in their direction, when they tried to board it.

"We are in the army," Avijit replied, a little irritated.

But they had to show their identity cards, before the two soldiers allowed them onto the truck. They didn't bother to apologize either. Ghoton decided to strike up a conversation with one of them.

"Will it be colder in the night?"

"This is summer. You have to wait another few months before the night is cold," the soldier replied.

"How cold?"

"Not much, just a few degrees below zero. I have seen worse near the international border."

"And how is the food?" Ghoton spoke of his main worry.

"The normal stuff."

Both soldiers seemed to be on a high alert and always kept an eye on the road, even when they spoke to Ghoton.

"Is there any trouble? You look tense," Avijit couldn't help but ask.

"There is trouble all the time," the soldier, who had sat stoically so far, replied, "this is not your training camp anymore. You are close to a war zone."

Avijit had read reports of insurgency and unrest all along the border areas in the papers, but had always dismissed them as exaggerated stories. He felt uneasy.

"I don't know why the Subedar is waiting this long," one of the soldiers looked at his watch and commented, "we will now have to move on the highway in the darkness of the night. This is not wise."

"Why?" Ghoton asked.

"Oh, you never know when the insurgents will throw a bomb on you. You might still have time to react in the daylight, as you can see it coming, but we are dead meat in the night."

"Does this happen often?"

"Almost everyday. Its like a hide and seek game. They hide when our strength is more and seek us out when we are lonely like today," the soldier replied casually.

"But can't they be stopped once and for all?"

"Yes, if the army is given a free hand. But then, the government would be accused of killing innocent people. People who live innocently enough, with fire power to blast out a whole city!"

"Don't worry. You will learn to live with it, like we have for the past one year."

There was a loud whistle and it seemed a train had entered the station. Ravi and a few others walked out a little later. They had a cheerful reunion. It had been difficult to stay away for two weeks, after their togetherness of the past months. The driver didn't waste another minute and they moved towards their new home.

The truck passed through a picturesque city, with wide and clean roads and small housing colonies. The city was surrounded by hills on all sides. The hillsides varied from a light green to a darker shade under the glaze of the late afternoon sun. The peaks were a dull brown, as they were devoid of the pines which covered the lower half of each hill. The city looked quiet and lonely, except for the army vehicles, which were parked at almost every street corner. The muzzle of light machine guns protruded from their covered hoods and conveyed a sense of danger all around. They were shortly on a highway and the driver pushed down on the accelerator, as the traffic reduced to a trickle. The city was soon behind and high mountains seemed to block their path. The wide road squeezed and curled through the mountains like a serpent. Avijit was mesmerized by the landscape and his fears of an attack on their vehicle evaporated. No one in their right mind, could think of bloodshed in this heavenly place.

"Why does one need such a wide road in the hills?" Ravi asked the Subedar, who escorted them from the station, "there is hardly any traffic here."

"It leads to the international border. The tanks and missile launchers can only go up this way."

They travelled for another hour, before reaching the regiment headquarters. Avijit always thought their training camp was big. But it got dwarfed in comparison to what lay in front of them. They went through a heavily guarded entrance and passed through row after row of staff quarters. Avijit counted three football fields and at least two basketball courts, before they reached a large building. It looked like the main administrative block and they were all herded into a large hall. Their personal details were noted down and a fresh set of uniforms supplied to them. They were shown their barracks, where they found most of their training mates. Guri was conspicuous by his absence and someone mentioned that he was expected the next day. The barracks looked a lot more comfortable than that at the training camp and the top of the toilets were thankfully covered. The food was also good and Ghoton was happy after dinner that night.

"This certainly is an interesting place. Good food to tickle your taste buds and the fear of the unknown to make your balls sweat."

"You know, I made it," Ravi told them.

"What?" Avijit asked.

"The girl I used to talk about. Her name is Saraswati and we really hit it off," Ravi sounded jubilant.

He was unstoppable for the next half hour. Both families had met and Ravi had spoken to her. He would marry her after her graduation in a year's time.

"I'm sure the *sardar* will realize now that I was not talking through my hat," Ravi referred to Guri and the latter's constant barracking, "he'll be jealous."

"He will be very happy," Avijit, corrected him, "he only made sure you didn't go overboard with your dreams. This world is a mad place and dreams die young."

"But you should never give up a dream. It has to materialize someday or the other," Ravi was too happy to be practical.

"A few fizzle out," Avijit sighed deeply.

"Did you love her very much?" Ghoton asked suddenly, after the lights went out and everyone was on the brink of repose.

"Who?" Avijit was surprised at his friend's question.

"Aunty showed me the photo of the girl Khokon is marrying. She came to meet you at the station last year."

So Ghoton had known all along. It also explained his strange silence, when Avijit's uncle had requested them to stay back for the wedding. Avijit didn't know what to say and kept quiet. He was fighting a terrible battle within to suppress the hurt and sense of betrayal.

"Look, relationships shouldn't rule life. I lost my parents. You lost your father. But we still have the zeal to live. Time has applied a balm to our wounds. I'm sure you will get a better girl someday," Ghoton tried to cheer him up.

Avijit knew he could never get involved with a girl again. He could never think beyond Sraboni.

The freshers gradually fell back into a routine life. They were initially posted within the campus and did not get any outside duty. Their day started early with physical exercises, followed by a long run all along the campus. Firearms training and target shooting were taken up after breakfast and lunch. The mandatory sports discipline was in the late afternoon. Their platoon now reported to Captain

Shekhar, who was a tough taskmaster. He was in his early thirties; a stubborn faced man with a waxed mustache, who had served a six-month stint near the line of control.

"You can't imagine what it is like up there," he would often recount his experience, "the enemy shells land without a warning. You are a dead duck, if you are not alert. But we can't retaliate, as then there might be a war. And the world community would come down heavily on our Government for jeopardizing their peace plans! Our army suffers like no other in the world. Our hands are tied and we watch helplessly, as the enemy shells and insurgents run riot with our security. We try our best to contain this impossible situation and there are almost a few thousand martyrs every year. But we haven't lost hope. We won't tolerate this rape of our motherland. A chance will surely present itself soon. The protagonists of peace need to embrace violence one last time, to bury the threat from the perpetrators of death. Then, all can live in peace. So we must be ready and that's why you need to train hard."

It was difficult to imagine a war like situation, less than a hundred kilometres away, sitting in the confines of a picturesque camp. Most of them yearned for an outside posting.

"Train for a few more months before we can place you outside. It's a crazy mess out there," the Captain would warn them.

They had telephone facilities within the camp and Avijit often called his mother. Khokon's marriage had passed off peacefully and the newly weds had gone on a honeymoon to Europe. His mother had finalized plans to shift back to Rajpur.

"Nalu has a phone in his home now. So you can call me there," she assured Avijit.

Ravi was spending double the amount on calls, as he had to call his fiancée prior to calling his parents.

"We must tell the Captain not to post you near the border. What if you lose your balls?" Guri would joke and Ravi joined him in a slanging match.

They got their first posting outside the campus, after almost six months. The winter had set in. Heavy pullovers were the order of the day and only a burning fire revived the chilled cells in the body at night. It was a simple enough job. They were to be posted in a temple city near the camp. Militants had threatened to blow up the temple and army help was needed to thwart their evil designs.

"Check everyone and never relax," Captain Shekhar warned.

The city was teeming with devotees, who had come to offer a prayer to the Almighty. Avijit often wondered why people went to temples, mosques or churches. God's presence was everywhere, but man had reduced Him to a mere idol. They were posted at a metal detector, near a gate leading to the temple. A few thousand devotees stood in a long queue and waited patiently, as Avijit and Guri checked each man thoroughly. Even the coconuts to be offered by the devotees were not spared. Avijit felt the militants had already won a moral victory. They had managed to create utter confusion by calling for the unprecedented security measures. The ladies were separated from the males of their family, as there were different queues for each gender. It also meant an endless wait for the devotees, who could have easily completed their visit within a fraction of the time, if the elaborate checks were not there. The queues lengthened and the crowd became restless as the day wore on, and Avijit had to use force on a couple of occasions to push back a few unruly ones.

"You think we are terrorists?" one of them challenged Avijit, "we are tax paying citizens of a democratic nation. Why should we face this nonsense? And your stupid security can lead to a stampede any minute. Let me go, as I can't take that risk."

Avijit tried to calm him down by explaining that it was all for the safety of the temple and the devotees. But the man wouldn't listen. His actions incited a few others and they suddenly charged through. Avijit and Guri were pushed aside and the devotees rushed in.

"Stop or I shoot," they could hear Captain Shekhar shout above the bedlam.

The crowd slowly fell back in line.

"How many had gone through?" the Captain hissed at Avijit.

"I couldn't count. Maybe a hundred, sir," Avijit stammered.

"Bloody hell," the Captain muttered and spoke urgently into his wireless set, "I will have your balls if anything goes wrong."

The Captain ran back towards the temple and Avijit and Guri carried on with their job. They were very tense and often harsh with anyone who jostled or argued. The Captain sent four more soldiers to help them. He was not taking any chances.

Luckily, nothing happened and the threat by the militants turned out to be a big hoax. But it ensured a strong reprimand for Avijit and

Guri from their section head.

"You acted irresponsibly," he shouted, "how could a few unarmed men throw you off guard? What will happen if you face the militants? I won't pardon a second mistake."

Avijit started hating the militants from that night. He also felt the devotees could have been a little more co-operative. It was all for their safety. But then most people put personal aims before public good. The incident left all the new entrants a lot wiser about human behaviour.

It was almost another three months, before they got a chance to prove their mettle. They had just finished their regular shooting stint, when their section head was summoned to the administrative office. He came back a half hour later and informed them that militants had been spotted in a village outside the city. A few soldiers were already there, but they wanted reinforcements.

"The Captain wants five volunteers from the freshers," he said.

Avijit hated the frequent reference to them as *freshers*. It was more than a year since they had joined the army and they were anything but *freshers*. It seemed they would have to wait till a new batch arrived, before the stigma wore off. Everyone volunteered for the job. Avijit, Guri and Ghoton were amongst the chosen five. They teamed up with ten other seniors of the regiment for the raid under the command of Captain Shekhar.

"Check your weapons and be ready. We start in five minutes."

They had never ventured this far out of the camp before and Avijit was struck by the pristine beauty of the area. The sun was setting and its last rays seemed to have lit a fire in the skies. The formless clouds darkened, as the sun sank; the birds hurried towards their shelter in the twilight, while the tall mountains watched silently, guarding the road to the unknown. The truck raced noisily along the road, winding its way through the green valley and the apple orchards. A few villages were scattered along the road and they stopped at one such village. An army truck was already there and Captain Shekhar spoke to the soldier standing near it.

"It seems they are holed up in the farmhouse there," the Captain briefed them, "two sepoys are standing guard near the gate. The militants opened fire, when the soldiers halted here to have some tea. Bloody fools!"

The farmhouse looked old, rickety and had a big lawn surrounding it, which was covered by shrubs and long grass. The house was a single storey one and its main entrance was closed. The entire village seemed deserted, its inhabitants behind doors the moment they had seen the army.

"Surround the house. Whistle once you are in position, but don't fire till I say so. I want them alive. Now go," the Captain ordered.

They had been trained for such situations before and Avijit had never been short on confidence. But he felt diffident at the thought of real bullets tearing through the air at him. He crouched and followed his colleagues at a fast pace, as they took up positions near the main entrance.

"You are surrounded," the Captain spoke into a microphone and his voice seemed to echo in the silent valley, "give up, as there is no escape route."

There was no reaction from inside the house and Avijit had a fleeting thought that it was again a hoax. Maybe the militants had managed to escape by the time they arrived. But a slightly built old man came out of the house, his hands raised, after the Captain had repeated his command.

"I'm innocent. Please don't shoot," he pleaded.

"Ask the others to come out," the Captain barked.

"There is only my family inside, sir. They are innocent," the man now stood under the glare of a spot light, which the driver of their truck directed onto the entrance.

"Why did they shoot if they are innocent? How many are there?" the Captain sounded harsh.

Avijit felt sad for the old man. He sounded true and it seemed there was a big mistake somewhere.

"There was no shooting. My two sons are inside, sir. They are both innocent," the man continued to plead.

"You have nothing to worry then. Ask them to come out."

"I repeat sir, they are innocent. I will ask them to come out, but please don't shoot," the man cried with folded hands.

"Okay, we won't shoot," the Captain assured him.

Avijit had read in the papers about army excesses in this part of the country. It seemed correct. A few young boys must have burst crackers and the soldiers mistook them for gunshots. A dozen guns were now trained on them. Avijit hoped the ordeal would end quickly.

The old man, who had disappeared inside, came out again followed by two boys, who looked in their early teens. They looked anything but militants.

"Put your hands above your head," the Captain shouted, "come forward slowly."

Avijit felt disappointed. He had expected some action, but it turned out to be a damp squib. He was convinced that the rantings about terrorism and insurgency were all exaggerated. A few incidents must have been blown out of proportion.

The loud explosion shook his senses. A bomb exploded near Captain Shekhar. Bombs were bursting all around them, before anyone could react. The distinct sound of rifle fire could also be heard and Avijit ducked for cover.

"Don't shoot. We must catch them alive," the voice of the Captain calmed him, as he had feared the worst.

Three young boys stood near the entrance and fired from automatic rifles. But they didn't hit anybody, as the soldiers had sprawled on the ground and were not visible in the darkness.

"Stop the fire or you will get killed," the Captain's booming voice warned again.

But the three decided to make a dash for it. They ran suddenly, in different directions, trying to catch the soldiers by surprise, clearly establishing that they had been trained for such eventualities. One came charging down towards where Avijit lay. Avijit waited till the militant was almost on him and then forcefully tripped him. The assailant had not noticed the soldier in the darkness, in his hurry to escape. He fought valiantly, but Avijit was too strong for the teenager. Avijit punched him a couple of times in the face and kicked away the rifle, which the militant lunged for. A few others soon joined Avijit and they dragged the militant out in front of the house. Guri and Ghoton stood over another one, but the third militant was nowhere to be found.

"We will get him soon. These two will lead us to him," Captain Shekhar observed.

Avijit looked around for the old man, who had been pleading innocence all along. But he also seemed to have vanished. They found him soon enough, behind a row of shrubs, lying dead in a pool of his own blood.

"Who the hell shot him? Who fired?" the Captain sounded very angry.

"He was shot by one of the militants. None of us had fired a single round, as you had ordered sir," Ghoton explained.

Avijit was shocked. The old man had pleaded that his sons were inside. The same sons, whose fingers didn't tremble, as they aimed death at their father. What had the world come to?

There was a stockpile of sophisticated weapons and explosives inside the house.

"Looks like they were planning a big assault. Thank God, we caught them," the Captain sounded relieved.

They pushed the two captured militants onto the truck and stood guard, as Ghoton and another soldier put the cache of arms and ammunition in the second truck. There was no one to claim the old man's body. The neighbours had bolted their doors on hearing the sound of the gunfire and no one ventured out.

"Let's carry him to the army morgue. We can hand him over to the local police tomorrow. It's getting late and there might be another attack. Let's move," the Captain ordered.

The two young militants sat between Ghoton and Guri, their hands tied behind their backs, their calm faces reflecting none of the violence they had unleashed a few moments back.

"Who gave you the guns?" the Captain asked one of them.

"What guns? I don't know of any guns," the young boy looked back at the Captain defiantly.

The Captain surprised Avijit. Any commander would have given orders to shoot, after the indiscriminate firing. But their leader had the patience to wait and catch the militants alive. He had risked getting killed in the process, as most of the fire was directed at him. Avijit also realized that all was not well in the valley. Teenagers picked up deadly weapons and showed no fear of death. But his surprise didn't end with the night.

They had just finished breakfast the next day, when Avijit, Ghoton and Guri were summoned to the office. They found that the others, who had participated in the previous day's encounter, had already gathered. Captain Shekhar came in shortly accompanied by a tall, well built man.

"This is Inspector Azad from the police station," the Captain introduced the stranger, "and these are the men who were with me yesterday. Ask them whatever you feel like, but don't make me more angry."

The stranger gave a wry smile and looked at the group.

"Who amongst you shot the old man?" he suddenly asked, the smile never leaving his face.

"He was shot by one of the militants," Guri answered.

The man was silent for sometime, as if in a deep thought, and then shot off his next question.

"But why would they kill him?"

Avijit felt the question was a stupid one. A stray bullet must have hit the old man, once the youths had started firing indiscriminately. It was as simple as that. He said so to the Inspector.

"But how do I know you are speaking the truth? You might have shot him as well," the Inspector smiled again.

Avijit was appalled! Each one of them had risked their lives in capturing the militants and this foolish man was accusing them instead. He wanted to reply to the charge, but kept quiet, once he heard the Captain's cold voice.

"I don't know how my seniors agreed to your request to question my team. This is beyond the normal protocol, but I will reply to your query. Get the bullet out of the man's body and send it to a forensic expert. He will tell you it was not fired from our guns, but from one of a foreign make. We have confiscated a stockpile of those. And I will roast your ass, if you raise another doubt about my men. It is because of your incompetence that the army had to be called in. We are trying our best to help you. Is this the way you complement our efforts?"

The Captain's last words were almost a scream. The policeman hesitated, before picking up the file he had kept on a table.

"Look, these are difficult times. You shouldn't have carried the body back, but called us instead. Then I wouldn't have had to file a report that the army had raided the village, shot dead an innocent old man and taken away the body to hush up the incident. Almost a hundred people along with a few Rights' activists, are sitting in front of the police station, demanding justice. I appreciate your concerns, but I also have a job to keep."

One had to acknowledge the finesse of the militants. They were trying to drive a wedge between the administration and the army. But what could they achieve except for killing a few more innocent individuals? Avijit also could not fathom why these human rights' organizations supported the inhuman militants at times. Was it deliberate or just an aberration? Maybe they needed a first hand experience like the previous day's encounter to get on the right side. The soldiers were dismissed shortly and they went back to their daily target practice.

Their evenings were dull, as they could not venture out of the army camp, except for outdoor duty, which was rare. They were still considered new and such critical duties reserved for the experienced. The Captain though had publicly appreciated their efforts in nabbing the two terrorists. The army provided them with all their material needs, as well as entertainment like the latest movies, within the camp. But they felt stifled. The boredom made them visit a tourist spot nearby. They hired a private car so that no one could recognize them as soldiers.

"It is safe," Guri assured them.

They forgot their worries, once they were out on the road. They were not in their drab uniforms and everyone was cheerful. The spot was a huge lake, surrounded by green hills, and snow-capped peaks peeped from behind them. There were a few boats, which took the visitors round the lake. It looked inviting enough and they would have taken the ride, but for Ghoton. He was hungry and coaxed the others to have an early lunch. They headed for one of the shabby food stalls, lined alongside the road leading up to the lake. They ordered their food and sat on the wooden benches arranged outside the kiosk. It felt good, sitting in the sun, with the snow-laden mountains within sniffing distance. The air felt fresh and the smell of spices rushed out of the metal pot in which their lunch was being cooked. Ravi broke into a song and the others thumped out a rhythm on the table. Guri danced his famous *bhangra.* A few young girls, who were sitting at a nearby food stall, soon joined in the clapping and cheering, and there was no stopping Guri. Ravi sang with gusto and the *sardar* danced as if possessed. The food arrived and they had a hearty meal.

It happened just when they were planning to take the boat ride. Guri had befriended a girl and they now walked side by side, the rest maintaining a modest distance. Ghoton seemed amazed at the ease with which the *sardar* could strike up a conversation with the opposite sex. But though he tried his best, none of the girls seemed keen to talk to him. Avijit was enjoying the pure beauty of the lake, which reflected the colours of the green hills nearby, the white mountains towering above it and the bright blue sky. They all stopped at the sudden commotion, which originated from one of the food stalls where a few tourists stood. The girls, who had mixed freely with the tough looking strangers, suddenly looked tense.

"Lets go back to the car and get out of this place," one of them suggested in a quivering voice.

"Don't be afraid. No one can hurt you, as long as we are here," Ghoton spoke out at the first chance to sound chivalrous.

They decided to have a look. Two soldiers were beating a young boy mercilessly, while an elderly man tried to stop them. He would have received a few blows too, had Avijit and Guri not intervened. The soldiers were upset at this, but calmed down, once Avijit produced his identity card.

"You don't interfere. Let us do our job," one of them tried to break free and attack the boy, who was kneeling and weeping.

"But you can't go on hitting him," Avijit stopped him, "he will die. What has he done to deserve this?"

"These tourists are from my hometown," the soldier pointed to a group, who stood nearby and enjoyed the episode, "this bastard won't serve them food. How dare he?"

"Sir, believe me. We do not have enough food to serve the full group," the elderly man intervened with folded hands, "we only told them to go to the next shop."

"He is lying. These are anti-nationals and they only serve the militants," the hometown hero was not to be out done.

"Well, let's find out," Guri ventured into the kiosk. "Tell me, would your friends from the home town be happy with three rotis, a plate of vegetable curry and a few pieces of chicken?" he shouted from inside, a few moments later.

"Are you joking? They are ten in number and famished."

"But that is all they have here," Guri came out.

"See! You didn't believe me! You unnecessarily beat up my innocent boy. What do I do, if he decides to take up the gun tomorrow? You mercilessly beat him. What for? You show your strength only in front of the weak and innocent like us. Shouldn't I be happy now, if the militants clobber you? Shouldn't I help them?" the elderly man gesticulated wildly, "but no. I won't. I believe in a man called Gandhi and whatever he espoused. He believed in non-violence and succeeded in securing our nation's freedom. I teach each one of my sons the same – the path of non-violence. We are sure that one day, we will also be able to drive both you and militancy out of our once prosperous state. Both of you are sheer evil for our well being."

Avijit wanted to hang his head in shame. Ravi helped the young boy to his feet, while Ghoton put the shawl, which had fallen during the scuffle, around the elderly man. The two soldiers looked unperturbed and only left once Guri threatened to report the incident at the headquarters. Normalcy soon returned with most of Avijit's colleagues taking the boat ride along with the girls. Avijit sat stoically by the lake. The old man's words troubled him. The behaviour of a few stray soldiers sent out the wrong signals about the army, demeaning it amongst the locals. He hoped a very strong punishment would be meted out to the two soldiers, once they reported the episode. But could it prevent the young boy, who had been tortured, from joining the militants? The latter thrived on such incidents, whipping up public sentiment against the administration and the army, and furthering their own cause. He was also moved by the elderly man's words, his determination to follow and make others follow the path of non-violence. Avijit couldn't help but wonder, as to why the whole of mankind was being wrecked by violence. There seemed to be no dearth of it the world over, once one went through the morning papers. It achieved nothing except destruction and decimation all over. But men still fought.

"Whew, that was great," Ghoton slumped on the grass next to Avijit, "I held the girl's hand for a full minute and she didn't protest. I can't believe it!"

Everyone sounded relaxed on the way back. It really was a welcome relief from their dull existence.

"Let's come again the next week. I'll ask the unit head to issue us an out pass. The girls promised to come too," Guri remarked.

"I think the girl is in love with me," Ghoton, who had been uncannily quiet throughout the evening, told Avijit before retiring to bed.

"Oh, really! What is her name?"

"I shall ask her the next time we meet," Ghoton sounded emphatic.

But the next time never materialized. They were assigned a crucial task towards the middle of the week. A few leading politicians of the country were to address a public gathering in the city and Captain Shekhar and his platoon were to escort them.

"I anticipate no trouble, as a security cordon has already been thrown all along the route. But be on the alert. These militants continue to spring nasty surprises on us," the Captain chuckled.

They started early that day. All of them had their automatic weapons at the ready and piled into two trucks. Captain Shekhar led the convoy in a jeep. The airport was almost forty kilometres from the camp and it took them an hour to reach it. A dense fog had enveloped the city and the plane was not expected before it cleared. The soldiers stood on the tarmac and waited for the VIPs.

"Well, only three more days before I meet her," Ghoton sounded excited.

He was infatuated with the girl and had hardly spoken of anything else, since they had come back from the outing. Even his endless obsession with food seemed to have ebbed. Avijit suspected that his friend was a little absentminded too and this worried him.

"Look, we have a job on hand. So don't daydream," Avijit warned.

The plane finally landed around noon. There were four politicians clad in khadi kurta-pajamas and waistcoats. The convoy started its journey, with the Captain in the lead in his jeep. A truck full of soldiers, the two cars carrying the guests and an ambulance followed him. The truck carrying Avijit and Ghoton brought up the rear. They had light machine guns fitted both at the front and the back of the hooded trucks. The soldiers kept a constant vigil on the road and its periphery. They reached the venue without any hurdles and the politicians moved towards the dais to address the sparse gathering. Avijit had seen a few political rallies in his state and the present one was a big letdown. The huge ground, where the dais had been erected, had only a few hundred people. It seemed most had remained indoors, fearing an attack by the militants.

"You idiot! We came all the way just to address these few jokers! Couldn't you get a bigger crowd?" one of the politicians was furious and shouted at what looked like their local representative.

"We will make sure party funds are not wasted on incompetents like you in the future," another threatened.

"What could I do sir?" the man pleaded, "the militants have threatened to blow up the dais during the meeting. We are lucky these few came."

"They will blow up the dais? Bloody hell! I'm not addressing the meeting," the politician, who had been threatening his colleague, now felt threatened.

"Not me either," another moaned, "let's get the hell out of here."

"No one is going anywhere," a voice suddenly thundered from behind.

Avijit, who had been standing near the politicians, turned towards the voice. A tall man with a bushy mustache stood behind him. He looked at the others in disdain.

"You are frightened? Why? Just because a few anti-nationals have made some stupid threats! You want to run away from reality? Then how do you expect these soldiers to stay on?" he shouted, "how do you expect them to stay on and fight, after setting such a sterling example? And what happens to the brave few who have come to listen to us? We will all stay and address them."

The man moved onto the dais with purpose and the others followed reluctantly. He started his address, while his colleagues sat stiffly on the podium, throwing furtive glances all around, expecting disaster to strike at any moment. The meeting lasted a half hour, with the senior politician speaking for twenty minutes, followed by a short stutter from the other three.

"We have arranged your lunch at the party office, sir," the local leader stated with folded hands.

"Well, thank you, but I'm on a fast today," the senior leader's statement brought relief to the faces of the other three visitors.

They posed for a few photographs and got into their cars.

"Be on the alert," the Captain reminded all of them, before jumping into his vehicle.

The convoy started its return journey to the airport. Avijit reflected on the half hour meeting. The private plane, the huge dais and the security arrangements would certainly cost the exchequer a fat amount. But was it justified? Or maybe it was all hogwash. The politicians just came down to demonstrate everything was normal in the valley. They would rave and rant at all their meetings about their experience. And life would go on. It was all a game of one-upmanship and the common man was a pawn.

The sudden blast took everyone by surprise. Their convoy was moving through a small stretch of forest area, when it happened. Dense trees lined either side of the road and someone had thrown a grenade towards the second car, from behind the tree line. The car swerved and hit a large tree on the opposite end. A shawl draped youth stepped out of his cover and ran towards the damaged car, an automatic rifle in his hand. He would have succeeded in opening the car's rear door and shooting the men inside, but for Ghoton. The latter reacted very fast and jumped out of their truck the moment it came to a halt. He raced towards the militant and hit him full in the face with the butt of his rifle. The militant collapsed and certain disaster was averted. But before Ghoton could move behind the cover of the car, a hail of bullets caught him straight in the chest. Avijit saw three militants firing in unison towards Ghoton and the felled militant, while a forth fired towards their truck, hitting the two front tyres. He aimed his gun towards them. But the militants ran back into the jungle, sensing a failed mission, just when Avijit's gun opened up, the bullets thudding harmlessly into the trees and beyond. Soldiers from the first truck, which had stopped a hundred metres up the road, came running down and crouched near the tree line, their guns at the ready. But the militants had fled. Avijit rushed towards Ghoton, who lay on the road, the black tar crimson from his blood. The medic from the ambulance came running and tore open Ghoton's shirt. Blood was gushing out from three bullet wounds around his stomach. The medic injected a colourless fluid and tried to stop the blood flow with thick wads of cotton wool, but it didn't help.

"Get him in the ambulance quickly," the medic ordered.

"Will he be all right?" Avijit was trembling with fear.

"We need to get him to the hospital quickly."

The militant, who had attacked the car, was dead. The soldiers kneeled down to raise Ghoton gently onto a stretcher and into the ambulance, but that was not to be. The two politicians, who were still inside the targeted car, cursed Captain Shekhar profusely.

"This is your fucking security!" one of them, who had a deep gash on his forearm shouted, "get us out of here immediately. I will have your head for this."

The other man and the driver seemed unharmed, and had no visible injuries.

"Someone stop this blood flow for God's sake," the injured politician shouted. "You soldier," he shouted at the Captain, "why don't you ask the ambulance to take us to the airport now? The militants surely won't target an ambulance."

The two politicians got into the ambulance without waiting for an answer.

"You attend to them," the Captain ordered the medic, "I'm calling for an ambulance, which should be here shortly." He turned towards the unit head and asked him to order a few soldiers to take up positions along the road. "The rest come with me. We must move immediately, as there can be another attack."

The Captain rushed back towards his vehicle. Avijit noticed that the other car stood just behind the Captain's jeep, surrounded by six soldiers. The senior politician, sitting in it, had not bothered to come out and have a look at the injured. He and his colleague must be discussing policies to take the nation forward, Avijit mused. The convoy moved away, leaving behind Ghoton in the midst of his convulsions. Blood was still oozing from his wounds, but he tried to smile at his colleagues.

"I'll be okay," he croaked, "I'll have to meet her after all."

His friends gingerly removed the antiseptic cotton wads from the wounds, once they turned red and pressed a fresh wad hurriedly thrown from the ambulance by the medic. But the blood flow did not ebb, nor did the promised ambulance arrive. Ghoton suddenly started having spasms and gasped for breath. Avijit felt helpless, standing on the road, all of them an easy target for the militants, if the latter bothered to come back. The ambulance arrived after another tense ten minutes and a full medical team poured out of it. Avijit thanked the Captain for keeping his word and hoped his friend would win this war against death. Ghoton smiled at him, a wry smile, and looked up at the sky, just before the doctors put him into the ambulance. The soldiers waited with the militant's body for a truck to arrive. They did not have to wait long, as a company of soldiers arrived and started combing the forest for the militants.

"I will kill every single militant, if anything happens to Ghoton," Ravi seethed.

Avijit only hoped Ghoton would be fine. He also felt sad for the dead militant. The young man would never know that he had been slain by his own comrades.

It took them almost twenty minutes to reach the army hospital. Ghoton had been rushed into the operation theatre. It was a long wait and the Captain soon joined them. He almost ran into the operation theatre, before a nurse stopped him. He was equally restless and lit a cigarette, something Avijit had never seen him do before while on duty. It was an endless wait, till the door to the operation theatre opened. They all rose expecting the good news. A doctor came out and spoke to the Captain in a low voice. Avijit wanted to ask how Ghoton was doing, but his heart sank once the Captain slumped onto a chair, his hands holding his head in agony. No one spoke as the truth slowly sank in. The clanging of the door made Avijit start. Ghoton's body, covered in a white sheet, was being brought out on a stretcher.

"No, no! This can't be true! You cannot leave us like this," Ravi's scream shattered the deathly silence. He wept inconsolably, clutching Ghoton's body. Guri had to use all his strength to separate Ravi from the deadbody.

"Bastards! I'll kill you all," Ravi continued to cry.

Avijit however shed no tears. He was instead consumed by a terrible rage. This was the second time that an assassin's bullet had taken away a dear one from him. It could take away more, if he wept and moaned. He decided to kill, to pay back the devil in his own coin. Ever since he had joined the army, ever since he had handled those deadly weapons, he had always been skeptical. He was not sure if he could actually kill one of his own race, even if it was the enemy. Now he knew for sure.

Ghoton's body was put in a coffin and they returned to their camp by late evening.

"Do you know his relations?" the unit head asked him.

"Why?"

"We have to return his body. Someone has to go with him. I thought you might volunteer."

Avijit was not sure it would be a good idea. He knew of Ghoton's uncle's apathy towards his nephew. Ghoton's uncle might celebrate the death. Also, Avijit had a job on hand and the record had to be put straight. He declined the offer, even though it would have given him a chance to meet his mother, and the unit head found someone else.

No one slept in the barracks that night. Death seemed to have suddenly muted the chatter, which was normally witnessed every night. The cot next to Avijit's looked empty, though someone had placed a wreath on it. Many recounted tales of Ghoton's pranks, over and over again. It was difficult to accept that the bubbly youth, who had risen with them in the morning and eaten at the same table, was gone. Avijit was repeatedly reminded of their first meeting and how Ghoton had tripped two competitors to ensure that he qualified. He stepped out of the barracks and stared at the night sky. The stars shoned brightly. He hoped Ghoton had found his parents. He looked up and vowed revenge. Violence could no more be willed away by non-violence. He came back and sobbed soundlessly into his pillow, his dear friend no longer there to console him.

CHAPTER Fourteen

They gave a tearful farewell to Ghoton the next day. Many wept openly, as the van carrying Ghoton's body slowly disappeared from sight.

Ravi blamed the Captain. "If only he had put Ghoton on the ambulance instead of those selfish politicians."

Avijit knew most shared Ravi's view, though he appreciated the Captain's dilemma. A soldier could be sacrificed, if it ensured the safety of the VIPs. After all, only politicians had the vision to run a country and a soldier was paid to die. It was all in one's destiny. But the anger in him grew with each passing day and he yearned for revenge. It was not a very long wait in the disturbed valley.

"A few militants have been spotted near the main town," Captain Shekhar announced one day, just after their morning run, "I need ten of you."

Avijit, Ravi and Guri immediately volunteered. The Captain relied a lot on them, ever since they had helped in the capture of the militants from the farmhouse.

"We need to catch them alive," the Captain reminded them on the truck during their journey, "no one shoots unless I say so."

The army had cordoned off the central part of the town and all vehicles were thoroughly checked, before being allowed to pass through. Even their truck was not spared, as the authorities were not leaving anything to chance.

"There are five of them. They are carrying bombs and automatic weapons. A bomb accidentally went off, killing one of their accomplices. That's how a patrol party spotted them and gave chase.

They went into that lane," a police officer briefed the Captain, "we have surrounded it from all sides, but the militants are not surrendering. Now you have to try and force them out. But be careful, there are a lot of civilians trapped in their houses in the lane."

The houses in the narrow lane stood so close to each other that one could easily jump from one roof to the next. Their job was made more difficult by the fact that they didn't know which house the militants were holed up in or the number of civilians they might have taken hostage.

"Give me cover," the Captain told Avijit and Ravi, "I will walk into the lane. You follow me a good twenty yards behind. Keep an eye open for any sudden movements. I'm sure they will open fire the moment I'm within their range. You have to figure out the house from which the firing takes place."

Avijit thought the Captain had gone mad. He was sure to be killed by this foolhardy act. What if the militants had separated and fired from different houses? Or what if they didn't fire at all? What purpose would it serve then?

"Can I make a request sir?" Guri suddenly asked.

"Go ahead," the Captain kept an eye on the lane.

"Can I walk down instead of you?"

"Why? You think I'm not capable! Or maybe I'm scared? Just do what I tell you," the Captain spoke rudely.

He picked up the microphone and started walking slowly into the death lane. Avijit and Ravi followed, their eyes darting all around, trying to detect the slightest of movements.

"This is the last call to you guys," the Captain's voice boomed out of the microphone, "give up and nothing will happen to you. But there is no escape route, as you are fully surrounded."

There seemed to be no life in the houses near them. The silence was broken by the shrill cry of a baby, but it stopped as suddenly as it had started. The mother must have stifled the cry to avoid drawing attention towards the house. Avijit wondered how the civilians accepted this frequent violation of their freedom. Fear of the militants would only prolong their agony, but no one came out or opened a window to tell them where the miscreants were hiding. He suddenly saw the Captain dive towards the right and roll over behind the cover of a dustbin. Bullets rained down on the spot where he had stood a few seconds earlier. Avijit and Ravi sprawled on the ground, their guns ready, but the Captain ordered them not to return the fire.

"Crawl back, out of the lane. I'll follow you," he whispered.

They managed to dodge the bullets and come out of the lane. The others immediately crowded around them.

"They are in the yellow two storeyed building and fired from the first floor. The adjacent house is a single storey one and they'll spot us now, if we try to climb up and attack from the roof," the Captain was deep in thought. "Well, we have two options," he finally looked at them, "either we go through the front door now and risk casualties, or wait for nightfall. It might be easier to climb onto the roof under darkness. The militants would certainly lower their guard by then, from anxiety and exhaustion."

Everyone was in favour of the first option, as it would otherwise mean a long wait of six to seven hours. The civilians would also be inconvenienced for that much longer. But the Captain didn't want more of his men to end up like Ghoton and decided to wear down the militants.

They waited for nightfall. The clock ticked over and the sun gradually sank to the horizon, till it disappeared altogether and veiled the sky in darkness. The soldiers were restless from such a long wait and Avijit was surprised at the doggedness of the militants. They had not made a single attempt to escape the death trap.

"I want these guys alive. Don't shoot unless absolutely essential," the Captain reminded them.

He led the way into the lane and the others followed. They crawled the last few metres to the house, to avoid being spotted. Luckily, no shots were fired at them. The Captain had planned the operation 'weed-out' meticulously. Guri and three others would climb up the drainpipes of the building and reach the roof. There was only one entrance to the house and the others would storm in, once those four were ready to attack from the roof. Avijit kicked on the thick wooden door with all his strength, when the Captain finally nodded his head, and rushed in. A lady suddenly appeared in front of him and he levelled the gun at her.

"No, no. Don't shoot," she whispered, "they are upstairs."

"How many are there?" the Captain, who was at Avijit's side in no time, asked.

Avijit lowered his gun just a fraction and kept a vigil on the stairway leading up to the next floor. They were standing in what looked like a small hall and a dim candle shed weird shadows on the wall. It was too dark for comfort and Avijit wondered whether the Captain's decision to cut the power supply to the lane was prudent.

"There are five of them. They are closeted in the room to the left of the staircase," the lady replied.

"Have they taken any hostages?"

"No. My daughters hid the moment we heard them come in. They have been good to me and looked very frightened. I don't blame them. Most are in their teens. May god punish the evil people, who are polluting their minds and forcing them to take up arms. Please don't kill them. They are good boys and can be reformed."

Avijit knew better and tiptoed up the stairway, followed by a few others. The Captain stayed with the lady, trying to assure her that normalcy would soon return. Guri and the other three had managed to come down into the house from the roof and stood near the staircase. Avijit indicated the left door and they inched towards it.

"Hey mates," Guri whispered to the others, "keep watch on the other doors too. They might surprise us."

Guri and Avijit looked at each other one last time, conveying an unspoken message, before kicking the wooden door open.

"Don't shoot! We are surrendering," there were five of them all right, the hands raised over the head, the eyes squinted to avoid the glare of Guri's heavy duty torch-light.

Avijit didn't wait. He let fly a heavy burst from his automatic weapon and Guri followed suit. There were a few sharp cries and then there was silence. Avijit's whole body shook, as if he was in the midst of a bout of epilepsy. He would have fallen down, had Guri not grabbed him by the arm.

"Who fired?" the Captain rushed in with a lamp and took in the scene.

The five militants lay in a pool of blood, no sign of life in their limp bodies.

"Why the hell did you fire? I asked you to get them alive," the Captain shouted.

They could hear the lady, wailing at the top of her voice.

"They tried to kill us," Guri replied flatly.

"Don't give me that shit," the Captain hissed, "their weapons are all stacked up in the corner. You two get out of here and wait in the truck."

"You killed them, you beasts," the lady shouted at them, when they came down, "such nice boys."

"Yes, we killed them," Avijit couldn't control himself any longer and screamed at the lady, "just like they killed my friend a few days back. Can you get him back for me? And your nice boys would have killed more if they had their way – maybe your daughters too. We *beasts* saved their lives today."

He spat on the road, once he was out of the house. He was sick and tired of these pious humans. They cursed the very people who risked their lives to protect them. It was indeed a crazy world. Avijit drank from a water bottle, his throat feeling parched even after he had gulped down the last drop from the full bottle. He looked upwards and searched the sky. Ghoton would surely approve of his action. There could be no mercy for killers. But the sky was cloudy and he couldn't see the stars. The siren of an ambulance startled him. It came and parked near the narrow lane, the medics and stretcher-bearers rushing towards the encounter site. Avijit wanted to kick himself. It meant someone was still alive and his job was incomplete. But whoever had survived the carnage would never again dare to threaten humans with violence and death.

"Don't worry, I made sure no one survived," Guri's cold voice surprised him.

It was as if his friend could read his mind. Avijit smiled weakly at him. He suddenly felt sick and vomited on the road. His head was spinning and he sprawled on the floor of the truck. He only felt better, after Guri and Ravi massaged his hands and legs.

"You disobeyed me," the Captain spoke, once they started their return journey, "and you killed in cold blood. You idiots! We could have got so much from them. But you were obsessed with revenge. Did it bring back your friend? And you might get court-martialled, if my superiors find out."

They completed the rest of their journey in silence.

"You did the right thing. I'm going to kill every single militant I can lay my hands on," Ravi said, when they were back in their barracks, "these bastards kill innocent people without pity and we are expected to be good to them! Take them into custody! What for?

So that they can enjoy two square meals a day in the prison and sleep a good night's sleep. I'm just not accepting this shit. Ghoton never killed a fly and they slaughtered him."

Ravi's words made Avijit fume, but he didn't feel any better even after killing the militants. He was also worried about his future in the army, as he knew that soldiers, who disobeyed orders, were sacked. What would he do then?

"Don't worry, nothing is going to happen," Ravi consoled him, after he had spoken his mind, "you'll never face a trial."

"But what if an enquiry is ordered?" Avijit was not so sure.

"Oh, don't bother," Ravi lowered his voice to a whisper, "I picked up one of the militant's gun and fired two rounds into the wall near the door. It will look as if they fired at you and you fired back in self defence."

"But how did you do it?" Avijit couldn't hide his surprise, "the Captain was in the room all along!"

"No, he had gone out. But I don't think he'll bother, even if he heard the gunshots," Ravi chuckled, "he still blames himself for Ghoton's death and I feel he appreciates our sentiment too. There is more to him than his tough exterior."

Avijit couldn't disagree. The Captain had taken the maximum risk, which he could have easily delegated to a soldier. But that was not how the army operated. The officers led from the front. He was reminded of the pot-bellied Mr Dayaram. In a similar situation, his ex-employer would have certainly fled from the rear. But then Mr Dayaram lived in a palace, with all the comforts of modernity and enjoyed life to the full, while the Captain slugged it out in a one-room hut, away from his family and faced death almost every day.

Sleep deserted Avijit for the next few nights. Five faces with their hands raised, seemed to haunt him every minute. Their cries of helplessness filled his mind, every time he closed his eyes. He lost his appetite and felt extremely weak. He wanted to call his mother and talk to her. But then, she would certainly ask about Ghoton, as she normally did and he couldn't continue lying that the latter was fine. He had decided he would only tell her about Ghoton, once he was with her. Now, he was not sure he could hold back much longer. His discomfort grew with each passing day. It became so unbearable that he paid their unit's doctor a visit.

"It happens when you face death from close quarters," the doctor, a soft spoken man, explained, after listening to him patiently, "but you have to overcome it on your own. I am giving you a few tranquilizers so that you sleep well. Try not to think of the incident. Why don't you take your annual leave and spend sometime with your family?"

Avijit thanked the doctor and collected the medicines the latter had prescribed. Though he did have a good night's sleep, he continued to feel he had sinned, and he shouldn't have killed those guys mercilessly. Guri too, seemed to have come around and shared his view.

"Ghoton will never come back. So I have decided to rein in my emotions. Let's take our annual leave and visit your place. I have heard a lot about Bengal and it's beautiful people. A visit to the place might help me forget this madness."

Their plans had to be altered slightly, as Ravi was getting married. It seemed his would-be-wife's parents did not want to delay their daughter's wedding any further and had threatened to find a new groom, if Ravi didn't marry her quickly. Hence the hurriedly fixed date. It would be held at their native place in Balasore, a small coastal town in the eastern part of the country. Ravi left for his hometown a week before the marriage, but not before both Avijit and Guri had promised to come down. The two had already applied for their leave and requested their unit head to push through the sanction. They were worried Captain Shekhar would not allow them to leave together, but the latter did nothing like that.

"Our country has extended a hand of friendship to our neighbours, who are believed to be instigating this violence. Trade channels are likely to be opened up, which should benefit both countries immensely," he told them, when they visited his office, "this could mean a temporary lull, if not a permanent end to the militancy here. It would be one big relief. So, go without a worry. I'll see to it that your leave is sanctioned."

And it was, within the next two days. They would spend a couple of days at Balasore, before visiting Avijit's mother at Rajpur.

Everyone in their platoon contributed money and left it to the two of them to buy the newly-weds a present. There was a lot of debate as to what could be a memorable gift.

"Give the bride a saree," few suggested.

Most turned it down, as the bride was sure to get plenty of them.

"Let's gift Ravi a suit," some others proposed.

But that too was turned down, as no one was sure whether he would wear it or not.

"Look, let's buy them a big box of condoms," Guri chipped in, "that way, the newly-weds can enjoy life for sometime without the wail of a child. The country will also be spared the burden of another idiot like its father."

They finally decided to buy a shawl for the bride from the local weavers, who had earned a name nationwide for their exquisite handiwork.

Avijit and Guri boarded the train three days before Ravi's wedding. They met a full company of soldiers, who looked jubilant. Avijit thought they had also been granted leave, but he was mistaken.

"Leave? No, no. We have been blessed with a new posting," one of them told Guri, "it's been two long years near the line of control. We can at last look forward to some peace and quiet."

Avijit looked back in wonder at the past many months, as the train gathered speed. There was indeed a war being fought but the outside world couldn't fathom its intensity. The local people, whom he had initially considered as timid and anti-national, were exemplary in their courage. All lived a life of uncertainty. They had to face the frequent frisking by the army, allow search parties to enter their bedrooms, face the prospect of getting injured or killed in the crossfire and adjust to the invasion of their privacy by gun toting militants, which often led to damage to their properties once the army swooped down. They braved it all, but didn't give up the zeal to live. The elders, like the man at the lake, had to watch helplessly, as a few fanatics lured away the teens from their normal life and transformed them into messengers of death. Avijit had heard from their unit head that the two militants, they had captured, had confessed to having received a week's arms training and orders to kill soldiers mercilessly. They were never told they would be pitted against the might of one of the largest armies in the world and a mere week's training couldn't save them from getting caught. And the reward for agreeing to the misadventure was a meagre sum of rupees two thousand and the promise of a job, once the fanatics took over the administration. Those youngsters died due to ignorance, whilst the Ghotons of the world laid down their lives, trying to make the ignorant see reason. And the fanatics rued over another failed attempt to destabilize peace and harmony, and sat down to plan a fresh one. It was a vicious circle and there was no easy way out.

C H A P T E R

Fifteen

Ravi was ecstatic when they arrived. They embraced like friends meeting after a very long time. Ravi introduced them to his parents, brother and wife, and six-year-old nephew.

"I'm really nervous," Ravi confided, once they had settled down in his room, "I've no idea what I'm supposed to do."

"Oh, don't worry. Its a one time experience, unless you plan to marry again," Guri tried to ease his friend's tension, "you should rather worry, as to what happens after the ceremony."

"What do you mean?" Ravi looked puzzled.

"I'm talking of your nuptial night, stupid. Don't forget to ask your wife, whether it is safe or not."

"What if it isn't?"

"Then don't screw without a condom. Or else, you might be a proud father, even before your next annual leave," the *sardar* chuckled.

"But where do I get it? I've never bought one before."

"You should be grateful to us for having thought of your problem in advance," Guri brought out the big box of prophylactics, "this should hopefully last you till the end of your leave."

Before Ravi could thank his friends, an unexpected thing happened. His nephew came running into the room and his eyes focused on the box that Guri had placed on Ravi's cot.

"Wow, another present!" the kid snatched up the box with his tiny hands and ran out of the room, before any of them could stop him. "Let me go and show it to Grandpa," he shouted.

There were a lot of guests in the drawing room, where Ravi's father sat. Everyone seemed to be enjoying themselves thoroughly, if their loud voices and laughter were any indication. But suddenly there was a hush.

"Look, look, there are so many packets in the box," the kid's voice paused, before it became a high pitched one. "See! Coloured balloons! I'll ask uncle to gift me this present. What will he do with all these? I'll blow them up and decorate the whole house."

Thankfully, they were spared further embarrassment, as the kid decided to take his uncle's permission and came back into the room.

"Uncle, blow this up for me," Ravi's nephew kept the box on the cot and held out the prophylactic he had opened.

"Hey! This is dirty and soiled," Guri seemed to observe it minutely, before speaking to the kid, "I think the entire bunch is spoilt. Don't worry, I'll get you a bigger pack of balloons in the evening. Let's throw this whole bunch."

Ravi was quick to seize the box and put it on top of the only cupboard in the room. He sighed deeply, certain that a major disaster had been averted. But he was wrong.

"What is this on your head?" the kid now pointed towards Guri's turban and tried to pull it off.

"No, no. Don't touch it," the *sardar*, who had faced many a militant bravely, looked helpless, "there is a devil inside."

The kid seemed to ponder for a moment and raced out of the room, only to be back within the minute with a plastic bat.

"Mom always tells Dad that she'll beat the devil out of him. Let me do it to you," and he hit Guri on the head with his plastic bat. Ravi came to his friend's rescue by picking up his nephew and going out of the room.

"What a kid!" Guri sighed in relief.

"Don't forget your promise or he might create a ruckus again," Avijit warned.

"Imagine how much Ghoton would have enjoyed himself if he was here today," Ravi remarked that night, the three of them cramped together on the bed meant for the newlyweds.

"Look, get the carpenter to tighten the screws on this bed," Guri tried to change the subject, "it creaks whenever I turn. I shudder at the thought of the noise it'll make, once its legitimate owners occupy it a few days from now. It could mean sleepless nights for all in your family!"

The groom had to reach the bride's place before noon the next day, for the marriage ceremony. Ravi, dressed in the traditional dhoti-kurta and leather sandals, got into the decorated car sent by the girl's house. Guri and Avijit got in on either side. The others from the groom's family followed them in a bus. It was a short distance, though it took them more than an hour to reach the venue, as the car followed a musical band at a snail's pace. The band played the latest musical hits. It attracted curious onlookers, who peered through the car's window to catch a glimpse of the groom. Ravi sat stiffly and grumbled with the driver for not bypassing the band.

"Hey, relax man," Guri tried to calm his friend down, "this is real fun."

Guri suddenly got out of the car and broke into a *bhangra* with the band. He danced well and a crowd soon gathered, stopping their progress altogether, much to the discomfort of Ravi.

"See! The idiot is showing off again, while I feel like pissing in my pants!"

Ravi's ordeal didn't end there, as hordes of people surrounded the car, once they reached the girl's house.

"Oh! He's so young," a lady commented, as if she had expected a worn out old man as the groom.

"And he has so little hair on his head! Is he going bald?"

"No, no. He is in the army. That is the army-cut."

"It'll be painful for Saraswati. Army men are supposed to be rough and tough."

Squeals of laughter followed. A few elderly ladies came out of the house blowing conch shells. Ravi squirmed and flinched, as they washed his feet tenderly with coconut water. He was finally allowed to get out of the car and made to sit in a room, where visits from strangers continued unabated.

"Looks like he's come with his bodyguard," a group of young girls smiled mockingly at Avijit.

"What is he afraid of? Saraswati has already slain him," another remarked.

"We need to decide what should be done to the bodyguard," a dark complexioned girl added.

She had a rustic beauty and Avijit couldn't help throwing a second glance at her, which didn't go unnoticed by its recipient. Avijit and Ravi desperately looked around for Guri, but he was nowhere to be seen. He was keen to observe the marriage rituals and had gone to see the puja being performed by the bride's and the groom's fathers. One pledged to give away his only child; the other accepted her as his son's life partner. Only Guri could match the girls, word for word, and Avijit decided to go and find him.

"Come back soon with the idiot," Ravi whispered, rubbing sweat off his forehead.

"Are you looking for someone?" the sudden question made Avijit turn around.

The dark complexioned girl stood behind him.

"I'm Nandita," she smiled.

"I'm Avijit. Have you seen my friend Guri? He should be the only *sardar* in the house."

"Come with me," she led the way.

She wore an orange saree and moved with a flaunting grace. They found Guri soon enough, intently watching proceedings from a corner of the hall, where the ceremony was going on. He came towards them, once Avijit beckoned to him. Nandita stared at the tall and handsome *sardar*, as he strode towards them.

"What is it?" he asked Avijit, looking back at the girl.

"Ravi wants you by his side," Avijit's remark couldn't break his gaze, "the girls are teasing him and he's scared stiff."

"We have not yet started," Nandita suddenly protested, "wait till the marriage is over. The real fun will begin then."

"Oh, really!" Guri seemed ready to take up the challenge, "then I must stay near my friend."

"It won't help," the girl replied, "you don't know us."

"I would certainly like to know more about a beautiful girl like you," Guri had put on his most charming smile.

The girl blushed and Avijit decided to go back to Ravi. The poor chap must be feeling deserted and Guri didn't seem to be in a terrible hurry to join his friend; some people were born lucky. Avijit rushed back. An old lady, squinted at Ravi's face, while holding up his chin with frail hands.

"Ah, you're like a prince. I would have married you had I been younger. Will you marry me instead of Saraswati?" she joked. Ravi's pale face turned a deeper shade of grey. He relaxed, once Avijit came and sat down next to him.

"Where the hell had you been and where is that fool?" Ravi sounded exasperated.

The bride's father came into the room before Avijit could answer. It was the turn of the groom to go to the marriage altar. Ravi was led out of the room and the others followed. The ladies moved their tongue against their lips in unison to create a sweet rolling sound. A few others blew the conch shell. Ravi looked terribly embarrassed when he had to take off his kurta and sit bare-chested in front of the swelling crowd, as the holy thread was first sanctified and then put around his torso. Avijit found Guri standing at the same corner. Only his attention was now divided between the ceremony and

Nandita, who stood next to him. Ravi slowly repeated the sacred text, read out loudly by the priests. Avijit moved towards Guri to catch a better view.

"He is being absolved of all his sins," Nandita was explaining each step to the *sardar*.

"Oh, he has never sinned," Guri replied.

"And what about you?"

"Me? Well, I'm tempted to sin right now."

Avijit was sure the *sardar*'s reply would invite a slap from the girl, but she simply smiled. They suddenly noticed Avijit next to them and concentrated on the ceremony. Ravi's part of the ritual ended soon and it was the turn of the bride at the altar. Ravi was led back to his room and Guri and Avijit followed. The three of them sat alone, as the others had gone to see the bride.

"So? How are you feeling?" Avijit asked Ravi.

"Yeah, on top of the world," Ravi grimaced, "I would have insisted on a registry marriage only, had I known of all this. I feel like a clown."

"Come on. Don't be a spoilsport," Guri protested, "think of the immense fun the others are having. You only marry once. I'm sure you will enjoy narrating this to your grandchildren. And if you ask me, feeling like a clown should not be new to you."

Ravi's patience was fully tested. All hell would have broken loose, had Nandita not come into the room just then. Ravi, who was halfway out of the chair, quickly sat down. Guri, who was running towards the door, stopped suddenly to avert a collision with the girl.

"What's going on?" she asked in surprise.

"Oh, the groom's dhoti has come undone. I was running out to call for help – get someone who can fix it. Can you help?"

"What?" the girl screamed and ran out of the room.

"You are not my friend, you ass. You are making fun of me. This is not fair," Ravi suddenly turned serious.

"I'm sorry pal," Guri came up to his friend, "I'm just trying to forget the madness of the past few months. I didn't mean to hurt you."

The two embraced and made up. Ravi was called back to the altar shortly and they had their first glimpse of Saraswati. She wore a bright red saree and seemed to droop under the weight of the jewelry that glittered all over her body. She was beautiful in a simple way, though she looked small next to Ravi. The priests tied the silk stole Ravi wore to a corner of her saree. They then circled the holy fire lit at the centre of the altar, seven times together, the bride leading the way and Ravi following with his arms wrapped around her. The priests chanted the sacred hymns loudly and the crowd threw flower petals at the couple. Each circle round the fire was supposed to make the bond stronger between husband and wife so that they could live happily ever after. The ceremony ended with Ravi putting sindoor on Saraswati's forehead, accepting her as his wife. A grand feast followed. They all sat on the floor on coir mats. Banana leaves, neatly cut and washed, were placed in front of them on which the food was served. There was rice, dal, crisp finger chips, a variety of vegetable curry, fish, prawn and meat. It was followed by chutney, curd and sweets. Avijit couldn't eat much. He was reminded at every point of Ghoton and how much he would have loved it. He ate with his head bent, so that no one noticed the tears welling in his eyes.

Ravi looked more comfortable after the meal. The newly weds sat together amongst the elders, who didn't bully the groom. Nandita sat next to the bride, while Guri and Avijit sat in front facing them. Ravi sang a few old hits after much persuasion and the *sardar* soon started his *bhangra.* Nandita was mesmerized and her eyes never left Guri for a moment. Avijit hoped it was nothing serious, as he knew his friend was not one to believe in a stable relationship. Guri was open to every beautiful girl in the universe. The newlyweds returned to Ravi's place in the evening. Saraswati's family bid her a tearful farewell. The overflowing eyes and constant sobs made it look more like a funeral than a marriage. Ravi looked upset and spoke his mind, once they were seated at the back of the flower-decked car.

"Holy shit! I feel like a thief!" Ravi remarked, after the car started its journey, "your parents were demanding till yesterday that I marry you immediately. And now, they put up such a show, as if I am taking you away forcibly."

"It wasn't a *show,*" Saraswati spoke in a sweet voice laced with sadness, "their most loved daughter is deserting them."

"Don't worry. I'm yet to get a family posting. So you can stay with them for sometime," Ravi made it sound easy.

But Avijit knew it wasn't easy. It was such a twister for the girl. She had to cope with the sadness of staying away from the people who reared her, while a new and exciting life beckoned to her.

The whole locality descended in front of Ravi's home, when the newlyweds arrived. The sun had set and darkness veiled the town, but it was banished under the bright lights of the video camera. Technology had ensured that Ravi's children could witness their father's marriage many times over. Ravi's mother, who had stayed home as per custom, came out to welcome the bride.

"Get it over with fast and let me into the house," Ravi snapped.

The ladies first placed a plate of milk on the ground. The bride was to put her first step on it. She was then made to hold onto a live fish for a full minute. Saraswati held on amid squeals of laughter, as the fish taken out of the bucket, wriggled and tried to escape death. It survived, as the bride gently lowered it back into the water, after the minute of test was over.

"Now your husband can never slip away from you," an elderly lady explained.

At night, the three friends again shared the same bed, as the newlyweds were to stay separate. Staying together till the second night after marriage was inauspicious in the Hindu custom.

"Who was the girl you were with the whole day?" Ravi asked Guri.

"Oh, she's Nandita, your wife's best friend. Don't you know her?"

"I'd never seen her before. We hardly had time for ourselves and you talk of friends!"

"She is a great girl. She works in a multinational and stays all by herself at Mumbai. It takes guts to do that," Guri was all praise.

"Look, don't do anything silly. I should not lose face in front of my in-laws," Ravi sounded out a warning.

"What do you mean?" Guri retorted, "I didn't even touch her. Don't be paranoid. Concentrate on what you'll do the day after."

"But what do we do tomorrow?" Avijit couldn't help but ask. They planned to leave for Rajpur, after Ravi's reception the day after.

"Why don't you go to the sea beach at Chandipur," Ravi suggested.

Avijit had visited Puri when he was very young. He remembered the huge waves crashing onto the beach. It was a splendid sight, but he had never managed another vacation at a sea resort. He agreed immediately and they decided to visit the beach after breakfast the next day.

Guri however changed his mind, when Nandita arrived unannounced the next day morning.

"I'm not feeling well," he intoned, "must have been all the food I had yesterday."

Nandita sat with Saraswati in an anteroom and the *sardar* stood guard near the door, waiting for a chance to talk to the girl. He didn't have to wait for long, as Nandita came out shortly.

"Hi there! How's life?" she asked Guri excitedly.

Avijit couldn't comprehend how life could change much during the short span the two had been separated. They started chatting animatedly, oblivious of the quizzical look from the elders.

"This place is too crowded. Why don't we all go to the beach?" the girl suggested.

Guri immediately agreed, brushing aside Avijit's reminder that he hadn't been feeling all too well just a few minutes back.

"Sick? Me? When?" he looked wide-eyed at Avijit.

They hired an auto-rickshaw and were off. It felt good to jump and roll in the small box of a vehicle, as the driver drove down the uneven road. Rows and rows of coconut trees greeted the eyes, whichever way one looked. It took them twenty minutes to reach the beach, but it was a huge disappointment. There was no water.

"The tide ebbs in the night and rises by the afternoon," their driver explained.

They paid him and moved towards a row of small buildings that looked like hotels.

"Cheap rooms available, sir," a thin faced man approached them.

"What has happened to the water?" Avijit asked in bewilderment, looking at the vast stretch of sand.

"It will come, sir. The tide is around a kilometre away now and should come in any time."

The three of them decided to take a walk down the sand bed.

"Please don't go far. The tide can come in very fast," the thin-faced man warned.

The sand felt hot under their feet and Nandita started picking up shells of all shapes and sizes. Guri walked with her, hand in hand, while Avijit followed close behind.

"So when are you marrying?" Avijit decided to strike up a conversation with the girl.

"Me and marriage?" she raised her eyebrows, "you must be crazy!"

"Why? What's wrong with marriage?"

"Look, I have changed three jobs in two years already. I can never tolerate anything for long. Marriage means living with the same guy for life. I don't think I can do that."

"But everyone does it. Your best friend just did it. You think she's crazy too?"

"No, she's like any other girl. Maybe I'm different. What about you guys? When are you getting married?"

"For me, it's equally difficult," Guri remarked, "how can you stay with one girl, when there are so many beautiful women like you all around?"

Avijit stayed silent, as the other two suddenly seemed to float away into a different orbit. Something glistened where the stretch of sand met the hazy blue sky and Avijit strained his eyes to get a better view.

"Look, that must be the water," Nandita also seemed to have noticed it.

It looked far away and they increased their speed to reach it. But it came closer with every step they took and their feet were suddenly wet. The water was coming in.

"Let's get back," Avijit looked back and realized they were a long way down from the row of buildings.

The water was already flowing in with great force and they could suddenly hear the roar of the approaching sea.

"Run back," Guri shouted and they started running, as fast as they could, both holding Nandita's hands, lest she fall.

But the sea was catching up fast and they had to wade through knee-deep water, with another fifty yards still separating them from safety. Nandita panicked and they had to catch her hands firmly and steer her towards the shore. They managed to reach it safely and all three flopped on the hot sand, fully drenched and breathless from their efforts. Avijit looked at Nandita, once he got his breath back. She was lying on her back, her wet saree clinging to her shapely body. She suddenly rolled over and started coughing.

"Let me rent a room. She can rest for sometime before we go back," Guri told Avijit, "Whew! That was close."

Avijit was too tired to bother and lay on the sand, while Guri took Nandita towards the row of buildings.

Avijit stared in amazement at this sudden change in the landscape. The innocuous looking stretch of sand of a half hour back now had high waves of water breaking and dancing on it. The froth almost touched his feet. The silence of the sands was replaced by the bellow of the salty waters. Small crabs peeped out of the sand bed all around Avijit; only to vanish back as a thin line of water crept up towards them from a dying wave. Avijit lost himself in the splendour and must have dozed off. He awoke with a start, as a huge wave broke near his feet and drenched him. He looked around for Guri and Nandita, but they were nowhere to be found. He suddenly felt concerned. Was she sick? She had fallen down and swallowed a lot of seawater, before they had pulled her up and reached the shore. He decided to have a look. The thin-faced man approached him again. It seemed he was the only other human on this lonely and tranquil beach.

"Are you okay, sir? I told you not to venture out deep. The sea is very cruel at times," the man smiled.

"Where are my friends? The lady was sick."

"They are in the cottage there," the man smiled again and pointed to a hut behind the row of buildings.

Avijit suddenly felt hungry. It was almost five hours since he had breakfast. He decided to call Nandita and Guri. The cottage looked dilapidated, with mud walls and dried coconut leaves as its thatched roof. Avijit pushed on the wooden door to find it closed. Nandita must be sleeping inside, he mused. But there was no sign of his friend. Had he gone to call a doctor? He decided to go back and ask the thin faced man, but stopped at the sound of sobbing. It seemed Nandita was crying. Was she very sick? He pushed on the door, but it didn't give in. He looked around and decided to peep in through a window, which was partly open. He caught his breath and couldn't believe what he saw. Guri and Nandita were on the bed, not a stitch of clothing on them! Guri lay on his back while Nandita rode him like a stallion-rider. She heaved and sighed and suddenly collapsed on Guri, as a strange spasm seemed to rake her. They stayed like that for a few moments, before Guri rolled her over and got on top. His eyes caught Avijit's, but he continued nonchalantly. Avijit couldn't see it anymore. He felt breathless, the hardness under his belly crying out for release, his hunger of a few moments back forgotten. He slowly trudged back towards the sea, his mind paralyzed. He took a dip, hoping it would cool his overheated senses. But the warm water made him more uncomfortable. He looked around and decided to give his body the much-needed release, as there was no one around. It mingled with the froth of the waves and was soon lost. But he couldn't forget what he had seen. Nandita was making a big mistake. Guri would never marry her. But then, she had spoken of not believing in the custom of marriage. How could strangers, who would probably remain so, indulge in acts meant only for people who lived as husband and wife? Khokon too had boasted of bedding girls before marriage. Maybe people like he and Ravi were outdated. Extinct. This was how modern people lived and enjoyed life. He thought of Nandita, the dark torso still dancing in his mind. Did she do it often?

"Sorry, I was feeling very sick and decided to take some rest," her sudden remark broke his thoughts.

She looked calm and the saree still clung to her body seductively.

"Aren't you hungry? I'm famished," she prodded him in the ribs.

Avijit got up. He looked at Guri, who winked and grinned back at him.

"The girl really needed it," the *sardar* told Avijit that evening, once they were alone in Ravi's room, "she said she had never bedded a *sardar*. I had to oblige."

"Bloody idiot! Have you thought of the shame it will bring on

Ravi, if word got out," Avijit felt angry.

"Only you know. She wouldn't tell a soul. It was nothing new for her."

"What if she gets pregnant?"

"We're not stupid."

Avijit didn't speak to Guri again that night. Ravi was too busy with the marriage arrangements and did not seem to notice.

"You're angry with me. But why? Break free from old shackles and enjoy life as it should be," Guri thumped him on the shoulder after breakfast the next day.

The whole house was preparing for the reception in the evening. The entire building had been beautifully decorated. New curtains adorned the doors and windows, and a thin strain of shehnai filled the air. Ravi looked a lot more relaxed and sat with Saraswati for the puja in the morning. It was performed to formally induct the bride into the caste of the groom's family. Guri looked bored and sat silently in one corner.

"Too many pujas," he observed.

His eyes lit up when Nandita arrived late in the afternoon. But she didn't seem to have much time for the *sardar* and helped Saraswati dress up for the evening. The reception was a grand success. The food was delicious and Ravi's relations coaxed them to eat every single dish. Most of the guests had left by the time they took leave from everyone in the house.

"Devil Uncle, can I sleep with my new aunty tonight?" Ravi's nephew asked Guri.

He had become fully obedient to the *sardar,* ever since the latter had given him a big chocolate bar and a packet of balloons.

"No son, don't do that or your mother will be lonely."

"But Mom doesn't care about me anymore. She clings to Dad the moment she thinks I'm asleep."

The *sardar* decided to throw in the towel and left the room, leaving it to Ravi to sort out the family matter.

"Do come again. We couldn't take proper care of you in the bustle," Ravi's mother said.

"We will definitely come," they assured her, before setting out for the station.

Surprisingly, Guri and Nandita hadn't spoken even once during the whole evening. The two, whom he had seen in the most intimate of embraces the day before, looked like total strangers.

"It happens," the *sardar* confided on the train, "we just satiated each other's bodily needs. There was nothing more."

Avijit could soon hear his friend snoring softly, but couldn't sleep himself. The rolling of the train as also the wisdom of a one-day relationship continued to disturb him.

They reached Rajpur around afternoon. It was almost two and a half years since Avijit had last set foot in his birthplace. Rajpur looked the same quiet city where he had nurtured and nourished all his childhood dreams. He was suddenly reminded of his father. That man would have been very proud to see his son a well-groomed soldier. Avijit had called his mother the previous day at Naluda's place to tell her of their arrival. His mother hugged him and her eyes couldn't hold back the tears of joy, the moment he set foot in the house. They had lunch together and Guri decided to take a nap afterwards. Avijit walked into his mother's room to catch up with her on the events of the past year. A huge garlanded photograph of his father stood on a table. His father seemed to be looking straight at him. Nothing had changed in the house and Avijit felt his father would walk in any minute and pat him on the shoulder, like he always used to.

"Where is Ghoton? Did he go straight to his uncle's place?" the sudden question from his mother broke his trance.

Avijit didn't know how to begin. His mother didn't seem to notice his dilemma and continued to admire the shawl he had brought for her.

"This must be very costly. You shouldn't have wasted money on me." She looked up at him and seemed to sense something amiss. "What is it?" her voice wavered, "has something happened to Ghoton?"

So Avijit told her. He also told her about the death of the five young militants. She sat stunned for a long time and wept silently, as the news sank in.

"What has this world come to?" she sobbed, "I knew something was wrong when his letters stopped but never this!"

Thankfully, she didn't comment at all on the killing of the militants. She apparently understood that her son's job was to defend the motherland at any cost. She sat morosely for the rest of the afternoon, till Guri spoke to her.

"I heard you are a great singer of Tagore songs. It'd be a great pleasure, if you sing a few for me now," Guri appeared to understand the cause of her melancholy.

She didn't disappoint and sang with total devotion. Her sadness flowed out through her voice and touched them. A few of Avijit's school friends called on him in the evening. A picnic was being organized the next day and both Avijit and Guri were invited.

The *sardar* wore a colourful kurta-pyjama for the picnic. There were quite a few families and everyone looked set for a day of fun and merriment. They boarded a battered bus and it started with a rush of white exhaust. It took them an hour to reach the venue, which was on the banks of the Bhairab. They disembarked in front of a bungalow. A huge lawn surrounding it was to act as the picnic spot.

"How do you find the place?" one of the organizers asked Guri.

"It reminds me of my home town – green fields, wide rivers and colourful people."

The organizers looked experienced and everyone was soon served a breakfast of bread and eggs. It was followed by sandesh and tea. Avijit introduced Guri to most of his neighbours, whom he was meeting after a long time. Many youngsters came up and asked him about life in Calcutta. They were planning to pursue their careers in the City of Joy and wanted a first hand account. A few asked him about football and the ideal practice schedule. But no one asked him about a career in the army. Serving the motherland was not a viable career. A musical band soon livened up the proceedings. Anirudha, his childhood friend, started singing a few fast numbers and there was no stopping Guri. Attention immediately shifted from the singer to the dancer and people cheered and clapped, as the *sardar* danced the *bhangra.* He had to continue till he could dance no more. There was an audible moan, especially from a group of young girls, when the *sardar* sat down exhausted.

"You were simply great," a good-looking girl complimented Guri.

Avijit had never seen the girl before and quickly looked around to ensure none of the elders gave them a stare. But Guri had already put on his most charming smile and was staring dreamily at the girl. Her name was Rupa and she looked infatuated with the turbaned *sardar.* They chatted for the next hour, in spite of Avijit's best efforts to separate them.

"Have you seen the river? The water dazzles like silver. Lets go," he suggested to Guri.

But the girl also got up to have a look. The beach incident was still fresh in Avijit's mind and he quickly sat down.

"What happened?" the girl asked.

"I don't think it's a good idea. There might be poisonous snakes," he made them change their minds too.

"Why don't you go back and sit with your friends?" Avijit suggested to the girl after some time.

"Why? Are you jealous?" she shot back and made him squirm.

He gave up and looked skywards. Relief came in the form of the call for lunch.

It was a simple but enjoyable affair. They were served hot rice with meat curry followed by tomato chutney, curd and sweets. Guri seemed to enjoy the meal immensely and Avijit hoped the *sardar* had forgotten the girl. But that was not to be. The girl joined them after lunch. Avijit decided to leave the two to their own destiny and moved towards where the last batch was having its lunch. He helped in serving the food, heaping it from the aluminium container onto their plates. Later, he sat with his friends and recounted tales of insurgency and the tension he had faced over the past one year.

"Have you killed anyone?" the sudden question from one of them surprised him.

He was not sure how they might react and thought for a long moment, before nodding his head, his eyes downcast.

"Wow! How many?" one of them asked excitedly.

"How did it feel?" another asked philosophically, as if it was just another normal human activity.

Avijit wanted to tell them it felt bad, that it was inhuman and he had sinned. But no one was listening to him.

"Shoot them at sight, the bastards. They think they can scare our great nation with a few guns. We can show them, how tough we are," one of them lectured knowingly.

Avijit wondered what his tough friends would do, if a militant suddenly put in an appearance there. It seemed no one understood the enormity of the problem. The country wouldn't have slept easy, if they did.

Guri had to dance again on public demand and the day was almost coming to an end, when they boarded the bus for the return journey. Rupa sat next to Guri, much to the annoyance of a few other girls.

"I'll come over tomorrow," the girl told Guri.

"What are you doing?" Avijit felt irritated, "I don't want a repeat of Chandipur."

The *sardar* grinned. They trudged down the road to Avijit's home silently. Avijit's mother stood near the door, as if she was waiting for them, her face heavy with worry. She silently handed over a small piece of paper. It was a telegram from their army head quarters! They were to report back for duty immediately. Both of them sat dumbfounded in the drawing room, unable to decide what to do next.

"Someone must have played a prank," Guri looked closely at the telegram, "let's go and call the unit head."

The phone booth was nearby and they got through quickly. Guri smiled and winked at Avijit, as he was being put through. But his face turned serious as the call progressed. He had disbelief in his eyes after completing it.

"What is it?"

"Thousands of armed militants have infiltrated the line of control. A war is imminent. We have to catch the first train back."

Avijit couldn't believe it either. It meant they had to pack and leave immediately. They hurried back towards home.

"What will you tell your mother?" Guri asked him just before they reached.

"The truth," Avijit knew she would come to know later. It was pointless to hide the truth. That would add to her pain and anxiety.

Avijit's mother broke down at the news.

"You can't leave me like this," she kept on repeating, "how can I live without you?"

"Aunty, you should be proud of your son. He is going to defend our motherland," Guri tried to calm her down, while Avijit packed, "don't worry. Nothing will happen to us. I will come back and listen to your singing again and again."

It couldn't cheer her up and she sobbed every few minutes. But like a true mother, she didn't forget her duties either and quickly packed dinner for the two of them.

"May God be with you," she hugged both of them and wept, when their time came to depart.

Avijit was too puzzled to react. He still couldn't believe what Guri had told him. How could someone ever think of invading a nation? It seemed these people never valued life and the fun of living. They always lived in the shadow of death.

CHAPTER Sixteen

They didn't have to wait for long at the railway station. A train rumbled in, moments after they had purchased their tickets. But they were in for a disappointment. The train looked full and their hopes of two sleeping berths were dashed, once they spoke to the train ticket examiner.

"Sorry, no berths," was the dismissive reply.

"Sir, we are in the army and have to report back to our regiment immediately," Avijit tried to explain by showing the telegram, "you must help us."

"How can I help? There are no empty berths," the man was rude, "why didn't your army organize a train if it was so urgent."

Avijit was on the brink of bursting out. What did the man think of himself? But a firm hand on his shoulder stopped him.

"Please, we can do anything for two berths," Guri whispered to the man.

The train was to stop only for a few minutes and the signal was already green. Missing it might mean waiting for a few more hours, till the next one arrived.

"But you said you were in the army?"

"No, no, my friend was just joking. We have to attend a friend's marriage and have to go. How much?"

"One hundred each."

The deal was struck. Avijit was not shocked anymore. It was indeed ironic that they might have to lay down their lives, for men like the ticket examiner to enjoy their democratic freedom.

Long live the nation!

"Just relax and concentrate on the job ahead," Guri tried to calm him down, "you have to accept such complexities in our society. Treat them as ignorant and you will feel no pain."

They quickly settled down on the two lower berths.

"Did he say a war has already broken out?" Avijit asked for the umpteenth time.

"No. But he said we are on red alert. I hope Ravi is spared," his friend sighed.

But destiny thought otherwise. Ravi was already there in the barracks, when they reached their regimental headquarters.

"Bloody hell man," he exploded, "couldn't these idiots find a better time to try out this adventure? I was packing for my honeymoon when the telegram arrived."

"How is Saraswati?" Avijit knew the answer, but still asked.

"Oh, she's fine. I just can't live without her," Ravi sounded cheerful.

But the news was pretty gloomy. Thousands of intruders had taken positions on the higher reaches of the mountains, inside the line of control. The army never maintained a permanent forward post, as the place was uninhabitable in the winter. No one in their right minds would venture up there in the cold, as they could be frozen to death. But the intruders had somehow survived. They were now attacking the soldiers, who were going up to resume their vigil after the snows had melted. Avijit was convinced these infiltrators didn't value life and thought of death as a reward. Only, they were sharing it with the soldiers, who had to respond to the call of their duty.

"We must be on our toes," their unit head told them, "we might be asked to join forces anytime."

They were put on a tough daily routine: physical exercises followed by small arms training. They also practiced a lot of rock climbing. Each new day brought news of more deaths at the frontier and a firmer resolve amongst the soldiers to avenge this unnecessary butchering of their colleagues. A few were scared too. But they remained silent fearing a court martial. There were conflicting reports on the intruder's identity. Some said they were mujahideens, while others confirmed them as an infantry battalion of the enemy.

"We have got our call," their unit head announced one afternoon, "get ready. We leave within the hour."

All of them assembled in the barracks one last time. They held each other's hands and stood in a circle.

"We will kill them, every single one," Ravi hissed, "remember how they killed Ghoton? This will be our answer. We will teach them not to bother us again."

They boarded their truck amidst loud cheering from the rest of the regiment, many unlikely to meet ever again. Avijit felt a strange sense of relief, as if the opportunity he had been waiting for since his father's death had finally arrived. There were loud chants of '*Jai Hind*' and '*Bharat Mata Ki Jai*', as their convoy moved out of the camp. It was a six-hour drive and they finally disembarked next to the last railway station. A temporary camp had been set up there to brief the soldiers one last time. The place was teeming with soldiers from various regiments, each from a different corner of the country, but all with a single mission – to defend the motherland from the evil designs of the intruders. They were ordered to attend a briefing at nine p.m. They had about an hour to kill and Avijit decided to take a walk with Ravi at his side.

"Let's hope this is over within a week. I can well imagine the tension and anxiety Saraswati and my folks must be going through, after reading the reports in the paper," Ravi remarked.

Avijit thought of his own mother and hoped the same. They walked along a railway platform. It was pitch dark and difficult to see ahead. They almost tripped over a box kept at the centre of the platform.

"Some idiot must have left his luggage behind," Avijit muttered.

But it was too large to be a normal trunk; it was a coffin. They counted nine others, all lined up along the platform, each draped in the national tri-colour. Two men suddenly appeared, carrying one more on their shoulders.

"Who's that?" one of them flashed a torch on Avijit's face. It was lowered, once the man realized who they were.

"They were amongst the first to be up there," he explained, after lowering the coffin with a lot of care, "killed in action. We're sending them home."

Avijit and Ravi stood there, mouthing a silent prayer for the soul of the departed, not quite sure whether one such coffin awaited them too in the near future.

They sat attentively throughout the briefing session, trying to memorize every single instruction, as it could well mean the thin line between life and death. They were provided special clothing against the near freezing temperatures in the battle zone.

"We start sometime tomorrow," Captain Shekhar informed their unit head after the briefing.

They huddled in a makeshift tent, the tension in their minds driving away sleep. Avijit had seen many a war movie in his childhood. He always believed a war was madness. Only the demented participated in it, people who didn't care if they lived or died. But Avijit feared death. He dreamt of his father. His father was trying to pull him out of a deep crevice. But the more he pulled, the deeper Avijit sank. He woke up with a start, his throat absolutely dry. He drank from a water bottle and peeped out of the tent. The sky had turned a hazy grey, heralding another uncertain day. He lazed on the makeshift bed for a few more minutes, not sure when he could do the same again. They spent their day doing physical exercises, checking and rechecking their weapons, and praying. Each one of them had to do sit-ups in their full gear under the watchful eyes of an officer. Soldiers from all communities visited a temple nearby and paid their respects.

"You will live long," the priest blessed them.

He must have blessed those ten dead soldiers too. Man was as good as his destiny.

They finally boarded their truck, which would carry them to the battlefront around evening. Their convoy moved through the night, the sound of the shells and gunfire increasing with every approaching kilometre. They reached a base camp at three in the morning. They covered their ears, as a battery of guns fired away continuously towards the invisible enemy.

"Rest now," Captain Shekhar ordered, "we meet again at five hundred hours."

It was easier said than done. Sleep was forgotten because of anxiety and tension.

"May God be with you," his mother's last words kept echoing in his mind. How could God be with everyone? Thousands of soldiers had spread out over the entire line of control. How could the Almighty keep track of every single soul? Or could he? Avijit must have dozed off, as Guri shook him awake. It was almost five o'clock and they assembled at the makeshift tent. The Captain was already there, looking smart in his uniform and sounding calm in spite of the din all around.

"The enemy is occupying a few strategic peaks. They are being able to direct artillery fire from across the border on our convoy along the highway below. We have been ordered to recapture one such peak – peak 4987 – immediately," he said.

As per intelligence reports, there were around twenty intruders, holed up with machine guns and hand grenades. They also had an intact supply line from across the border. The air force was unable to cut it off, as it could mean violation of the neighbouring nation's airspace. The army planned to attack the intruders from the three sides of the hill. They would be attacking from the steepest side.

"We need to walk all the way up, around fifteen kilometres, to reach the base of peak 4987," the Captain continued, pointing at a map with red and green circles, "the mountains will be a natural cover from the enemy fire till the last few kilometres. Collect your rations and snow boots from the store. We start at eight hundred hours so that we reach the base by nightfall. Any questions?"

The Captain looked closely at the men sitting in the room, searching for a hint of nerves or indecision, which could put everyone in danger later. But the soldiers were resigned to their fate and stared back at the Captain.

"I want all of you with me for the celebrations, once our job is done. So don't get shot. I'll haul you out of hospital, even if you have four bullets in your ass," he joked.

They had a bath in the river that flowed by. Some sang, while a few, including Guri, danced. They checked their weapons and rations one last time, before reporting back to the Captain. It was a minute past eight, when the platoon started marching towards the invaders. They walked at a brisk pace along the pristine valley, their heavy boots trampling over a few flower buds, the sound of their marching drowning the sweet gurgling of the river. They walked along the river bank for almost an hour, before following a narrow path up the mountains. A small hill had to be crossed before they could go further. They slowed considerably in trying to scale the hill, but more worry awaited them at the top, once they reached it.

The soldiers halted on the hilltop, a few catching their breath from the effort. A long line of snow-clad peaks greeted the eye. They had a panoramic view of the valley too, the green shaking off its cover of snow with the approaching summer. Avijit's eyes strained to catch a glimpse of the intruders, once the Captain pointed out peak 4987. It was half covered in snow and looked imposing. The thought of climbing it sent shivers down Avijit's spine. He wondered how the intruders had managed to survive on the beautiful but forlorn peak. A sudden blast broke his thoughts. A shell had landed on their right from nowhere!

"Get back behind the cover of the hill," the Captain shouted and they ran.

The intruders must have spotted them on top of the hill and radioed their position to the artillery behind the enemy lines. Shells were now raining down on the area, where they had been relaxing a few moments back. But they were out of harm's way. The intruders could not see them any more, as they had moved back behind the cover of the hill. It resulted in a detour and an extra three hours of traversing through rocky terrain.

"Bastards! Just let me get my hands on them," Ravi muttered under his breath, "it's easy to shoot from the top. They'll know what it means to have a bayonet up their ass, when I catch them."

They rested for a half-hour on the edge of a small lake. The hills surrounding it were almost barren and partly covered in snow. The air was icy and the tea had to be gulped down quickly or it turned ice cold within the minute. They also had a quick lunch of dry rotis, boiled eggs and cauliflower curry from their rations. It tasted horrible, but would be their sustenance for the next few days. Only the chocolates were delicious and Avijit was overjoyed at the sight of the ten bars he had been given at the base camp. He had fought many a war with his parents for a bar of chocolate in his childhood, but had never been this lucky.

"Look, someone is coming," Guri suddenly pointed towards the far end of the lake. The soldiers scrambled for their guns and aimed at the target. Avijit squinted his eyes and could see a few men trudging towards them.

"They are our soldiers and look wounded," the Captain observed, after looking through his binoculars.

He ordered a few men, including the medics in their forward platoon, to go and help. Avijit ran along with Ravi and reached the men first. There were five of them, four carrying the other on a stretcher. They collapsed after the medics gently lowered the stretcher and attended to the critically wounded soldier. Avijit couldn't make out whether he was unconscious or dead. One of the four grabbed the water bottle Ravi offered and drank thirstily.

"We've been walking since early morning," he remarked, "he took four bullets and the rest in our platoon are dead. We had no option but to retreat."

The medics covered the body on the stretcher with a plastic sheet.

"Couldn't survive the cold," one of them shook his head sadly.

The soldier, who had spoken earlier, broke down at the news.

"We tried our best," he sobbed.

The other three recovered faster and gave them an account of what had happened.

"We tried to climb up to the peak at night and surprise the enemy.

But those bastards seemed to know all our moves. Two of our soldiers were crushed beneath the heavy boulders they pushed down from the top," the soldier closed his eyes, as the horror of the event seemed to make him breathless. "We thought we had them, when ten of us reached within fifty metres of their bunker. But they opened fire suddenly. Our Commander and the others died on the spot, while we came down with him."

The four men pleaded to be included in their team, their tiredness forgotten at the thought of a chance to avenge the death of their colleagues. The Captain agreed, as he realized they could provide vital intelligence on the exact location of the intruders. He kept in touch with the base camp and herded them on.

"We're behind schedule," he barked, "the other groups are ready at the flanks."

They marched on, panting, their lungs straining for oxygen in the high altitude, and reached the base of a bare and rocky hill around four in the afternoon. Their final destination rose high just behind it, its peak invisible from the ground, as were the intruders.

"We climbed it from there," one of the four soldiers indicated a narrow crevasse on the face of the mountain.

The intruders on the top couldn't see them, as the small hill in front was a natural cover. They would be within range, once they stepped out of its shadow and continued upwards.

"We wait till nightfall," the Captain said, after consulting his superiors at the base camp, "the other teams are already in position and our artillery will start shelling the peak after nightfall. We need to climb up before the enemy recovers."

So they waited, ready for any eventuality. No one spoke, as if even whispers might carry to the peak and alert the enemy. It was bitingly cold and the wind penetrated through the layers of leather, silk and cotton, and hammered at their ribs.

"Drink this," Guri brought out a small bottle of rum and handed it to him.

Avijit looked around and made sure no one was watching him. He quickly had a sip. It warmed his body. He remembered the first time he had sipped a drink at Ujjal's house. He was full of remorse after the first sip, as he believed it was an act of transgression against the divine law. Today, all his worries seemed to dissolve with the one swig. He was going to succeed in his mission. Yeah, that would be it. He had accepted too many failures in the past. But he wouldn't fail again. Avijit willed his fear away and waited for the night.

CHAPTER Seventeen

The stars shone brightly. The silence of the night was broken by the roar of water rushing out of the barrage. Avijit was standing on the edge and a thin wisp of vapour blew against his face. Avijit looked up and saw his father. His father smiled at him.

"You have done well so far," he told Avijit, "try a little harder and you'll reach the finish."

"You're happy but I'm lonely," his mother interjected, "don't take away my son."

"It was all because of Roy," his father said, "he was greedy."

Mr Roy stood near his father, a gun in his hand.

"I'll put you in jail," Mr Dayaram threatened, "you refused my wife."

"Please love me," it was Mrs Dayaram. The others had disappeared and Avijit was left with her. She stood bare, longing for his touch and he obliged. Only Mrs Dayaram seemed to change to Nandita and then to Sraboni. He was making frenzied love to her. Or was it Khokon?

"Wake up," Ravi shook him awake, "the shelling has started."

It had indeed. The entire horizon was veiled in darkness and orange fireballs rushed out of nowhere. They sailed over their heads with a whooshing noise and thudded onto the mountain peak in a deafening sound. Avijit wondered how he had slept amidst the din. But it had revived his numb nerves and he felt ready for action.

"We need to cover an open area of around a hundred metres before we can reach the base of the mountain. Then we climb up,"

Captain Shekhar told them, "we charge towards the mountain in groups of four. We start in five minutes."

Ravi, Guri and Avijit huddled together, waiting their turn to charge. They peeped out from their cover at the open area they were supposed to cross. It looked innocent and had a barren serenity to it. A few boulders seemed to have stuck on the flat stretch, after rolling down from the top.

"Okay guys. Let's avenge Ghoton's death," Ravi hissed, "may God remind us of him every minute so that our hands don't waver while shooting the buggers."

The Captain rushed out first along with three other soldiers and sped towards their target area. They reached safely and signalled to the next group to follow.

Avijit ran out of his shelter and his friends followed closely. He tried to run fast through the near darkness and had almost reached the other end, when he took a tumble! The others would have reached the safe zone, had they not halted to help him. Ravi and Guri hauled him up, while the third soldier looked back. But he didn't see the bullets, which darted through the still air at him. A few intruders must have come down. He died even before he realized what had hit him.

"Run towards the left," Guri pointed towards a large boulder a few feet away.

They ran and reached it, just before a grenade exploded where Avijit had fallen down.

"Get back here," the Captain snapped at them, "before its too late."

They ran with all the strength in their bodies, expecting a hail of bullets to cut them down any moment. But they reached safely. The gunfire and the pounding of the grenades continued unabated for the next few minutes, before it stopped all together.

"It was all my fault," Avijit lamented the death of his colleague.

He was one of the four soldiers, who had been there the previous night. Avijit hardly knew him. But the man sacrificed his life trying to help a careless junior. He lay on the barren stretch, at peace with all the bombardment that shook the valley. The Captain didn't allow them to retrieve the body.

"I don't need more casualties," he stopped them, "we can carry him back, once our job is complete. Let him rest in peace."

He waited for another half hour, before asking the rest to come over. The bombardment had stopped entirely and an eerie silence had descended on them. The others in their group slowly came over, each soldier more watchful while traversing the open area. But the attack from the flanks must have started as they heard a lot of gunfire above them, though none was directed downwards. Avijit wanted to get up there fast and fight face to face with the vandals.

They started crawling up the hard rock face. One had to be careful not to step on a loose rock. It would mean a fresh effort to crawl up from the bottom, if one survived the fall. It was difficult climbing up the sheer rock face with their rifle and rations slung on the back. But the nation had to be defended and its citizens ensured a good night's sleep. They climbed and crawled for the better part of the night, the gun battle above deafening, till they reached a small plain area on the face of the mountain. The mountain had risen again after a flat stretch of a few metres and a thin layer of snow covered the rock face. The soldiers exhausted from the steep climb wanted a rest, but the Captain would have none of it.

"We can't stop till the job is complete. Move your ass," he ordered and allowed them to rest for only the few minutes it took him to radio headquarters.

"The two other groups have suffered heavy casualties and reinforcements are being rushed in," he informed them, "so only we can win back the peak tonight. Otherwise, it will be delayed till reinforcements arrive."

"Let's win it back, sir," Ravi seemed eager for an early finish.

The others echoed similar sentiments and they started their crawl again. Captain Shekhar led the way, as he had been doing, since they had ventured out of the base camp. They had climbed around a hundred metres, when hell broke loose. The mountain face sloped to a gradual incline for the next hundred metres or so, before going up again. The peak was not clearly visible, as the rocks stood like huge pillars, guarding the entrance to the unknown. Avijit's lungs were on fire and his muscles felt as hard as bones. He had never trained for this nightmare. Most of the soldiers were trying to get their breath back and it was extremely difficult to cling to the snow-covered surface. There was every chance of slipping back over the edge into oblivion. The dark night was giving way to a grey and misty morning.

The sudden gunfire caught them unawares. It came from behind a boulder.

"Get down," the Captain roared.

But it didn't help. The bullets tore through three soldiers, who had crept a little ahead of the others. They died without a whimper. The others tried their best to lie below the bullet's trajectory and avoid certain death. More would have died, had not a soldier shaken off his fear and fatigue, and run towards the enemy. Ravi always hated vandals and the death of Ghoton was still fresh in his mind. He roared and ran towards the boulder, avoiding the bullets, as if by a miracle. He hurled two grenades from close quarters and the gunfire suddenly stopped. Avijit rushed up to Ravi, who had collapsed, seemingly from exhaustion.

"I did it!" he shouted jubilantly, "I killed the bastards! I have avenged the death of Ghoton."

He collapsed again, with blood coming out of his mouth. The bullets had not entirely missed their target. Though most had sailed past harmlessly, two small holes were oozing blood just below Ravi's chest.

"We need to shift him to the base camp immediately," the medic whispered to Avijit and Guri, who were crouching next to Ravi, "ask the Captain to radio for a chopper."

Avijit ran towards the boulder where Captain Shekhar and the others stood. It was carnage! Five mercenaries had been manning the gun. Now there were four burnt bodies and a lone survivor, who had miraculously survived with a minor injury. The stench of burning flesh made Avijit cover his nose.

"Please don't kill me," the man pleaded repeatedly, "treat me like a prisoner of war."

Captain Shekhar rushed back with Avijit, with a clear order to the others not to kill the prisoner. He radioed for help but had grim news. A chopper would not be able to reach them immediately, as the weather was bad.

"We need to wait," the Captain tried to keep the frustration out of his voice.

Ravi seemed to be in a trance, calling out for his parents and wife in his delirium.

"He must be shifted down immediately," the medics warned again, "oxygen is scarce at this height and he can die."

The three soldiers, who had carried down one of their colleagues the previous night, were prompt to respond.

"We know the way down," one of them pointed towards a narrow ledge, "it is a gradual slope and we can have him down within two hours and await the chopper."

"But be careful. The enemy might have more forward posts like this one," the Captain warned.

"He'll be fine," the medic assured Guri, who had sat stonily all through, his injured friend's head in his lap, his ears straining to pick up the words that Ravi mumbled.

The three soldiers put Ravi on a makeshift stretcher and started the journey back to the mountain base with one of the medics. The rest watched silently, as the four men disappeared.

"Please don't kill me," the prisoner was still pleading with the stony faced soldiers, who stood guard.

"Don't worry, we will put you on the next plane back to your hometown," one of them assured him.

That seemed to calm him down.

"We'll set you free, if you give us the exact location of your colleagues," the Captain crouched in front of him and added sweetly.

"I'll tell you everything, but please don't kill me."

The man told them that they had been manning the forward post for the past two days, as they had received a tip-off about an army attack. There were thirty others, a mix of mercenaries and enemy soldiers, holed up on the peak in a huge bunker. They had come up from across the line of control during the height of winter, when the army had abandoned its vigil and gone down to more inhabitable heights. More teams had followed and occupied other strategic heights all along the border. The intruders had travelled at night through thick snow and blizzards, and only forty out of the sixty-five in their team had survived the ordeal. They had rations to last another week and enough ammunition to blow up the mountains. They took turns in manning this forward post and the next team was expected within the hour. It was unlikely that the people in the bunker knew of their state, as the spot was not visible from the top.

"Get into position," the Captain ordered.

They took up their position behind boulders strewn near the path along which the mercenaries were expected.

"What do we do with him?" Guri asked the Captain, "he might try to alert his colleagues when they come down."

They looked at each other silently and the Captain finally nodded his head. Guri grabbed the intruder and forced him to stand up.

"Please don't kill me," he started sobbing.

"Don't worry. I won't waste a costly bullet on scum like you. I am just taking you away from the action."

Avijit joined the *sardar* and the two pulled the man towards the edge of the mountain.

"Tell me, what did you gain from all this?" Avijit couldn't help but ask the bewildered man.

The man stayed silent for a long time before answering.

"It is a fight for our identity, for our freedom. The freedom, which had been snatched away from us. You may kill me today, but it won't stop others from continuing the fight and achieving it someday."

"You kill people and then talk of freedom! Did those dead soldiers pinch your freedom?" Avijit kicked the man in the groin.

The intruder doubled over in pain and lay silently. He got up slowly, only after Guri prodded him in the ribs with his boot.

"I'm sorry," the man spoke with difficulty, "I'm sure God will understand and pardon me."

"I hope not. May you rot in hell," and with that, Avijit pushed the man with all his strength over the edge.

The man's shrill cry was soon lost, as he fell into the ravine. The two of them took up their position behind the boulder, where the intruders had set up their guns. It was not a long wait, as they could soon hear the murmur of voices. The enemy didn't fear to announce their arrival, as they never believed it possible for the army to capture their forward post. Anyone, who managed to come up from the sheer rock face, could not avoid death from the volley of bullets that would be racing towards him. But Avijit and his colleagues had achieved the impossible thanks to the Captain, who had coaxed and cajoled them all the way up.

"Drop your guns," Captain Shekhar bellowed, as the five men walked into the trap, "you're surrounded from all sides."

But they were soldiers too; ready to die for their cause. They opened fire from their sophisticated automatic weapons instead of surrendering. It was over within the minute, as Avijit and his team were too good for those five men caught in the middle. There was only a single injury on their side – Guri took a hit in his left forearm. The lone medic attended to him, quickly bandaging the wound.

"You're lucky, the bullet grazed your arm," he told the *sardar*, "you stay out of action for now. You might aggravate the injury otherwise."

But Guri wouldn't listen.

"I can move the arm and hold my rifle straight. So you can't stop me. Nothing will happen," he was firm.

The five intruders lay in a heap, their arms and legs entangled with each other in the agony of death. They seemed to be in the prime of their youth and a college classroom would have suited them better. Avijit was also surprised by his own action. His hands didn't waver, when he had pushed the enemy soldier over the edge. These were strange times. He wondered whether he could live a normal life again, if he survived the ordeal. Humans were behaving like animals on this serene land.

"Let's wait for nightfall," the Captain said, "the enemy will know shortly that something has gone wrong down here. They will surely watch the approach roads and we could be sitting ducks, if we try to go up in the daylight. We can wait here instead, if a few come down to look for their missing colleagues."

And so they halted there for the day. Each ate sparingly from the already dwindling rations and took turns in getting some rest. Water was available in plenty. They just had to collect ice in a saucepan and heat it. The bodies of the intruders were shifted out of sight. They would be taken down later and returned with full honours. After all, they were also soldiers who didn't shirk their duty, however weird it might have been. Avijit thought of Ravi and how he was doing. There was no way of knowing, as their wireless set had malfunctioned and they had been cut off from the operational headquarters since early morning. He hoped his friend had already been taken to the hospital and was safe. Avijit slept soundlessly for a full three hours, in spite of the cold piercing like a double edged sword through the thin plastic sheet on which he lay. He felt refreshed afterwards and gratefully accepted the hot mug of tea offered by one of the soldiers. Guri was already up and looked cheerful, though his arm didn't look too good. His jacket was stained with blood and Avijit requested the medic to have another look.

"Don't exert pressure on your arm and don't expose the wound to this cold," the latter warned the *sardar*, while injecting a painkiller, "you would be better off at the base hospital."

"No way," Guri protested, "I've to finish my job."

But the end looked far away. It was only afternoon and a full five hours, before darkness would once again envelop the misty sky. Their operation could start only then. The mountain played hide and seek, once revealing itself in front and vanishing the next moment behind a cover of fine mist. It looked innocuous enough, with no clear view of the messengers of death, who breathed within its folds. The intruders also seemed to be waiting for the skies to darken, before they resumed their acts of barbarism.

Avijit's platoon crouched on the snow covered surface, lying on plastic sheets to avoid getting wet, their guns aimed at the narrow path along which the enemy had descended. But no one came down. Each one of them managed some sleep and the entire team was refreshed and ready for the final battle as the skies started to darken. Sounds of shells and gunfire echoed sporadically across the mountain range, but it was nothing compared to the din of the previous night. An uneasy silence had descended all around them. The wireless set was still not functional and Captain Shekhar had no way of knowing, whether reinforcements had reached the flanks and were ready to attack. He wanted to wait a little longer, before deciding to move forward.

The shell destroyed the silence of the mountains. It was fired by the enemy and landed a few hundred metres to their left. Avijit felt a terrible urge to relieve himself, but the Captain's instructions were firm. No one was to leave his position without informing the latter. Avijit decided to do it lying on the snow, as the Captain was far away to the right. Another shell landed nearby, a little too close for comfort. The intruders at the top must have given the artillery behind the enemy lines their exact location. It was no longer a secret that the army had captured the enemy's forward post. None of the intruders had come down to look for their missing colleagues. But Avijit was equally surprised by the inaction of his own artillery. They had not fired back at all. Were they sleeping? It was not safe to remain in their position any longer. The next enemy shell might be racing towards them already. The Captain seemed to read his mind and ordered them to move forward. They spread out in a small semi-circle and started crawling forward, their rifles at the ready, their eyes straining for the smallest of movements to press on the trigger. Shells started pouring down on the merceneries' forward post, which they had left behind; the snow-clad surface erupted into fireballs, as the shells exploded harmlessly. It took them the better part of an hour to come within striking distance of the peak. Enemy shells from behind the border continued to pound harmlessly below them. But surprisingly, there was neither any response from their artillery nor an attack from the flanks. It seemed their own army had abandoned them. The intruders were also strangely silent and not a single gun fired, as they inched closer and closer. Maybe, the intruders didn't want to waste their bullets and would only fire once the target came within sniffing distance. They could now see the bunker, but it seemed devoid of life. Captain Shekhar fell back, as they approached the peak, and coaxed them on from behind. He ordered them to open fire, when they were within thirty metres of the bunker. The guns blazed in unison, their tension and hatred of the past few days pouring out. A soldier lobbed three grenades into the large bunker and the explosion lit up the sky. Any life form, which might have survived the bullets, would surely be annihilated under its impact. But it looked too easy. There had been absolutely no resistance from the intruders.

"Stop the fire," Captain Shekhar ordered, "I want three of you to go inside and check. Move."

No one moved an inch and the Captain had to shout out his order for a second time. Avijit got up cautiously and crawled towards the bunker. What were the others afraid of? There were no intruders alive for sure. He found only Guri alongside him and they peered over the edge of the bunker. It looked empty under the beam of their torchlights. There was no one, not even a dead mercenary! Avijit jumped into the bunker and looked around. It was built all around the mountain peak and he moved towards the other end. The stench of cordite filled his nostrils. The enemy seemed to have abandoned the post in a hurry. Burnt clothing and bedding were scattered all over. The sudden searing pain took him by surprise. It seemed a ray of white light erupted from the floor of the bunker and engulfed him. A hot blade tore at his left leg and he collapsed.

A Month Later....

The nurse raised Avijit's bed, after placing the food on the stool. It was dinner-time. Avijit hated the food, as much as he hated everything else.

"You must eat," the nurse knew her patient and remarked softly, "only then can you regain your strength."

Avijit knew better and kept quiet. He opened his mouth after the nurse tore the roti, rolled it over a small quantity of the curry and touched his chin with her hand. He chewed on the tasteless food and gulped it down, once the nurse had the next bite ready. She looked calm in spite of the sporadic cry from an injured soldier in the ward. Avijit had strange company. Some had lost an eye, a few had lost limbs and none would ever be fully fit. But their zeal for life had not ebbed. They cried out only when the pain became unbearable.

The nurse lowered Avijit's bed after he had finished dinner. She handed over a sports magazine, which he had asked for, and moved to the next bed. She was young and Avijit wondered what made her waste her youth in this godforsaken place. He turned the first page of the magazine and immediately regretted it. It had the picture of a football player. The player's eyes were fixed on the ball in front of him. Avijit felt a sudden sadness. It could so easily have been him in the picture. But luck had never smiled on him. Otherwise why had he stepped on that bloody mine? The blast though had alerted the others and there had been no more casualties.

"Our government had decided to allow the intruders to go back safely," Guri had announced glumly, after he had met his friend at the base hospital, "a ceasefire had been announced that morning. The mercenaries must have received news and moved away immediately. That's why our artillery didn't fire when we were expecting it."

So the wise old men, who started the conflict, had signed their truce, after a few thousand young men had sacrificed their lives during the war games. Avijit hardly remembered anything though. It was all like a bad dream. Only the sound of the explosion beneath his feet shook him out of his sleep at times.

There was still no news of Ravi and his four stretcher-bearers. No one knew their fate, as they had neither reported to the base camp nor had their bodies been found. Avijit still remembered the shy bride holding the squirming fish for a full minute, as that was supposed to ensure a long and happy life for the newly weds. He still believed in folklore and hoped Ravi would come back. Maybe, he had been taken prisoner and would be released soon.

Most in his ward felt that the job had not been completed.

"The lunatics might be encouraged," he heard one soldier tell another, "they now know that our government can never declare a war to weed them out, under pressure from the international community. So they can always come across the border and get some target practice. And retire just before their asses are on fire!"

Avijit hoped it wouldn't be true. The intruders had suffered heavy casualties all across the terrain. Guri had mentioned that many bodies still lay unclaimed as the fanatics who had backed the intruders, no longer owned them up, Their designs had been laid bare to the whole world. It made Avijit ponder how the families of the dead mercenaries were taking it. Were they enjoying sumptuous meals from the money their young boys had earned? Or would they question the wisdom of these fanatics, who were a threat to the peaceful coexistence of mankind?

"You know what," Guri had summed up, "it makes me wonder whether we're civilized only because we cover our genitals in fabric and do not copulate in public."

Avijit's mother had broken down when he had spoken to her a few days earlier. He could now walk with a crutch and the nurse had led him to the phone booth near the ward. His mother was happy to hear her son's voice. She had been strangely silent though, when he had spoken of his fate. She had spoken after a long pause and assured him that everything would be fine, once he went back home. But was everything really fine?

Where the mind is without fear,

And the head is held high.

He remembered his father quote Tagore. Was it true anymore? The common man now feared the unknown. Their heads were always bent, lest some hooligan chop them off. The people who had killed his father roamed around freely and the Dayarams cheated the nation's coffers dry. The Ghotons sacrificed their lives to ensure freedom and democracy for such people. Would they ever change? He was also amazed at man's eternal quest for extinction. Man created boundaries all around. Mankind fought over barren land, as they had been doing for the past few days, little realizing that Mother Earth had resources to accommodate all.

It was all so meaningless. Futile. The pain shot through his body like lightning, as he tried to roll over on his left side. He often forgot in his hurry that he no longer had the support of his left leg. The blast had ripped it apart and left only a small stump of flesh as a souvenir.

A Year Later...

Saraswati still puts sindoor on her forehead every day and awaits her husband Ravi's arrival. According to army records, Ravi is still *missing in action.*

Guri has been promoted to Lance Naik and is presently fighting insurgency in the north-eastern tip of the country.

Major Shekhar was awarded two citations for his gallantry in leading the assault on peak 4987. He is posted near the southern fringe of the country, away from the madness of insurgency.

Avijit runs a tea stall in Rajpur. No one can say that he has an artificial leg, but for his slight limp. He still polishes the regiment's emblem on his torn uniform everyday.

And life goes on.

Last summer I had a dream,
I dreamt of people sad and grim,
A few without limbs and a lifelong scar,
They had just been back from a war.
They thought they fought the Nation's worry,
Though it meant a meaningless boundary.
They couldn't shirk the superior's order,
As they were soldiers and paid not to bother,
So they embraced pain, death and fear,
To ensure sleep for the Nation's peer.
There were martyrs, orphans and widows,
As the soldiers kept on fighting shadows.